Pictures from a Brewery

ASHER BARASH

*Pictures
from
a Brewery*

A NOVEL

TRANSLATED FROM THE HEBREW BY KATIE KAPLAN

*Introduction by
Israel Cohen*

PETER OWEN · LONDON

ISBN 0 7206 0092 8

UNESCO COLLECTION OF REPRESENTATIVE WORKS
ISRAEL SERIES

This book has been accepted in the
Israel Literature Translations Series of
the United Nations Educational, Scientific and
Cultural Organization (UNESCO)

PETER OWEN LIMITED
12 Kendrick Mews Kendrick Place London SW7

First British Commonwealth edition 1972

© 1971 Massada Press Ltd

Printed in Great Britain by
Lowe & Brydone (Printers) Ltd London

Asher Barash

I

Asher Barash was one of the greatest short-story writers in modern Hebrew literature, his work forming a cornerstone of that genre. The subject-matter of his fiction, which was his main interest, can be grouped under three headings: the life of Galician Jewry, the new Jewish community in Eretz-Israel (Palestine), and episodes selected from history.

Within the short story he blazed a trail that was entirely his own. He described the Jews of Galicia, deeply rooted in their environment, burdened by the need to earn a livelihood and by worldly concerns, busy and harried, yet at the same time retaining their self-respect; Jews who had adapted themselves to their Gentile neighbours, and who in the lulls between tempests would meet cordially to deal with matters of commerce and trade. Folksy Jews, who, while burdened with anxiety and suffering, had a rich Jewish way of life that was steeped in faith and light, during the six days of labour as well as on Sabbaths and holidays.

Barash was not the only author nor even the first to describe this milieu. S. Y. Agnon, his contemporary, painted a broad canvas of the life of this same community in Galicia. But Barash occupies a special niche, just as the subject of his depiction and the means he used are unique. His stories do not possess the mythical, romantic aura of

Agnon's. Barash lays bare the realistic background, and strives to describe the actual setting as it appeared to him in terms of his own experience.

The Jews of Galicia, who lived under the protection of the Emperor Franz Josef, led a generally tranquil existence. Whether they were merchants, land-owners, religious functionaries or pedlars doing their rounds of the villages — they felt stable and secure. They could move freely throughout the country as well as beyond its borders, completely unmolested.

His *Chapters of Rudorfer* and *Stories of Rudorfer* seem more like biographical notes than stories, describing lively excursions to various places, full of vigour and insight, and sketching Jewish and Gentile types. The travel-hungry Rudorfer tours as a carefree citizen, meditating about everything he encounters on his way, about instances of good fortune and about minor mishaps, and describes the various characters in his stories. He is a person born beneath the star of wanderlust, who lives on the move, reaching his destination by chance changes in the direction of his walking. Rudorfer is not a frivolous, irresponsible person, but an admirer of beauty and splendour, who loves life and at the same time is bemused by everything he encounters in his rambling. And numerous phenomena do await him on his way, so that it is with a sense of gratitude that Rudorfer remarks: "Such wonders must have been prepared for me in heaven." But finally he wearies of this purposeless and insecure life and decides to emigrate to Eretz-Israel (Palestine) and find normalcy there. About this book Barash himself said, "I depicted a few episodes from the life of the small country of my birth — a land abundant in natural charm and vitality even if it is not widely recognized as such—insofar as I had been permitted to enter its realms and observe its ways."

The unique character of Galicia is described primarily in the stories: "Pictures from the Brewery" and "Strange Love." In these stories Barash painted, with the brush of an artist and in the richest of colours, the Jewish community of that country, both in its light and shade, the older generation and the new, the Jews and non-Jews, the religious and the secular, the mundane and the festive, its men, women and children. "The Brewery" will be discussed separately below, and here we need only consider the character of the milieu described. The first impression is that Barash had described a way of life almost idyllically tranquil. To be sure, the plot does seem to be smoothly interconnected, without superfluous psychological analyses, without leaps in time and without the introduction of miracles. Jews go about their business in collaboration with Gentiles, there are occasional passing tensions, but everything works out in the end. Even the "Strange Love" between Peretz Segal and the Christian girl, Frania—which might constitute a perilous breach and is potentially earth-shaking—while it does terminate in a rift between the two, does so in a sequence of events that is quite smooth in comparison with the seriousness of the situation. In the course of reading, a powerful sympathy for Frania's true love is frequently evoked. Barash the storyteller retains his equanimity even when describing the rift, and the way the anti-Semitic venom again begins to poison Frania and the members of her family. It may be that there is present an implicit, unarticulated moral: that there are here two fundamental emotional temperaments which will never achieve lasting communion.

Nevertheless, the perceptive will be aware that beneath the surface idyl lie depths of agony, though it may appear that a canopy of tranquility is spread over them. Baruch Wilder, whose life had been as calm as a bed of flowers, having once glimpsed the real life of his friend, the priest: "there fell upon him a great fear, like the fear that had engulfed him when he had stood lost and naked in the moving water of the river." And there is heard a loud weeping, as well, like that of Brachele (from "In the Brewery"), which is unforgettable. This is the weeping of a daughter of Israel in the face of the destruction of the paternal home, the pillar of security. Incidentally, in the midst of this seemingly well bastioned, stable existence, the premonition of future terrors is granted chiefly, although not exclusively, to the young: Brachele had an intuition and even warned against the two devoutly pious Jews who brought down catastrophe on Mrs. Aberdam and her enterprise. The "lad with the delicate face" in the story "A Jew is Delivered from Trouble" was also granted such intuition about the evil approaching from afar. And Libke, the hunch-backed boy in "From the Lot," "had a clear feeling that evil was imminent" and would befall his admired Pablo.

Hence, not everything in these stories is level, tranquil and pellucid. Here and there the gloom crouches, and in the clear skies threatening clouds suddenly loom. But over all the instances of catastrophe and injury, at the hands of heaven and at the hands of man, hovers a sort of sublime resignation, an indulgent smile.

There was no prejudicial impulse clouding Barash's vision. Never did he discriminate against the Gentile, but depicted him with both his shortcomings and his virtues.

In the fine story, "A Jew is Delivered from Trouble," Barash showed the beauty of the priest's mansion, and in other stories he drew portraits of Gentiles free from any negative bias: simply the Gentile as he is, entirely human despite the darker sides. In the story, "From the Lot," Pablo Stap is depicted as a Gentile of distinguished virtues, whom all the vicissitudes of fate, from poverty to wealth, and from wealth to destitution, never weakened in his grace and his charity. And it is a Jew, Shlomo Chaim, who benefited from his ruin. In "From the Life of Baruch Wilder," too, Barash endowed the Polish priest Victor Mienkienski with an attractive humanity, and so forth.

II

From the time Barash emigrated to Eretz-Israel (Palestine), he went about listening attentively to the rhythm of its upbuilding and to the sounds of rebirth and renewal. As a storyteller, Barash cultivated the new section of the young Jewish settlement in the country. In three long stories ("Gardeners," "Man and Home Blotted Out" and "Like a Besieged City") and in sixteen short stories, he wove the tapestry of the milieu coming into being in Tel Aviv and elsewhere. In "Like a Besieged City" an attempt was made, as the author himself wrote for the dust-jacket, "to paint a comprehensive picture of the suburb of Tel Aviv and the spirit that moved within it during the time span that began with the sailing of the last ship from Jaffa Port, when the sea was closed against the Jewish settlement, and which terminated after the expulsion of all its inhabitants by decree of the Turkish authorities." This story is populated by numerous people, for each of whom Barash not only carved out a face of his own, but captured each gesture and feature of his character. The Turkish rulers, and those being expelled, the attitudes of the communities and the staffs of the foreign consulates, the distribution of support and the divided opinions, the terror of decrees and the subterfuges of those fleeing the suburb — all is painted with an artist's hand, in high relief and bold colours, and with a humour that clothes the hidden sadness that shows through the highly suspenseful situation.

In the story "Gardeners" are described two brothers, Menashe and Ephraim, who have left Galicia and their traditional environment to become gardeners in Eretz-Israel (Palestine). The contrast between the gentler soul and his materialistic brother did not hinder them from settling down in Tel Aviv and making their livelihood from a fine farm. At the start, the marriage of the older brother, Menashe, with Mira from Grodna turns out quite well, and they even have a daughter. But ultimately Menashe's wife rebels against the life of the small farmer. She becomes intimate with a young man from a well-to-do Australian family. His manners and ideas fascinate her, and she is caught up in a dream of a pleasurable city life. After an intense struggle with herself she parts from her husband and her small daughter and follows her lover to Australia. But fate is not kind to her there, and six years later she returns to Eretz-Israel alone, her entire world in ruins, and commits suicide by drowning herself at sea. In this story, which might seem to have an ordinary plot, there is a very surprising development. The beginning and middle have an idyllic air, while the end is charged with the tragedy of a woman, unaccustomed to a life of toil, who is led astray by the call of her blood.

In "Man and Home Blotted Out," too, there pass before

the reader's eyes a variety of people from the period of "Little Tel Aviv," and a detailed view of their life. The hero, who comes from the neighbourhood of Odessa, is a man of colourful contrasts, which soften and sharpen by turns. He is rash and yet calculating, goodhearted and cruel, shrewd in his dealings yet finally a bankrupt, captivating women with his charm yet deceived by them, optimistic and — a suicide. By his cruel behaviour he has put an end to two wives, and he has married a third. He is always reaching a peak, in order to plunge to the depths. At first, fate offers him his fill of pleasure, in order to give him his fill of bitterness afterwards. Finally, his strength gone, he commits suicide in Roman fashion, which has for some reason quite often preoccupied his imagination: by slashing his wrists. There is something strange and symbolic in his dialogue with an ape he sees opposite himself outside, a sort of preparation for his suicide. He is buried next to the wall of the graveyard, and his third wife is subsequently found on his grave, mortally stricken.

III

A unique category, in which new aspects of Barash's literary talent are manifested, is occupied by his historical stories, which have been collected in the volume *Talk of the Times*. The subject-matter is drawn from various periods: the downfall of Saul in the battle with the Philistines ("Saul and the Asses"), the decline of Jerusalem after its conquest by the Roman hosts ("Even to the Foundation"), the uprooting of the Jewish community in Spain ("The Last in Toledo"), the banishing of the Regensburg Jews in the sixteenth century ("At a Certain Inn"), the annihilation of the Jewish communities by the Haidameks in the eighteenth century ("Before the Gates of Heaven"), the destruction of the Jewish way of life in Galicia in World War I ("The Bones of Reb Shimshon Shapira"), and the horrors of the Nazi extermination of German Jewry ("In Marburg"). It is a longitudinal section of Jewish history, of both significance and depth.

The story, "Before the Gates of Heaven," stands out here as intrinsically original. When "Papa" Gonta's Cossacks burst into the town of Tetayev, they seized the beadle of the synagogue and flogged him viciously, for having attempted to defend the House of God singlehanded, lest "the unclean Gentile hordes...defile the House of the Lord, and bemire...the sacred books..."But while the brawny Zorbilo was standing over the elderly beadle and flogging him relentlessly, it was the Gentile flogger and not the flogged beadle who became weary unto death. The beadle, seeing how fatigued he was, soothed him: "You are tired, my son. Rest, rest a while, rest..." David had bested Goliath, matter had flinched before spirit. For the beadle was bereft of any sense of pain, and he "felt himself being taken up and borne aloft, higher and higher, to the gate of Heaven, to the eternal serenity and the Hidden Light beyond."

"At a Certain Inn" also has a marvellous plot. Two *yeshiva* boys risked their lives in order to bring back from Regensburg copies of the Holy Writ which the principal of the *yeshiva* had entrusted to a righteous Gentile ten years before, on the day the Jews were expelled. While conveying the scrolls hidden in tar barrels, the two fell into the hands of two hoodlums in the woods. The hoodlums, upon seeing the barrels, were certain they contained valuables and broke them open. Having discovered only the scrolls inside, they brought them to an inn where two Christian scholars, Desiderius Erasmus and Willibald Pirkheimer, happened to be, so that they might examine whether the two Jews were engaged in spying or in libelling Christianity. The encounter between the two Jews and the two Christian scholars is of the greatest interest, and their discourse on Judaism and Christianity is magnificently conveyed.

In these and other stories, although the realistic description suffices in itself, in combination with the characters and the action it transcends its bounds to symbolize the life of the Jewish community in exile.

IV

Barash began writing "Pictures from the Brewery" at about the time of his arrival in Eretz-Israel (Palestine), while still poised between the old and the new. The experiences of his youth were becoming crystal clear, while his impressions of young Eretz-Israel were beginning to inspire him with the force of their novelty. This is the apex of Barash's work.

"The Brewery" tells of a patriarchal Jewish family, or more correctly a matriarchal one. It is deeply rooted and entrenched in an economic enterprise humming with business activity, but it is also steeped in the nobility of Jewish tradition. The central figure of the story is Mrs. Channa Aberdam, a woman of valour in the tradition of the Biblical matron, but at the same time a woman of her own era. Her impulsive drives are balanced by her moral strength, and her material affairs are immersed in an aura of spiritual uplift. Her sense of proportion is not blunted either during her greatest prosperity or in time of decline.

There is something majestic in her cast. Her first husband, Reb Shlomki, whose sole passion had been the study of the Holy Writ, had been compelled by the advice of her two brothers-in-law and her father to engage in commerce against his inclinations. As they became more demanding, he proposed to them that he travel to Hungary to buy cattle for fattening. Initially, they had been afraid to entrust money to the "idler" lest he be swindled or robbed on the way, but ultimately they agreed to his proposal. Miraculously he concluded the purchase felicitously and returned home safely. But after this successful transaction he had closeted himself in his house, fallen into a decline and died.

Two years after the death of her first husband, she remarried, this time to Reb Naftali Zvi Aberdam, a respectable shop-keeper, though Reb Shlomki still occupied her mind and her world. After several unsuccessful attempts at business deals, she got up one day, sold the shop and her jewellery — and leased a brewery owned by the agents' representative, Pan Grabinsky. To be sure, it was Mrs. Aberdam who oversaw the conduct of the entire brewery, and everything was done her way. And indeed, her intelligence, her manners, her remarkable virtues, her industry, and her practical talent stood her in good stead, and fortune was kind to her. She was an educated woman, spoke excellent Polish, was good with figures and had a marvellous memory. Not only was she diligent in the affairs of the brewery, but she also gave to charity, entertained guests, and inspired a Jewish atmosphere in all her surroundings.

She had a daughter named Brachele, who was "the complete opposite of her mother: fragile, shy and melancholy." She married the son of the Rabbi from Radichov, but only after being with her husband for fifteen years of aching sterility did she bear him twin girls, and a boy who resembled her in the complexity of his mind. But the many years of sterility had killed the mother urge in her, which only flickered into life from time to time. She was the only one who was not dwelling in a nest of felicity. She used to burst out crying, and her weeping was not merely an emotional outlet, but an expression of her premonitions of the impending tragedy that threatened the entire house of Aberdam.

Barash proceeds to describe the workings of this economic enterprise which fed and supported almost all the Jews of the vicinity, and he conveys the wisdom of Mrs. Aberdam, the builder of this stronghold, parading before his reader a variety of characters, Jews and Gentiles, children and old people, each modelled with an artist's hand, till the time arrives for the fall of the house of Aberdam. This decline seems to be caused by human agency, instigated by the two dishonest Jews and the greed of the landlord's new agent. Nevertheless, we entertain the feeling that the collapse is the fruit of cumulative change. Conditions have altered, the brewery needs new initiative and different supervision. Not only have the bonds of the family been sundered, but the bonds of the enterprise as well. Everything which had at the outset seemed to be firm and immutable since Creation, has come apart. An invisible hand has written on the wall of the brewery: "The end has come." The swindlers and all the rest of the speculators have been but the scourges of an angry fate.

The story, "The Brewery," is composed of consecutive

scenes and episodes which would not seem to be cast as one piece, but this is only on the surface. They are a single unit from which emerges, with gradual moderation, a highly suspenseful and mutable Jewish reality. It is this moderation on the part of the author, this narrative restraint, that is the secret of Barash's unique art. Just as Barash never sought to portray the great personages of the world nor the luminaries of nations, but caught in the snare of his vision the ordinary man, the small hero, so he made no attempt to depict climactic situations or world-shaking events. However, in Barash's hand, the mediocre person performing his role in the brewery and the seemingly ordinary situation become memorable, clear-cut figures functioning in devasting circumstances. This ordinary existence, which has no lofty mountains nor deep abysses, is enveloped in a warm, human aura, which touches the heart. Within it we sense the mystery beyond. The Brewery is a fine example of this.

Barash's style is neat, precise, without redundancies or belaboured linguistic mannerisms, but at the same time permeated with a lyric vitality. The garb of language is very closely fitted to the characters and the events. There is in it an inner rhythm. The poet in Barash can be sensed in this prose fiction as well.

Israel Cohen

Pictures from a Brewery

I

The Burning Bed

I shall begin with the story of Mrs. Aberdam — Mrs. Hanna Aberdam — lessee of the brewery in the little town of L. these thirty years or so (which means that she is an old woman by now). The full extent of her warm-hearted personality will not be evident from this story, but it will serve to sketch the environment within which she flourished. The rest will fall into place piece by piece.

This is the story as she told it in her unassuming way:

My father, may he rest in peace, was a rich man and one of the leading merchants in the little town of K. near Cracow, the capital, and a close follower of the Hassidic Rebbe of Belz. We had a house of ten rooms with a large yard, storerooms and cowsheds. I was the child of my father's old age and his love for me knew no bounds. There was nothing too fine or too expensive for his Hannele. And when the time came for me to wed, he journeyed to one of the largest yeshivas in Lithuania (he himself came of a Lithuanian family that had settled in Poland and embraced Hassidism) and there he picked me a bridegroom called Reb Shlomke, of blessed memory, a poor man though of great learning and piety. After the wedding, my husband came to live with my father, together with two other sons-in-law, husbands of my older sisters (my father had no sons), who were partners in his livestock and forestry businesses. From the

3

moment I set eyes on my husband's pale, gentle face, saw his large, honest eyes, and heard his modest, soft, sad way of speaking, my heart went out to him, to honour and love him with all my soul. He was, in my eyes, like a man of God whom I had been called upon to serve. Day and night he would sit alone in the room my father had allocated to him, studying the Torah in a sadly sweet and yearning chant. My whole life hung on this chant.

Five years went by. I had already borne him two daughters—Judith, who died while I was still a widow in my father's house and Brachele, the one who is with me now. The first few years, I helped around the house as I used to before my marriage (and I dislike being idle, as you know). But when the two little girls came into the world I devoted most of my time to them, like any other young mother that finds it a difficult and burdensome job to bring up children, and was no longer able to carry out all my housekeeping duties. Then my sisters, who were already burdened with families of their own, began to grumble and grouse as married sisters do when they live under the same roof. And suddenly the husbands began to get jealous too, though they were actually mild men by nature and honest merchants, and they began to rant and rail against my husband—at first in asides and afterwards openly—for eating without working, for consuming what they produced with the toil of body and soul. And complaints, as you know, are like the opening of flood-gates... At first my father would dismiss them with a rebuke, or calm them down by reasoning with them, taking care not to let what they were saying reach my husband's ears, for my father respected him and added to his collection of books whenever he had an opportunity, either with what he brought from Cracow or what he bought from book-pedlars who came to the town. "To me, he is like a Holy Ark in the house," he used to say. But as time went on, the complaints of my brothers-in-law grew more persistent. My father was beginning to age and the reins were getting a little slack in his hands, so he summoned my husband and spoke to him as follows:

"You are certainly aware, Reb Shlomke" (that's what they used to call him at home. Even my father addressed him that way) "that study without work leads to idleness and can end, God forbid, in sin. The time has come, in my opinion, for you to do something for your household. As you can see, I've grown old and I haven't the strength I used to have for business, and my sons-in-law are tired of carrying the burden of feeding you and your family. So my advice to you is that you take time off from your studies for some secular occupation. For *Who is righteous at all times? He who feeds his sons and daughters,*" and so on and so forth...

These words must have sorely grieved my late husband, whose sole desire was to study the holy books, but he didn't refuse, God forbid! He just asked my father to give him a few days to think it over. One morning, two days later, when he returned from his ritual bath at the mikveh, he called me to his room and asked me to tell my father the following: "Autumn is approaching and someone has to go abroad to buy oxen for fattening, just as we always do." (I wondered how he knew this, as he seemed to know nothing about our business, being always immersed in his Talmud.) "So let him give me five thousand roubles and I will go and bring him the number of oxen he requires." Having spoken, he removed his kerchief from the open Gemarrah and began to read in an unusually loud, clear voice, a voice that frightened me a little.

Naturally, I immediately told my father what he had said, word for word. Pandemonium broke loose in the house. Everyone was excited, maintaining that such a thing just wasn't possible. My brothers-in-law objected most of all, declaring that you can't entrust such an enormous sum to an inept idler, a *batlan* (it was the first time I had heard this derogatory term applied to my husband and I was shocked) who doesn't even know what a coin looks like and knows nothing about cattle, and they were certain that thieves and robbers would waylay him and take all the money from him; and even without thieves and robbers, there are the dangers of the road and he has to go through foreign lands and cities and he knows nothing about travel and doesn't know languages. His Talmud won't help him there. In short, they were worried about my father's money, which was as important to them as their own, and maybe they were even a little concerned for my husband's safety, who knows? My father, may he rest in peace, tried to calm them all down and suggested some other transaction to my husband, something easier, which involved less danger and less responsibility. I no longer remember what it was — but he turned stubborn and refused to budge. My father must make up his mind: either let him study in peace — or send him to buy the oxen. Then my father proposed that one of my brothers-in-law go with him to help him out on the way. He wouldn't agree to this either. He would go alone and buy alone and God would help him. What could man do for him?... My father finally understood that that was that, and then he too turned stubborn and informed my brothers-in-law that his mind was made up. He would send him on his own responsibility and if any mishap occurred, God forbid, and the money was lost he would bear the whole loss himself. And as for Reb Shlomke's personal safety, he has a pair of legs to stand on, thank God, is neither deaf nor simple-minded and is not a minor who needs a guardian.

In short, they had no alternative but to agree. So I began to prepare him for the journey. I mended his linen, cleaned and pressed his clothes, gave him his ritual garments to check (he had a scribe check his phylacteries), and on Saturday evening, I remember as if it were yesterday, Reb Shlomke set out in a waggon that took passengers to New Tzanz, to proceed from there through the mountain valleys to the foreign land from which they would bring the good oxen. We all saw him off to the waggon and my father fussed over him more than anyone else: he helped him into his fox-fur overcoat, pulled his Crimean fur hat down over his ears, and cautioned him about the packet of money in the leather purse strapped to him diagonally across one shoulder under his caftan. It was the beginning of Succoth. The roads had been damaged by the excessive rains that had fallen over the holidays (I remember we couldn't eat in the open Succah most of the time) and cold autumn winds were blowing. By all accounts, he needed five or six days to reach the market in B. for they had to use horses all the way (there wasn't a railway line in that country yet) — and two weeks for the journey back because of the slowness of the cattle and the many stops on the way. All in all, we reckoned he would be away for about three weeks, and if he was held up for any reason — another week, at the most; in short, we were prepared to wait for a month.

You can well imagine what I went through after my husband left. Although I knew very well that he wasn't due back yet, my heart was full of dread all the time and I remember that I hadn't a wink of sleep for nights on end. I tossed on my bed imagining all sorts of frightening things that grew worse from night to night. I controlled myself with all my might so as not to groan out loud and give my sisters satisfaction, for they had adopted their husbands' attitude, but my suffering was unbearable. I said to myself more than once: "Hanna, you silly fool. You know by now what kind of man he is and if he was so adamant it means he knew what he was doing." But everyone knows that reason cannot prevail over a fearful heart. At first, my brothers-in-law, who seemed to haunt the house from the day my husband left, kept mumbling and grumbling against my father between themselves (openly, they wouldn't dare show disrespect), but as the days went by they too fell silent and it was evident that they were growing uneasy and apprehensive, in self-reproach over some calamity for which they somehow felt responsible, although they could not have objected more than they did at the time. Even my father, with all his confidence, paced the house silently all the time, sometimes stroking his grey beard, or nervously chewing strands of it. The whole house was in a state of expectation, as if waiting for something that was to happen and no one dared conjecture what it was going to be. I felt as though I was a widow already, God save us! And when I looked at the children — the little one hadn't started to walk yet — my eyes filled with tears. I attended to them with infinite compassion and took care not to raise my voice to them. What frightened me most was my husband's empty study. When I went in there in the mornings to dust, I couldn't bear the sight of the books standing silent and forlorn in the cupboard and on the wall shelves that seemed to be gazing at me reproachfully.

Until one day — it was a Thursday afternoon as I recall, not quite three weeks since he left — above the sound of the wind and the pouring rain outside, we suddenly heard a cart draw up in front of our house. The wheels sounded different from those of the waggons that usually came to us. I rushed to the window, and through the pouring rain that pelted on the window-panes I saw my husband, Reb Shlomke, dismount from the cart wrapped in his overcoat, the one with the fox fur, that was all wet and shiny with the rain. My father happened not to be at home at the time. My brothers-in-law too had gone to a nearby village to collect some debt or other and were due back towards evening. I and Judith (Brachele was asleep in the bedroom), my mother (may she rest in peace) and my sisters and their children all rushed to the door and flung it open and — together with the wind and the rain that lashed our faces, in came my husband, the water streaming from his coat, from his fur hat, from his side-locks and from his beard, pale-faced and weary-eyed, his lips — I noticed — pressed tightly together as if in anger or deep grief. My heart pounded like a sledgehammer and I couldn't get a word out to ask about his journey. Only my sisters, who were very elated for some reason, bombarded him immediately with questions. *What? How? Did he buy? And why did he get back so soon? And where were the oxen?* And he, bless his memory, answered shortly: "In half an hour's time." He asked me to bring him some dry clothes. I handed the child, who was shivering with cold and excitement, to my sister and ran to the cupboard and brought him a clean shirt, underwear, a pair of white stockings and the blue

9

alpaca that he wore for his studies. I helped him remove his sopping-wet coat, which was difficult to lift because of the weight, and his caftan, and after changing the rest of his clothes in the bedroom·he went straight to his room, closed the door, and sat down to his chanting where he had left off, as if nothing had happened.

Treading carefully so as not to disturb him I brought him something to drink. I wanted to ask him how he was but I could see that he was engrossed in his books so that I shouldn't try to draw him into conversation. I put the glass down on a corner of the table and turned to slip away unobserved, when he called my name. I turned to him with a questioning look. He said:

"When Father gets back, be so kind as to tell him in my name that the good Lord has blessed my mission with success. The oxen, together with the travelling expenses, cost exactly the five thousand roubles that I received from him and all accounts are thereby settled between us. The profit he will make on this purchase will suffice to support us for several years and I am now exempted from any secular occupation. So from now on, I would ask him not to take me away from my studies, not even for an hour, not even for a minute."

When I went to the window afterwards to see if the cart was still standing in front of the house, it had vanished as if it had never been. But the clouds parted and a strip of clear blue sky showed through, and the rain which was still coming down heavily, glistened white in the sunlight as in summer and soon stopped altogether. The clouds dispersed and the sun shone down as it does in the days preceding Shavuot. It seemed like a miracle to me, for it had been raining steadily for two days and the wind hadn't died down for a single moment and the ground was covered with mud.

I busied myself with one thing and another, but before long I heard the voice of my eldest sister (she was holding Brachele who had woken up in the meantime) calling to me from the window:

"Hanna! Come and see. Here come the cattle. A whole herd of them!"

We all went outside and saw a large herd of reddish-grey long-horned oxen coming up the road, plodding along in the mud and splashing mire and water with their hooves; and the herdsmen dressed in sacks, barefooted, calling to them noisily and driving them with the long sticks that they carry. In a few minutes the oxen reached the house, where they were stopped by the herdsmen who quickly blocked the road before them. One of them, an undersized Jew, a midget of a man with a red beard and one blind eye, addressed himself to us and asked:

"Is this the house of Reb Elhana Bardash?"

"It is," we all answered in chorus.

We had barely managed to answer when my mother ran out in slippers into the mud in the yard (she was light-footed, bless her!) and opened the big gate and the little man ordered the herdsmen to drive the cattle into our large yard. After they drove all of them inside, we saw that there were some two hundred large, tall oxen, fearsome with their long, straight horns, a veritable forest of horns. We invited the Gentiles together with the Jew to come into the house and have something to drink. But the Jew said he was in a hurry to get going: he had to drive another herd twice as large as this to another town, and the cattle and their drivers were standing and waiting for him at the

wayside inn. He added, however, that if we would like
to give him and his men a little brandy and be so kind as
to bring it out to them, they would drink it standing and
go on their way, as they were in a hurry, a great hurry. He
repeated the last words several times, fixing us with his
one eye and smiling into his mustache as if he was con-
cealing something.

I hurried inside and brought out a bottle of brandy with
some glasses and some good egg *kuchen* that we always had
in the house, and offered them around. The Jew asked me
to serve the drivers first and they said "good health" in
their language as they raised their glasses and wished us
success in fattening the oxen. The Jew drank to our health
and added: "A toast to Reb Shlomke too!" That's exactly
what he called him. And that too struck me as a miracle.
My sisters, who stood beaming happily all the time, plied
him with questions: *Where were the cattle from? When and
how were they bought? How was the journey? Didn't any of
the animals fall, God forbid?*

The bizarre little stranger only smiled, his eye boring into
us, and answered briefly:

"Why the questions? Everything turned out for the best,
thank God, for the best."

He tucked the muddy ends of his capote into a rope around
his thighs, took up his knotty cane, said goodbye and went
off with his five goyim. As they went out of the gate, they
all turned and bowed: the Jew, I noticed, inclined his head
in the direction of my husband's room. Then he put his
hand through the hole, bolted the gate behind him and
disappeared the way he had come.

About half an hour later my father came home in his little
horse-and-trap together with my brothers-in-law whom he

had apparently met on the way. As they came along, they saw the hoofprints of the cattle and when they came nearer they caught sight of the enormous herd standing closely packed in the yard. My father paled; then his face suddenly began to glow. Even my brothers-in-law were pleased, though worsted. What a herd! What horns! My father jumped from the trap with an agility not at all in keeping with his years or his weight, and with shining eyes and outstretched arms he called out:

"Where is the *batlan*? Bring him here! I must see him at once. He must come at once!" — while my brothers-in-law ran into the yard to get a close view of the animals.

I called my father aside and told him what Reb Shlomke had said. But he dismissed it with a wave of the hand. Overjoyed, he ran into my husband's room. He came out a moment later shrugging his shoulders.

"Oh well, he doesn't want to talk — so he needn't. Let him keep his secret, the genius! The main thing is that he has outdone the professional merchants. He can put them all in his pocket!" And he too ran off to see the oxen.

In brief, my brothers-in-law (their jealousy notwithstanding), my father and other experts who came to see the marvel, were all of one opinion: the oxen were a wonderful bargain. If they were to sell them as they were they could make fifty percent on them without any difficulty. It was simply a gift from heaven. What a herd!

Next morning they sent the animals to the sheds near the distilleries and began to feed them up and they grew stronger and fatter from day to day.

But not so my poor husband (a thousand pardons for the comparison!). From the day he got back from his journey he changed very much for the worse. He cut himself off completely from the rest of the household and never left his room, except (excuse me!) to relieve himself or to go to the prayer-house. He avoided talking even with me and would pass by the babies without a glance, as if they were strangers, as if he didn't see them at all. On the Sabbath, at my father's table (on weekdays I brought his food and the water for washing his hands to his room), he would sit there sadly with his eyes closed, rocking lightly back and forth, humming over and over again some secret tune without words. And if anyone asked him a question he would rouse himself with a jolt and answer a startled "yes" or "no", but mostly he only nodded his head. It was evident that he didn't see the person addressing him at all. And as for me, my heart grew heavier and heavier as the days went by. The rest of the members of the household hardly noticed anything. Everyone was intoxicated with the successful business deal and my father was beside himself with happiness. He kept repeating the story of the oxen that had been bought for next to nothing and were now stuffing themselves and putting on flesh before his very eyes. All this, his unworthy *batlan* had done, the one that didn't seem to know what a coin looked like. *How was it? Tell me again about the little Jew with the red beard and the one blind eye* . . . 'Everything turned out for the best!' . . . *Ha! Ha! Ha! 'Why the questions?' 'It turned out for the best!' Ha! Ha! Ha!* He even buttonholed strangers, in fact anyone who came to the house, well-wisher or otherwise, and told them about the miracle that had happened to his *batlan*. He made up endless saws and proverbs, his face alight and shining with enthusiasm. My sisters stopped quarrelling and did a lot of frying and baking and tried to help me all the time and relieve me of the heavy work, as if I had suddenly become someone of importance. And my brothers-in-law, when at home, would sit down with pen and paper and make calculations, expatiating with relish on the profit expected from the cattle for them, the owners.

And I was the only one in the house who could take no part in all this rejoicing, for my heart, my poor heart, was heavy with foreboding. I saw my husband, his pale face growing longer and thinner every day, his blue alpaca hanging on him and the creases multiplying around the belt; only his dark eyes burning like the sacred flame, his hollow cheeks alarmingly red and flushed. His appetite deserted him entirely and he ate like a day-old chick. Only his voice, as he studied, grew stronger, more ecstatic, as if the ministering angels — as it were — were listening to him. And so it continued for several months. All the while, I felt so forsaken and alone, like a condemned woman moving amongst carefree strangers who are unaware of her thoughts and of what lies in store for her.

One hot summer night (the oxen had already been sold and with the money my father and my brothers-in-law had bought a large forest and the three of them were busy there setting up a saw-mill) I woke from a heavy dream — and there was a great light in the room like the blaze of a fire, God help us! I turned my head to my husband's bed against the opposite wall. The whole thing was in flames, real flames. A bright silent wall of fire surrounded it, rising to the ceiling, and through the fire I saw my husband lying stretched out under the sheet, limbs extended, eyes open, his face peaceful, soft and smiling in the great light. The fear of God came over me and I began to cry out in a voice I didn't recognise as my own: "*Shalom,*

Shalom! What's the matter with you, Shlomke!'' He raised himself slightly and answered me in a voice that was both annoyed and soothing at the same time.

"Nothing, Hanna, nothing. You've been dreaming. Go back to sleep. It's nothing."

And indeed, in a moment, the fire went out and it was dark in the room, the darkness after a great light, a light not of this world. As you can imagine, I didn't close my eyes again that night. All kinds of weird thoughts kept running through my mind, and I kept seeing the picture of the bush that burned in the wilderness and was not consumed; and it seemed to me that I could hear from far away a voice calling from within the bush, not *Moses, Moses!* but *Shalom, Shalom!* I don't quite know how to say it, but I seemed to feel two different things at once (I don't know myself what possessed me!): a sort of deadly fear and a sort of sublime joy, a joy not of this world. I covered my face with my pillow and prayed, the tears streaming down my cheeks: "God in heaven, don't take my most precious possession away from me. Don't take him from me as you took Enoch in the Bible. Oh Lord, oh Lord! why didn't you strike me with blindness so that I should see nothing? Why did you wake me from my sleep? Why was it given to me, a simple sinful woman, to see this? What will happen now? What is the meaning of this vision?" And I went on praying and crying, controlled myself, then cried and prayed again — till morning.

And when in the morning I tip-toed up to his room, the Torah room, and listened at the closed door, I heard groaning, subdued but heartrending. And when I went in, almost paralyzed with fright, I found him sitting at the table, his head on the open Gemarrah, and burning with fever with his eyes turned up, God help me! I alerted the frightened household with my cries. They came and took him to the bedroom and laid him on his bed, the bed that burned in the night. We quickly summoned Reb Yossel Schoub to whisper to him. In time of trouble, he always used to come and whisper. After that the "healer" came and then the doctor. They brought ice, they cupped him, they bled him, they applied mustard poultices — nothing helped. His doom was sealed.

At twilight he delivered up his pure soul. Like Enoch "...he was no more, for God had taken him."

The Brewery Establishment

C ount Stefan Molodetzki, scion of the Zamoiski family, lives in Paris, capital of the world, and his estates, which extend over one eighth of the area of East Galicia, are ruled over and managed by agents. Most of the estates are leased to Jews, the rest being worked by Ruthenian villagers who appear to love their masters but in their heart of hearts are waiting for their downfall and are prepared to help it along when the time is ripe. The Count himself comes once every two or three years to make the round of his property, to hunt in his forests with a party of friends and participate with them in a royal feast which his sycophantic agents prepare in his honour — the rest of the time he is busy squandering his vast income, in Paris. But when he dies (he is a confirmed bachelor who leads a wild life, rides like a madman, and will certainly suffer an apoplectic fit one day), they will bring him embalmed and disembowelled in an expensive glass coffin and lay him to eternal rest in the tomb of his fathers next to the ancient monastery in the little town of L., as they have done for generations.

The little town of L. is the most important of the Count's estates. In the palace, splendid still in its semi-ruined state, sits the head agent, Pan Grabinski who lives like a vice-regent. He is a noble and courtly gentleman, kind to all under his patronage. Apart from his wife and three grown daughters, he has several sisters and sisters-in-law living with him. They are all advanced in years, and they go riding on fine horses through the town and its environs. The lands are all worked by farm-labourers under a sort of feudal tenancy and the distilleries and the brewery are rented out to Jews: the distillery to the old skin-flint Reb Aryeh Leibush, and the brewery to the gracious Mrs. Hanna Aberdam, the heroine of this story.

The little town of L. (a small Jewish community dwells in the centre of it like the tiny mite of cheese in the middle of a poor man's big potato pancake) is surrounded by cultivated fields, grassy meadows, and dense forests growing up the hillsides and down into the valleys, to gladden the eye of the beholder. Beyond the Sabbath limit, near the swamp, runs a swift stream which, as it passes the bridge, turns the three wheels of the flour-mill leased by little Reb Michele. With its houses set apart from one another, its shady green trees and blooming gardens, it looks more like a country village. In the middle of the town, there is a large stretch of water, like a dividing zone between the circular shopping area (the "Ring" as it is called) which is tenanted exclusively by devout Jews, and the bath-house quarter where there is a mixed population of Jews and Gentiles. It is a fragrant lake with hidden springs, tucked away among reeds and weeping willows, fenced around with thin strips of wood, and swarming with the choicest fish that have been brought there for breeding purposes from rivers far away. A special expert has been appointed to take care of their food-supply and breeding. Officially, fishing in the lake is forbidden except on days when the Count is there and the fish are needed for the dinner table when he is entertaining. But actually, the palace officials send servants out every Sabbath with rods and nets to do a little fishing (the overseer purposely goes to sleep in the warm drying-house), and the fat, thrashing carp with the golden striped scales are afterwards shared out among the officials according to their rank. But the more experienced servants hold back a number of good specimens, hiding them in their high boots, and later exchange them with the Jews for brandy steeped in wormwood or a glass of strong rum, and it is well known that there is no fish anywhere in the neighbourhood like the Sabbath fish of the Jews of L.

On the shore of the lake, to the left, rises a multi-storeyed structure like a tower, known as the drying-house, where they dry the husks of the fruit and take out the seeds for replanting in areas where the trees have become depleted. Beside it, there is a road leading to the distillery with its large cowsheds. The building rises up in the distance at the far end of the lake recognizable by its red roof and enormous chimney-stack. On the right of the lake, beyond the wide, well-trodden dirt road and the mighty avenue of chestnut trees that cast a perpetual shadow on the wooden sidewalk that has rotted in many places, stands a long, ancient building with a wall around it, like a fortress. A large wing projects at right angles from one end of it, in such a way as to form an 'L'. Inside the 'L' there is a big courtyard always bustling with activity and movement. Wood-piles, tubs, barrels, iron hoops, plugs, wood-shavings, heaps of barley and hops — compel the labourers to zig-zag through it all or go around, thereby adding even more to the bustling scene. Opposite the main building, the whole length of the yard, there is a fenced-off vegetable garden on about a hectare of land, and beyond the vegetable garden there are more buildings: wooden outhouses, cowsheds and a stable; building next to building, shed after shed.

This structure is an ancient brewery which is not particularly noted for the quality of its brew. On the contrary, the light beer produced there sometimes has a slightly bitter taste, but as it is sold cheaply and as there is no other brewery for miles around and as the roads are bad and as Gentile throats hate being dry, the brewery has to work at full capacity almost every day except during Lent when strong drink is forbidden. Then they only brew once or twice a week. And Saturdays and holidays of both religions, they lay off work altogether.

Next to the brewery, on the garden side, there is a little villa. There Pan Yashinski the forester lives, with his family. A very refined family, as I shall describe later.

All three large business establishments that embrace the lake in a triangle, draw their essential water from its gushing springs in thick pipes: the first, during a few months in the summer; the second only in the winter months; and the last, as mentioned above, most days of the year.

The traffic, the bustle of work, and the noise of wheels coming and going fill the air of the brewery yard and its environs up to the bath-house quarter on the one side and the Ring on the other. The smell of malt cooking, a warm smell, sweet and satisfying, pervades the whole town on brewing days. The Jews dilate their nostrils and inhale it with relish. *Ah, it's good!* Afterwards, they send the little children accompanied by the bigger ones, carrying jugs and flasks, to get some of the warm malt brew which they call *menthe*, or — in the language of the German brewer — *wirze*. They drink their fill and make the rest into a kind of honey to flavour babies' food. Mrs. Aberdam, lessee of the brewery, has given Reb Israel Elia, the trustee, instructions to fill the vessel free of charge once a week for any Jew that asks, and this rule has to be strictly observed. The pollen of the hops, the main condiment of the beer, carries quite a distance in the air and often makes passers-by sneeze. But no one minds. On the contrary, it is generally believed that this sneezing is good for the health. *A — tshoo! A — tshoo!. Long life to Mrs. Aberdam! She is a mother to big and small.*

An old cooper, one of the Gentile heroes, stands outside at the work-bench with his two stalwart sons, a coarse linen apron around him. Bare-armed, they saw and plane, mend and fasten hoops all day, and their big wooden mallets beat on the empty barrels, producing a booming, ear-splitting sound; but the people in the town are used to this too, and nobody is disturbed by it. Along the garden fence, inside the yard, there are rows of oaken barrel-staves and new bases propped up one against the other, so arranged as to dry well in the wind to prevent the barrels from cracking afterwards. Vanka, a short, bald Gentile, red-eyed from too much drinking, stands there bent over, pulling plugs out of the empty barrels with an implement specially made for the purpose. Every plug he extracts makes a noise like a shot. Five or six labourers groan and curse raucously as they roll full and empty barrels back and forth: from the waggons to the brewery, from the brewery to the ice-house, and from the ice-house back to the waggons waiting to be loaded, their horses tethered to the rear of the waggon champing fodder out of tripods as at Fair-time. A short, stocky Jew with a reddish greying beard, red neck and red eyes (possibly from drinking), Reb Israel Elia the "bailiff" — called Srael by the labourers — moves around among them, swinging a heavy bunch of keys with an authoritative air. He peers at the waggons and counts the loaded barrels; he lifts up the hay and pokes around to see if the goy or even the tax-gatherer himself has not hidden something away "by mistake". If he finds anything he calmly removes it — sometimes even without the knowledge of the pilferer — as if it were a matter of course and no reason for surprise.

Next to the ice-house in the angle of the 'L', up to the part beneath Mrs. Aberdam's apartment, runs a sort of high cellar. This is where the malt is made. A huge hall with rough columns, always warm and damp. A spiral staircase leads up from it to the drying-tower consisting of several storeys. The smell of the drying grain and the slightly scorched seedlings rises from there like the smell of tobacco. In the brewery itself, that dark, dank building which you enter by going down a few wooden steps, three different noises are being produced simultaneously: the noise of the large wooden wheels revolving on ratchets and belts; the noise of the fire crackling in the giant furnace that lies at the bottom of the building and looks like a flaming scene out of Hell and the bubbling noise from the huge copper vat called the "shooter", which straddles the furnace and is reached by means of a straight iron ladder fastened to the side. Wooden vats as wide as pools stand under a deck suspended on poles which is the "cooling basin". Some of the vats are filled with water which looks black in the gloom, with a cold and baleful gleam on the surface; others contain a strong concoction that bubbles and effervesces all the time, with scum floating on the surface. Heaps of red, damp wood-shavings lie on the cold, stone floor; leather straps and ropes are stretched from wheel to wheel; and heavy, iron-studded doors lead to dark recesses and cellars, deep down and frightening, which no stranger may enter.

About twenty permanent employees work there, sturdy peasants with fair skins, wearing linen shirts fastened over their hips with a broad leather belt. In charge of them is Herr Lieber the brewer, with the bristling mustaches that stand out straight on either side like a pair of horns. When the brewing is in process, he clambers up the iron steps every few minutes to the "shooter", draws a little of the brew in a large ladle, pours it into a long glass tube and, closing one eye, holds it up to the light that comes through the space between the suspended roof and the walls. He dips his little finger in and takes a lick in order to test the taste of the brew, the *menthe*. Suddenly he gives a mighty shout, with an answering echo from the vats, the barrels, the niches and the cellars, the hollow ceiling and the cooling basin: "Quench the fire!"

Everyone starts running. Out in the yard, the workers stop what they are doing and stand still as if expecting some great event. After a moment or two the voice bellows again: "Raise the lock!"

All at once the whole brewery is filled with a white vapour, warm and heavy, which wafts up from the cooling basin area, forcing its way out in swirling columns through the gap between the walls and the roof. Through the thickness of the cloud can be heard voices calling, the clatter of feet, wheels turning, hammers pounding and the sound of running liquid — a mixed hubbub.

The brewing is now finished and the malt has been set to cool. The aroma carries far and wide and men, women and children begin to stream towards the brewery with their jugs and jars.

That is when Mrs. Aberdam's husband orders the windows to be closed. He is a sick man and the vapour makes it difficult for him to breathe.

III

Mrs. Hanna Aberdam and her Household

I n the wing of the building are located the living quarters of most of the brewery people. Next to the angle of the 'L', in a perpetual shadow, a few stone steps lead between two crooked old bushes, to the apartment of the owner of the business, Mrs. Hanna Aberdam.

How did she get here?

After losing her saintly first husband, she stayed on in her father's house for about five years while he was still alive and for two years after his death. Then a proposition was put to her to marry the childless widower, Reb Naftali Zvi Aberdam, a worthy shopkeeper in a distant town of East Galicia, and having no other course she reconciled herself to marrying him.

When her father died, it transpired that his various businesses had declined in his latter years (there was a firm belief in the household that this collapse was somehow connected with the tragedy of Reb Shlomke). What was left would just be sufficient to cover the debts. The brothers-in-law parted company and each went into business on his own, with a good deal of effort but little success. Then she, the young widow, also tried to do business in a small way to keep herself, her old mother (who refused to be separated from her) and her little daughter Brachele, who was all she had left after the elder daughter, Judith, had died of the

27

croup; but she had little to show for her work. She couldn't compete with the other energetic and enterprising shopkeepers. So she decided, after giving the matter considerable thought, that she would remarry. She wanted someone respected and well-to-do, learned and religious, even if a little elderly, in whose home she would find a haven for herself and her only child, and be able to devote her time to prayer and charitable work, so as not to have to meet her first husband in the world to come "with empty hands". Throughout the years following his death, it always seemed to her that she was not worthy of him and had to improve herself through good deeds so that he should not be ashamed of her when the time came for her to leave this transitory world. In the hidden recesses of her heart she was still with him and he filled her whole world. Whatever she decided to do here in the interim was just a temporary necessity dictated by circumstances.

The matchmaker, who was a Belze Hassid and one of her late father's acquaintances, described the 'groom' (how strange and offensive the word seemed!) as a well-established storekeeper comfortably provided for, a good Hassid even if he had Husiatinic leanings, a scholarly and God-fearing Jew. But when she came there she saw immediately that there had been some tampering with the facts; the shop, a grocery-store, was very small and the shelves poorly stocked. The turnover was slight and depended on the season, and the season depended on the situation of the farmers in the region; there were many debts; and Reb Naftali Zvi himself—a childless widower, pleasant-looking and honest though made of ordinary stuff, a bit of a glutton, ineffectual in business and given over entirely to continual prayer, to dabbling in the lighter parts of the Talmud, and to carving religious ornaments, a labour of love that absorbed him for hours on end. Nevertheless, she accepted it all dutifully and no word of complaint passed her lips. And she honoured and respected her second husband with all her heart, as behove a good daughter of Israel. Her mother had to remain behind with the eldest sister, where she died two years later, and Brachele, who was dearer to her than anything else in life, stayed with her. She regarded her as a sort of brand rescued from the burning pillar of fire of her late husband and therefore treated her like some sacred vessel.

After some time, Reb Naftali's business declined even further because of a Russian Jewish refugee called Spodik, a stutterer, as cunning as a serpent and greedy for gain, who came and opened a store just like theirs right next door and sold at cut prices giving credit right and left, to the amusement of the older so-called "experienced" shop-keepers. But it soon became apparent that he had out-smarted them all, for he drew most of the customers away from them and did a lively trade. Reb Naftali did not apply his mind to improving his position in any way because he was stolid and imperturbable by nature, and from the day he remarried and saw what a strong personality his wife was, he was content to leave everything to her provided he got his meals on time, could go to the prayer-house every morning and every evening, sleep in the afternoons, and carry on with his carving. He saw right away that this was not a woman who would pester the life out of him with her complaints and her grousing as his first wife did. And Hanna saw that it was decreed from Heaven that she would have to take care of their needs, not just their bodily needs but also the spiritual side of things — the charities and other

good works without which life was no life. She developed
an energy and enterprise in commercial matters that
amazed even her at first and she began to try her hand at
various small business deals without succeeding at any of
them, as if a curse (Heaven forbid!) lay on everything she
did. So she went to see the Zaddik of Belz with all kinds
of complaints and demands, on the strength of her late
father's close association with him, and he advised her to
rent the derelict brewery in her town (how he knew that
such a thing existed there remains a mystery to this day).
She sold the shop and the jewellery she brought from home
and also borrowed a certain sum of money and rented the
brewery. From then on, suddenly, success came her way,
and the load was lifted entirely from Reb Naftali Zvi for
the rest of his days, like a man who wins a lottery and is
henceforth free to do whatever he likes.

As the years went by, his copious beard grew white (he
was ten years older than his wife) and he took to wearing
an expensive robe on weekdays as well as on the Sabbath.
A satin sash as thick as a towel girds his waist and the
fringes of his ritual garments seem to caress him lovingly.
His striped trousers are tied close to the knee and his thin
legs are encased in white stockings and soft woollen
embroidered slippers. He himself is a Hassid of the Husiatinic sect but as he is loath to face the inconveniences of
the long journey he has to make to visit his own rebbe, he
goes with his wife on her pilgrimages to Belz twice a year
and just pays his dues (for his own rebbe) once a year to
Reb Hirschel Merubeh. He spends all his days in a spacious
room, specially set aside for him, smoking a long pipe and
reading (he has recently bought from an itinerant book-
seller a number of books on ethics and sermons which he

30

only half understands). Or else he makes holy ornaments in the form of wood-carvings or paper cut-outs for the house or for the prayer-room on the premises. When he passes through the yard on his way to relieve himself, his pipe goes with him and gives him an air of venerableness and distinction. But in the affairs of the brewery he is a complete ignoramus and takes no part in it at all, as if it is no concern of his. The general impression is that of a pleasantly painted, finely moulded household vessel placed there for decoration, not for use. Early every morning, after washing his hands, he drinks a glass of cold water, a proven remedy for constipation and other abdominal ailments, on the advice of Reb Aron Schoub who is an expert on medical matters. After that, before prayers, he sits and recites a number of psalms and daily selections from the Bible, Mishnah and Talmud, while his wife is busy outside with the staff. That is his daily routine. Hanna is the one who supervises the entire running of the brewery. Everything hangs on her word. She is about fifty by now, but she is by no means old: her carriage is erect, her face smooth and unwrinkled and she is a picture of energy and efficiency. In her clear, steady eyes there is still a youthful sparkle, a freshness that is to be found in the pure of heart or the strong in will. Although she has already been living in East Galicia for about twenty years, she has not entirely cast off her West Galician ways: she still speaks a sing-song kind of Yiddish interspersed with words peculiar to West Galicia — the heart of Poland. Not because she is trying to put on airs, but simply from force of habit. This too gives her added importance in the eyes of her acquaintances, because people are impressed with anything foreign. Every Saturday evening, when the

Havdalah service has marked the end of the Sabbath and the workmen have been paid, she closets herself for hours with the accountant, Reb Simha, to go over the books and he, smart lazy fellow that he is, pretends to listen to everything she says and defers to her opinion as to that of an expert in accountancy, whereas in actual fact he knows just how far her so-called knowledge goes of what is contained in the pages covered with his fine, round handwriting; except that here and there her phenomenal memory produces support for some figure or other and helps her maintain the impression that she is actually checking. For the main part, this inspection is just a put-on show, enabling her to go through the motions required of the head of the concern, for she has complete faith in Reb Simha, a confidence based on instinct and experience. And he, for his part, doesn't mind being put through this fictitious inspection as his conscience is perfectly clear. For miles around, Mrs. Aberdam is known for her unparalleled ability, charity and hospitality. Beggars and vagrants, people of standing, public-spirited women collecting for indigent brides, and such like come flocking to her, eat and sleep in her house, and avail themselves generously of the contents of her cash-box. The cash-box never empties, and she firmly believes that there is a charm on it, first of all because it has been blessed by the Zaddik of Belz; and secondly, because of her own good deeds; and also — she fervently believes — thanks to her daughter, Brachele, who is the image of her late father. Two large rooms in her apartment have been set aside for accommodating guests for the night, and in them are ten comfortable, solid straw mattresses with good, soft featherbeds — fit for the rich.

Besides the two guest bedrooms which are not for use when there are no guests, there are three other large rooms in the apartment in which she and her husband live but they still seem half empty. There are several old, massive pieces of expensive furniture in them which she bought from the previous occupant, but in their bare, solid bulk they seem to be part and parcel of the thick, grey stone walls. It is all made of heavy, dark oak and when they have to move a piece of furniture from its place to clean the house before the holidays it takes four hefty labourers to do it, with a lot of perspiring and grunting.

So, too, the small items: the pitcher on the ledge in the vestibule, beside the tub of water covered with a wooden board, is made of copper lined with tin and weighs a couple of pounds; a big Russian samovar made of nickel (a family heirloom dating back several generations) reposes on a small, marble-topped table; an enormous mortar stands on a wide cupboard occupying half the wall and seeming to threaten passers-by with its sloping pestle; copper pots of all sizes line the top of the entire wall in the dining room, apart from those in the kitchen for everyday use; a high-topped ornamental clock with heavy, polished weights, hangs on the wall between two windows, ticking quietly away with measured beat; even the cloths on the tables and the blankets on the beds are of such imposing weight and thickness that anyone who sees them is struck speechless with awe and wide-eyed wonder.

The rooms are divided up in the following way: from the steps we enter a wide vestibule where, as I have mentioned before, there stands the barrel of water with the jug and basin on the shelf for washing hands (from time to time, Mrs. Aberdam checks to see that the rim isn't chipped) and a towel hangs on a wooden peg above it. On the right there are two doors, one leading to the spare bedrooms and the other to the kitchen, the domain of Pearl, their cook; and on the left there is a door leading into a large room, which is the dining-room, from which there is a door to their bedroom, and only after that comes Reb Naftali Zvi's own room, the room specially set aside for him so as not to disturb his rest. In the dining-room and in Reb Naftali Zvi's room there are wide, cool sofas upholstered in black leather. The rooms are cool in the summer and warm in the winter, so that the people in the business like to come in sometimes for a chat over a glass of tea with some good biscuits, or simply to sit there for a while. And although Reb Naftali Zvi's room is far away and well insulated against sound, Mrs. Aberdam asks visitors to speak in a whisper lest their voices reach her husband's room and distract him from his studies. In asking this, she has the pleasant feeling that in spite of everything there is someone who sits aparts from the rest of the world, occupied with the Torah — something like it was then...

This world and the world to come are not entirely separate domains, after all.

IV

Brachele and her Husband

A t the end of the wing that touches the garden fence (the entrance to the garden lies in the shade of a thick chestnut tree) live Brachele and her husband.

Brachele, a perpetual source of pride and anxiety to Mrs. Aberdam, is the exact opposite of her mother: delicate, reticent and of melancholy disposition. Her skin is amazingly fine and white and the women of the town ardently declare that one can no more look into her face (touch wood!) than into the face of the sun. Her eyes, in which wonder alternates with fear, are large and black; so are her eyebrows which meet prettily over the top of her finely-chiselled nose with its narrow nostrils. The contrast between the whiteness of her skin, tinged with a faint flush like the bloom of certain exotic fruits, and her black eyes and eyebrows has a strange effect on people who see her for the first time, arousing neither warmth nor a feeling of attraction, but surprise and a certain excitement — as if she were something unreal.

Years ago, when she was a young girl, she had a mass of beautifully braided hair which reached below her waist, black hair soft and shining as if it was always oiled. Her forehead was straight and smooth, covered by her tresses only at the corners, where her hair draped charmingly over her ears, with only the tips of the unadorned pink lobes of her ears showing. When she came with her mother from the magic distances she was about ten years old, delicate and small for her age, and her arrival was an event that brought radiance into the busy though humdrum and colourless lives of the children of the town. She did not mix with them and was to be seen in the street only in the company of her mother, as if a little afraid, but the thoughts of the children always turned to the miracle in their midst, first in the town itself in Reb Naftali Zvi's house, and later a distance away in the wing of the brewery. She was woven into their thoughts and their meditations like some angelic creature who had come from heaven to scatter radiance and enchantment. But old and young alike watched her development with considerable uneasiness, and even after she grew up the feeling still persisted with many of them.

The day she turned eighteen (it was a spring day full of sunshine, the birds were singing, the brewery rested from its labours and the chestnut trees were laden with heavy clusters of flowers) Mrs. Aberdam remarked to her husband after breakfast (Brachele had been sent to Henche the hunchback for an embroidery lesson), as she ran her fingers up and down the tablecloth:

"The time has come for our Brachele to marry. The son of the Rabbi of Radichov has been suggested."

Reb Naftali Zvi, who had finished reciting grace and had already lit his pipe, answered between puffs without removing it from the corner of his mouth:

"How old is she, did you say? Eighteen? It is written that a boy should marry at eighteen; from this we may learn that a girl should too, *puff-puff*... Very well, let's have a wedding feast, *puff-puff*."

36

And he got up to leave the room, all flushed, with his skullcap askew. He was satisfied that everything would be taken proper care of and he could take his half-hour nap as he did every day.

Six months later, at the beginning of the winter, with great pomp and ceremony Brachele was married to Hirtzel Pallan, a boy her own age (a question was raised as to the possibility of an objection because of the similarity of the names of the groom and the stepfather-in-law, but the Zaddik of Belz gave his permission at once). He was the son of the Rabbi of nearby Radichov, a sturdy, good-looking young man who had been redeemed from military service by payment of a large sum of money; a bit of a student and a good mixer. After his marriage he gave up studying the Torah altogether, and devoted his time to the wood and produce business with a good measure of success. The morning after the wedding, the aunts of the groom, resplendent in all their jewellery, cut off the bride's hair. They were a bit nervous before the shearing, but she did not refuse to let them do it nor did she cry, as Jewish brides with lovely hair usually do. Only the sparkle in her eyes died a little and the sadness in them deepened and she stopped singing to herself as she used to do as a girl. She loved her handsome, charming husband in a quiet, restrained sort of way, part admiration part gratitude (for what, no one knows), but in front of people and even in front of her mother she put on an air of indifference and mentioned him only rarely, as she might talk of someone akin to her whom she respected. And he on his part, whose moral stature and sensitivity became more and more apparent every day, treated her with care and fatherly affection to a point of courtly tenderness. He did not call

37

her by any names of endearment, but when he asked her for anything he never failed to add the words: "If you would be so kind..." or "If you'll forgive me..." And when she did what he asked, he would bestow on her a long look full of feeling. He absolutely forbade her to do any tiring work around the house, and the brewery workers who feasted their eyes on her in silent admiration from afar when she passed through the yard, used to vie with one another to perform some service for her. Her frail build, her rhythmic gait and the transparency of her face aroused in them some deep humanity which had to find an outlet.

The first few months after their marriage, Hirtzel would sometimes be perturbed by her appearance, and pick her up and carry her from room to room in his arms like a baby. She would lie close up against him but never made a move to put her arms around him. He began to sense that she was not happy. As time went on, when he was away on business, for the first day or two he had a feeling that he was more at ease away from her, but after a few days an urgent need would come over him to go back and be with her. She began to frighten him. He tried to get her to open her heart to him by speaking to her, but after the first few unsuccessful attempts he left her alone. On moonlight nights he would sometimes wake up, lift his head from the pillow, and gaze at her sadly; also in the mornings, while she still slept and her breathing was so light as to be almost inaudible. The barrier between these two remained there day and night, very thin and very cruel.

Bracha couldn't endure the chatter of the ladies who came to the place every day to make up to her mother and dip into her coffers for their charities; and the sight of the bustling activity and all the traffic in the yard made her feel weak and slightly dizzy, so she used to shut herself up at home most of the day and busy herself there with arranging her fully-stocked linen cupboard, wiping the dust off her handsome furniture with a fine, clean cloth, or sitting at the window that overlooked the garden embroidering in silk and satin with her long, transparent fingers, the way the hunchbacked seamstress had taught her. But sometimes the "work" would suddenly slip from her fingers and she would sit there motionless, gazing idly with veiled eyes across the yard and the houses, the hills and the fields, and the woods shimmering in a blue haze at the edge of the sky. She sits listening, then, to the hidden springs of her heart, like the gushing springs on the bed of the lake that lies at the foot of the brewery. The curator of the lake has given her permission (and a key) to come inside the fence any time she likes and stroll along the edge of the water. And on summer mornings, when her husband, Hirtzel, is not at home, she walks there alone in a light frock, bending as she passes under the willow branches, holding on to them as she skips over the pebbles washed by the tepid water, lifting her long skirt with one hand; or else she sits on a stone or a tree-stump in the high grass, watching the fish at play in the water. This behaviour, her remoteness and her aloofness, could have made many people suspect that she was haughty, but her gentle expression and her shy voice immediately obliterated any such thought.

Her apartment, too, is altogether different from her mother's. Her rooms are small, light (she sees to it that they are whitewashed three times a year) and almost square. About two years after they were married, after a transaction that brought in a handsome profit, Hirtzel Pallan went himself to the capital, Lwow, stayed there a week, and came back with three vans full of furniture packed in straw. Some curious villagers who came to the yard to see the wonders from the city, gathered around the goods, fingered them cautiously, passed their hands over the lacquer, made wild guesses at the price and argued among themselves over the kind of wood, but when Brachele came out of the house they grew abashed and made off one by one. A few of the labourers, under the supervision of Reb Israel Elia, the bailiff, moved the old furniture out of the house (it was distributed free among the brewery workers) and put in the new; but the arranging of it was done by Reb Hirtzel himself in accordance with Bracha's taste and wishes. It was then that she displayed an animation and energy most unusual for her. When she finished arranging the furniture, the rooms were laid out in the following way:

The bedroom was all white: a wide linen cupboard with two doors on either side and a chest of drawers in the middle; white wooden beds with pretty night-tables; a white quilted couch, small and dainty, and on it an embroidered mat, narrow and very delicate, which was called a "runner"; a washstand with a marble top and a polished mirror at the head; a few lovely landscapes in white wooden frames; and on the three windows, white woven curtains reaching down to the scrubbed floor boards, yellow as the yolk of an egg. Besides all this, there were two tall, slender pedestals with ornate flower-pots, one in each corner. The sitting-room was dark green plush: two sofas, one big and one small, three carved, upholstered chairs at a round table covered with a heavy, velvet cloth, heavy drapes on the walls, pictures in olive-wood frames, a three-tiered plant stand and an expensive lamp hanging from the ceiling in a bluish sheath transparent as a cloud at sunset. And in the dining-room: a brown leather sofa, a wide, carved cabinet of superb craftsmanship, full of gold and silver-ware, a large table with six heavy-backed chairs, a clock in a case and a bronze standard lamp.

After the rooms had been furnished in this way, a different mood came over Bracha. She felt that only now had she come into an atmosphere congenial to her. More than anything else, she loved the white bedroom where every-thing was so light and pure and gay in its place. Especially when the windows were open and the breeze made the light curtains billow into the sunny air of the room with their copper rings tinkling, and flicked them lightly over the ends of the gleaming beds. Her heart was so full of gratitude to her husband that on several occasions she could not contain herself, opened the cupboard, buried her face in his Sabbath caftan and wept silently into it. But Hirtzel knew nothing about this.

In addition to all the furniture, Pallan also brought a complete set of kitchen utensils and tableware, but those were redundant for the time being and served only as ornaments as they both ate with the old people at Mrs. Aberdam's insistence.

When Reb Hirtzel negotiated with the Polish squires in the vicinity his clothes were always clean and well pressed, his sidecurls and beard neatly combed. He always behaved with decorum and politeness and spoke a good, fluent Polish (when he lived with his father, the Rabbi, before his marriage, he paid great attention to his dress and his speech and acted as interpreter for all the Jews who received "documents" from the authorities). He was extremely well-liked and respected by them and they pressed all kinds of gifts on him. In this way he received from a certain Graf, a renowned huntsman, a pair of superbly-branched deer-antlers mounted on costly wooden boards, and they hang on the sitting-room wall. Another gentleman gave him a fine wolf-skin, and it lies at the foot of Brachele's bed. Once he bought a forest from a wealthy Bishop, and the old priest took such a liking to him that he gave him as a gift a large portrait of himself in his ceremonial robes, in a heavy gilt frame, with an inscription and a dedication at the bottom in his own handwriting. This picture hangs in the sitting-room. And if some Jew happens to look inside by chance, he recoils in amazement, but Reb Hirtzel smiles and says: "I shall respect those who respect me. As he gave me his portrait, that means he would like it to hang in my home and I am obliged to give him the satisfaction. Like the antlers that Graf Uyeski gave me, this is not a living object and just serves as a decoration."

And no one dares argue with Reb Hirtzel. He is a good Jew who knows his Torah, a successful and charitable man, and if he has any faults — his wealth atones for them. With the rich, one is not so particular; and also Mrs. Aberdam's standing comes in useful.

Reb Hirtzel is away most of the time because of his many business dealings, so Brachele sleeps the night sharing the same bed with her mother, as she used to do when she was a child, and nestles up to her as if she is still a little girl. Next morning, she spends several hours out in the open, strolling along the edge of the lake on the road to the distilleries. At such times her apartment is closed up, and in the slumbering rooms which now look like a furniture storeroom, orderly and abandoned, all one can hear is the ticking of the clock, a forlorn, anxious kind of ticking, and a lone fly, hungry and desperate, buzzing endlessly away at it, to no purpose and to no avail.

Perhaps an infant could revitalize the somnolent atmosphere, but several years have gone by and Bracha is still childless, to the sorrow of her husband and her mother.

V

Israel Elia the Bailiff and his Good wife

I srael Elia, or Srael as the Gentile labourers call him, is a distant relative of Reb Naftali Zvi, and immediately after he married Sosele, the orphan, Mrs. Aberdam appointed him "bailiff" of the brewery, a position which she had filled herself till then. He was put in charge of everything: barley, malt, hops, wood, ice, barrels and the finished brew. And he is, indeed, wholeheartedly dedicated to his work — diligent, energetic, running from storeroom to storeroom, his heavy bunch of keys rattling importantly in his hand, reprimanding and scolding the workers with and without reason. If he thinks someone is not doing a job exactly the way it should be, he throws the keys on the ground, snatches the tool from the man's hand, pushes him aside, and works at it himself for a moment with a speed and a zest as if to say: "See, this is the way we work here." It happened more than once that he struck a labourer across the face, or a waggoner from the outside who was caught stealing, and afterwards got agitated and confused and dashed from the place as if it were he who had been hit.

He is a simple man: apart from a few chapters of the Psalms learned by heart, a hastily mumbled prayer and going over the weekly portion of the Law, he has no learning to speak of. But his memory in worldly matters is phenomenal. He always knows exactly the number of full and empty barrels, the weight of barley and hops, the quantity of wood and plugs, although he never writes anything down. Like Mrs. Aberdam, his strongest point is his memory. And since he regards himself as a relative of the owners of the business (he is the only one who sometimes refers to the brewery by Reb Naftali Zvi's name), he performs his job very strictly and irascibly. He watches every penny and takes the careless and the negligent to task just as if the place belonged to him, with the result that he is thoroughly hated by all the brewery employees, from Herr Lieber the "brewer" to Vanka the "extractor". Everyone regards him as a sort of destructive angel whose eyes take in everything and who does not give a moment's respite. A few times, the labourers wanted to gang up against him and beat him up one night when nobody could see until they broke his bones, but they were afraid of Mrs. Aberdam. On the other hand, they are not afraid to bring their complaints against him to her, and she, the mother of the brewery, who dislikes fuss and likes to make everyone happy, takes him to task in front of them and tells him somewhat sternly not to be overanxious about her property, for she has no desire whatsoever to get rich; not for that is she keeping the brewery running, but so as to be able to give to charity, to public needs and to the "Zaddik", and also to make a decent living — that and no more. And she concludes with a verse from Proverbs condemning riches. But actually, she is well pleased with him, because his devotion keeps the business running.

Sosele, his wife, is an awkward, pale-faced woman, sickly, self-indulgent and childless. The whole year through, she pesters the old Jewish doctor of the town with questions, goes to every Zaddik in the vicinity and even to the Gentile miracle-workers — for she very much wants to have a child. But all her efforts are in vain. The greater part of her husband's weekly earnings she distributes among the poor, demanding of each recipient as she hands him the money that he make a wish for her; point blank, without beating about the bush: "Say to me: 'May you be blessed shortly with a male child'." She also gave some costly offerings to the town synagogue once or twice a year: a mantle for the Scroll of the Law, a pointer; and once she gave an embroidered curtain for the front of the Ark and as she handed over the sacred object she laid down a condition to the Lord that he would "visit" her soon. She treats Him like any other beneficiary. Reb Israel Elia indulges her and gives away practically his last penny. They hardly spend anything. On whom and for what should they spend? Mrs. Aberdam makes fun of them a little, particularly in her conversations with that jester, the accountant, but she doesn't try to stop them from doing what Sosele wants (after all, is what she wants a bad thing?) although she treats them like family and visits them out of affection, and, at the same time, a little patronisingly.

One day, it occurred to Reb Israel Elia to arrange a permanent prayer group, or 'minyan' on the brewery premises. At the end of the building, there was one floor with several unoccupied rooms. Reb Simha, the accountant, had his office there, where he worked on his accounts, wrote chits and letters to the tax-collectors, and paid the workers their wages every Saturday evening. The Customs Police used to come to this room to see the production and sales accounts, and record in a book with a red seal the amount of excise due to the Authority. Next to his room were two more rooms, empty and neglected. They were closed up

47

and full of cobwebs. Broken bits of equipment and tattered sacks that no one had any use for, possibly still from the days before the brewery was leased to Mrs. Aberdam, lay around there. It was these rooms that Reb Israel Elia had in mind for his minyan. A small Ark with a Scroll of the Law stood in Reb Naftali Zvi's room and it could be moved to there — in which case all they needed was a table, a reader's stand and a few benches. All this could be produced on the premises of the brewery within a few days. Reb Naftali agreed with pleasure for it was convenient for him to pray on Saturdays at his own place, especially in the evenings, and not have to go out in the rain and the cold to the synagogue in town. Mrs. Aberdam was even more pleased: it seemed to her that only now would the brewery acquire the standing it merited. In a place where Jews pray together, the holy spirit abides.

Reb Simha, the accountant, although he lives in the lane next to the Ring, undertook to come there on Saturdays and conduct the service (he has a very pleasant voice and is not one to refuse). At first, he had to ask a few men from the bath-house quarter to come and make up the minyan, but from Sabbath to Sabbath the number of worshippers increased, and some beggars also came from the town, until eventually the big room filled up with men, and the small room next to it — with women. It is very pleasant to pray there: in the summer, the windows are kept wide open; outside, the thick chestnut trees rustle, birds twitter gaily, and a cool, fragrant breeze blows in from the lake through the windows, ruffling the prayer-shawls and playing over the faces; and in winter the rooms are well-heated, bright and comfortable, like at home. After the service, while the worshippers are still folding their prayer-shawls, holding them under their chins as they straighten the folds, and murmuring the final prayer *Aleinu*, a big-bellied green bottle full of good strong liquor for the Kiddush and a silver tray heaped with delectable egg wafers to go with it, are brought from Mrs. Aberdam's house. Even the clean fringed cloth hanging over the edge of the tray is pleasant to look at and adds to the Sabbath delight.

This minyan has become Israel Elia's whole world, and he does everything in his power to improve it and keep it in a proper state of repair. From Reb Naftali Zvi he orders for every holiday new carvings for the reader's stand and the walls. From his wife he frequently extracts new gifts. He has to use subtlety because Sosele, for some reason, treats this "synagogue" with disdain, doesn't believe in it and maintains that it is a pity to give anything there because it isn't a real synagogue, just an ordinary room, and anything given there is just thrown away. But he approaches her indirectly and with all sorts of blandishments until she succumbs, for she hasn't much will-power. First, he simply suggests that she should give something to the synagogue. She naturally agrees at once, but on condition that it goes to the real synagogue this time, the one in town — the Belzian one or the Husiatin one, it's all the same to her. "Very well", he says. "To me it certainly makes no difference. Give to anyone you like, as long as you give. You haven't given anything for ages." But after the article has been made and lies ready in Sosele's box, he begins to protest. "How can we possibly do such a thing? It is a slight towards a relative, a member of the family. What will our minyan think when they see the wife of Israel Elia leaving the premises carrying a new 'mantle' to another synagogue? They will never forgive us. It is forbidden to

c

offend a holy place, it is a risky thing to do." She still tries to insist and says she will not give it under any circumstances. Have you ever heard of such a thing? She stints herself and spends a fortune and now she'll go and give to some minyan in an ordinary room in a place where Gentiles work all week. No. Better she shouldn't give at all than give to such a place. And her eyes with their thin lashes fill with tears which will run down her cheeks in another minute. But in the end she softens, and consents on condition that Reb Israel promises her that he will open the Ark and tell the Scroll of the Law in no uncertain terms that this is the last time. If she doesn't become pregnant this year, she won't give another thing. Her patience is running out... And Reb Israel promised, naturally, and once when he was there alone he did so, but he didn't tell her because he was embarrassed.

In the minyan he serves both as beadle and *gabbai*, the lay head of the congregation who supervises the public reading of the Torah, calling each man up in order of importance, and it must be admitted that he shows a fine sense of discrimination in apportioning the honours and does it very well without offending a soul. But the one who dominates the show is the accountant, the scholarly Reb Simha. Although in everyday conversation he is flippant and always joking, here, in the minyan, he comports himself with the utmost decorum. Reb Naftali Zvi is content to sit on the east side of the room, behind the "sheviti," where the Rabbi sits in the town synagogue, and to be called up sixth. Moreover, the prayer-leader adapts his performance to him (or rather, to his appetite), either gabbling off the prayers or drawing them out as the case may be. When Reb Naftali Zvi is hungry, he raps on the reader's stand and calls out sharply:

"Nu! It's late." And the reader begins to race through the prayers. On the other hand, when he isn't hungry, he lowers the embroidered edge of his tallit expansively over his shoulders, waves his hand to the reader and calls out with a benign smile: "What's the hurry?" Then the reader warbles gaily away at the repetitive phrases at his leisure, and Reb Naftali Zvi nods his head in satisfaction.

Israel Elia would have liked to have prayers in the minyan on holidays too, but Mrs. Aberdam objected, Reb Naftali Zvi naturally following suit. Reb Simha made fun of the bailiff for being so easily satisfied with so little. In fact, the whole thing didn't matter to him at all. For his part, the minyan could have been abolished altogether.

For some years now, Reb Israel Elia and his wife have been bringing up a small orphan girl in their home, and they care for her with the utmost affection and devotion. The bailiff regards her as a daughter, but Sosele does not forget for a single moment that an adopted child is not a daughter (just as she does not forget that the minyan is not a synagogue), and she must go on striving until she eventually conceives. The little girl, a sad and modest child in all her ways, takes to no one but always hangs on to her "auntie", and knows very well that she is not their daughter, for Sosele talks to her about her affliction as if she were an adult, and tells her about all the medicines and potions that she has used without results. The child understands very well that a terrible "tragedy" has befallen her "auntie" in that she has no child of her own and she sympathises with all her little heart; and at night, in bed, after saying her prayers, she adds a secret prayer to the Lord to give her auntie a son this year. She too wants a brother, like other girls have.

VI

Herr Lieber the Brewer

The brewer is a German Jew, not very young, and his name is Herr Lieber, the "Herr" being pronounced with two "r"'s.

It has always been customary among those who run breweries in Galicia that the brewer must be a "German": that is, a Jew who speaks German and is clean-shaven and plump, eats *treif* and commits every possible abomination in public. Him, they forgive everything. They look upon him the same way as they look upon the doctor, the pharmacist, and the Jewish clerk in the tax-office: that is to say, as a sort of flagrant apostate. Herr Lieber wanders around the premises or strolls in the chestnut avenues on the Sabbath smoking a fat cigar; he puts the steaming coffee-pot on the sill of the open window just when people are praying in the minyan; he openly squeezes the *shikses* that work in the yard or in the garden and makes them squeal with laughter and enjoyment — for him, everything is permissible. He can't even speak Yiddish properly, and makes people laugh. And when he comes to the synagogue for an hour or two on the High Holidays, the worshippers look with mingled surprise and derision at him and his bristling mustaches, his frock-coat tight to bursting point, his flimsy *tallit* lying like a kerchief across his broad shoulders. Herr Lieber was born in the town of Satz in

Bohemia and has been working in Mrs. Aberdam's brewery from the year it was first leased, having worked prior to that in several other breweries in the vicinity. She is satisfied with him because of his naturalness and his loyalty and devotion to his work. He occupies two clean rooms in the centre of the wing of the brewery. He sleeps in the larger one and his servant in the other. Being alone, he took a servant, a Ruthenian hunchback without family, who cleans and tidies his rooms and, every evening, presses his clothes and polishes his shoes, prepares his breakfast and his supper and brings him his lunch from the only Christian restaurant in the town, of all places. The rest of the time he lies sprawled on his folding canvas bed in the ante-room, having filled his paunch with liquor, and snores summer and winter.

The brewery workers are very much afraid of the brewer because he is so strict and exacting but they also like him for his reticence and his straightforwardness. A smack in the face from him is regarded almost as a compliment.

Only when an expert on beer happens to come to the brewery does he become a little more communicative. Then he begins to expatiate on the quality of the malt, on the "fundamentals" in the preparation of the yeast, on the boiling time of the herb, on cooling the brew and steeping it in the hops, on its colour and its flavour and how long it can stand. "D'you understand? Beer is just liquid bread. Bread, for all purposes. With the addition of a bit of alcohol, of course. In Germany there are people who live on beer only. Take their pint from them and they die . . . Liquid bread and nothing more." He is almost an old bachelor. Almost; because some years back he had a wife—for two whole days. Everyone knows but they don't talk about it.

54

It was like this:

When he had been at the brewery in L. for about ten years and was already over forty, he suddenly began to feel the lack of a helpmate. What did he do? He sent his hunchback servant to summon Moshele, the village matchmaker, and told him that he wanted "to order" a wife from him. The shadchan was a little taken aback by the German's way of putting it and stood there blinking for a moment or two. But when he grasped the idea he took out a small, well-thumbed notebook and began to leaf through it rapidly. Finally he poked his finger at one of the pages and looked at the brewer triumphantly: he had found just the thing. Since time immemorial she had been intended for him. The same day, he got his travelling expenses from Herr Lieber and went to Zlotchuv and a few days later the brewer received a "kartl" in pearly lettering, to this effect:

"To the distinguished and most worthy Mr. Zeev Wilhelm Herr Lieber, may he live to a hundred and twenty. Having greeted you, I am able to inform you that the Blessed Lord sent his angel before me and I have found a perfect gem for you. (The Lord bestows and may he continue to do so!) The highly-lauded maiden bride, Miss Freda, long may she live, has, as stipulated by Your Honour, an amount of 200 roubles in cash, besides clothing and a royal abundance of various other things. She is an orphan (may we be spared a similar fate!) having lost both her parents more than twenty years ago, but she has an uncle, one of the leading citizens of the town, who takes the best possible care of her. God willing, but with no guarantee, next Tuesday you will take a small cart and come over to the village of Haritzivali, which lies exactly halfway

55

between our town and Zlotchuv and there, with God's help, we shall write out the terms of the betrothal, may it be with luck. This has been settled on the bride's side, that is — with her important uncle.

> Yours most humbly, who prays for
> you and greets you,
> Moshe Weintraub.

P.S.   For God's sake, don't forget to come because we shall be waiting for you impatiently at the Haritzivali village inn.

> Yours as above-mentioned."

When Herr Lieber received this flowery epistle, he held it up straight and then upside down with trembling fingers, and when he read the name 'Weintraub' on the back of it in Latin characters, he blushed like a little boy caught in the act, but couldn't make out a word of it. For several hours he paced the room (it was the Christian Sabbath and the brewery was closed), his heart pounding with excitement. He felt in his pockets, rubbed the back of his neck, and didn't know what to do. Eventually, it occurred to him to turn to the accountant who knew all about the small, unvowelled letters. Reb Simha received him with a broad smile and invited him to be seated. A kartl in the holy language? It will be a privilege, a great privilege. He deliberately went through some preparatory motions, and finally read the letter to him, explaining everything written in it very seriously, and in great detail. The brewer's face went every colour of the rainbow. He was so excited that he even forgot to say "thank you".

Next morning Herr Lieber shaved in front of the mirror and cut himself in several places because his hands were shaking, but he rubbed the cuts with alum until the bleeding stopped. Afterwards he waxed his mustache and fastened it down by means of two sticks tied with a thread behind the ears, put on the frock-coat he had had made fifteen years before in Prague (it was tight enough to burst), and put on his round hat which sat on his ears like an upturned pot. When he had removed the sticks and smoothed his stiff mustache with his finger, he took a last look at himself in the mirror and went to take leave of Mrs. Aberdam and the rest of the people on the premises. Then, accompanied by his hunchback servant, he set out for Haritzivali in the small cart they had in the yard, as instructed by the shadchan. The brewery would be closed only one extra day, as he would return on the morrow.

When he returned with the shadchan the following afternoon, his face was radiant and his mustache somewhat in disorder, and to those who enquired about his bride he replied with a happy gleam in his narrow eyes, half-hidden in the network of tiny wrinkles around them:

"Sehr fesh, sehr fesh!" (an expression with a double meaning: very beautiful or — very fat).

One month later, he went to get married. Everyone in the house gave him gifts and the finest of all was that of Mrs. Aberdam: a silver spice-box which she had brought specially from Brod. He accepted the present with thanks, kissed her hand and said he once saw a thing like that in his late father's house when he was a child, but didn't remember what it was. The people standing around laughed, and Mrs. Aberdam explained its purpose to him very seriously and expressed the hope that from now on he would use it on Saturday evenings.

Two days later the aforesaid groom returned with a

woman of about thirty-five. She was short and plump with an after-shaving stubble forming a shadow around her double chin; her eyes were tiny but alive, inquisitive and very bright as if thirsting for something rare. She entered the brewery like someone returning to home and family after a long separation, fell upon the necks of all and sundry, embraced them and kissed them over and over again and clung to them with her lips like a leech. Afterwards, she told them she wanted to live there with all of them like dear relatives. She herself, she said, was an orphan these thirty years and had been brought up in the house of a rich uncle, an extremely wealthy man who owned a house with a wall around it in the very centre of Zlotchuv, although she didn't get anything out of it at all. She worked, oh how she worked! She didn't want to live on charity. She worked for a specialist, a kind of specialist for those sorts of belts (at this point she raised herself on her toes and whispered something in Mrs. Aberdam's ear). In short, she thinks and hopes and prays that she will see a life of happiness, love and enjoyment with her beloved and charming Lieber (she peers at him through a sea of adoration), here, among such loving and delightful people... And she fell upon Mrs. Aberdam again and gave her a resounding kiss.

Her words and her behaviour, it must be confessed, made an impression on all the brewery folk. But the first night of their arrival, at about midnight, when the large courtyard was sunk in silent slumber and there was a lovely moon and angels seemed to dally in the dewy vegetable garden, suddenly a terrible wailing sound was heard coming from somewhere. Everyone on the premises was startled out of his sleep. At first they thought: cats on the prowl. Then they listened for a few moments, heads raised from the pillows, to try and make out where it was coming from. And when the sounds grew louder, the energetic ones jumped from their beds, grabbed some outer garment, and rushed outside. Within a few minutes, Mrs. Aberdam, Brachele, the bailiff and his wife, the maid-servant and the hunchback (who had been sent to sleep in the hay-loft), were all crowding around the locked door of the brewer's apartment.

Eventually, the agitated hunchback, unable to stand it any longer, seized an iron hook and broke open the door. There, in the long passage, they saw Herr Lieber in his shirt and underpants fleeing before his wife, who was chasing him in a long nightgown, wild-eyed and dishevelled, screaming at the top of her voice and throwing at him whatever happened to come to hand: slippers, clothing, utensils.

Everyone stood by stunned and uncomprehending. But the bride, catching sight of Mrs. Aberdam, threw herself at her with all her weight and clasped her tightly in her soft, strong arms, sobbing on her shoulder and beating her head against her like a slaughtered goose.

"Dear lady! Upon my soul, what a catastrophe! Oh, oh, oh, what a catastrophe! Who would have imagined...I thought—a red-faced fellow with such a mustache...and here, such a catastrophe! It's enough to drive a person crazy, dear lady. Oh, oh, oh! That cheat... such a mustache... what a catastrophe! enough to drive you out of your mind!" It seemed as if her whole, ample body was crying and sobbing.

The onlookers began to scratch themselves, pulled their wrappers closer around them and dispersed to their rooms, and from the distance one could hear their whispers and their stifled laughter. Only Brachele stood by, frightened and trembling all over, holding on to her mother's skirt, and asked with chattering teeth:

"Mother, what happened? Why is she all cross and crying?" Mrs. Aberdam, who had managed to extricate herself with difficulty from the strange woman's embrace, said to her daughter:

"Nothing, Brachele. Go back to sleep. Just an evil spirit... That's all. There are cases like that, Heaven protect us! It will pass. Go to sleep, my child, or you'll catch cold, God forbid. Go along now, and good-night."

She adjusted the wrap round her daughter's shoulders. She herself remained a little longer and calmed down the desperate creature as best she could. Then she took her into the apartment, closed the broken door, chased the hunchback back to the hay-loft and went back to her own house.

The following night the same thing was repeated, only worse. Everyone heard the noise but no one got up this time. And on the morning of the third day the couple went to the Rabbi, remained there for a few hours, and in the afternoon the bride packed her few belongings and went back to Zlotchuv in the brewery cart without saying good-bye.

Herr Lieber became a bachelor again and the hunchback came back to sleep in the small room. He was the only one who benefited from his master's misfortune.

Everyone knew about the incident but it was tacitly agreed not to talk about it. I hope the living and the dead will forgive me for having broken that agreement now.

VII

Reb Simha the Accountant

As a young man, he had been a successful and highly respected merchant, but his luck suddenly turned and he lost everything he had: first, in the heat of the summer, a tract of forest land extending over many miles burned down, and a few months later, in the heavy winter rain, a big water-mill of his was washed away. The two catastrophes coming one after the other, made a changed man of him.

He was one of the élite of Brod, an eminent scholar who knew his scriptures and had an excellent head for figures; an intelligent man, industrious and responsible, but the troubles that fate suddenly inflicted on him broke him completely. His business came to a standstill and he was left with a heavy debt without the money to settle even an eighth part of it. His wealthy relatives reached a compromise with his creditors and also let him keep his little house in the village. For a few years they even supported him in the hope of putting him back on his feet, but he was beyond help. The damage was in the backbone. For a year or more he was steeped in melancholy. Then he threw off all responsibility and became so lazy, frivolous, and irresponsible that people who knew him were astonished and asked: Is this Reb Simha?

He had a tall, refined wife and two slim daughters who resembled their mother, but he didn't bother about them

He seemed to be completely alienated from his family Were it not for the position of accountant which he obtained with Mrs. Aberdam at the brewery — who knows what his family would have come to. Even when he started to work, his attitude towards the women of his household didn't change. All he did was go home every day to eat and sleep, and bring his wife his salary every week — less a few pence which he kept for pocket money. He didn't care how things were at home, not even in cases of illness, and hardly ever enquired. At first, this surprised and grieved his womenfolk, who did not understand the profound change that had come over him. But gradually they grew used to the situation and accepted it without complaining. They accepted it submissively as just another one of the calamities and even pitied him in their heart of hearts.

Of his studies and his erudition all that remained was what his superb memory retained, for since calamity struck he hardly read a book. When, on the Sabbath, he opens the Bible with the Alshech commentary which he liked so much in the past, he closes it immediately no longer finding any interest in it. It seems to him that everything written there is long familiar and trite, and there is no room for innovation. And where does innovation get you? The foundation of wonder, which motivates all man's activities, had been cut away from under his feet. His extensive, thorough knowledge of figures had been preserved intact, although he handles relatively simple accounts. It is pleasant to see him sitting with his small skull-cap pushed to the back of his head, working at his figures, chatting, laughing and joking with one eye on the books, his short, stubby finger moving from the bottom of the page to the top (for some reason this is the way he adds) and when he gets to the top he whispers the total to himself and starts the next column from the bottom again. He never goes over it again, for he has full confidence in himself and is certain that he won't make a mistake. Checks made by others, just out of curiosity, have shown that his calculations are absolutely correct. Between the pages of his ledger hairs from his beard are stuck, as between the pages of a holy book (if you'll pardon the comparison) and he enjoys seeing them there.

He is still a Hassid and journeys once every year or two to Belz, but he also treats his Hassidism lightly and jokes about the Zaddik and his doctrines. His paunch is round and his beard thick and broad, golden with silver threads here and there, and when he yarns with someone and begins to chuckle, his whole body shakes in the chair and his small white teeth gleam delightfully. It is told of him that the Zaddik once took him to task in the presence of the Hassidim for his irresponsibility in not making any attempt to marry off his grown-up daughters, and he replied:

"Never mind, Rabbi. You are well enough and strong enough to bother about them when you are bothering about the rest of Jewry."

The Zaddik laughed, slapped him on the back and said:

"It's a good thing they called you Simha" (which means Joy).

He has one craving that he can't overcome. A childish craving. He adores sweets and is not ashamed to go into the grocery store on his way each day to buy a few pennyworth of sweets, and take them out of his pocket one by one afterwards and suck them while he works, while he talks, and even — you won't believe it! — while he prays. "I sweeten the material," he says and everyone laughs.

Actually, he finds considerable satisfaction in leading the prayers, but he is never over-eager to do so as other people with voices are, and he pokes fun at the cantors. When he speaks, his voice is soft and low and insignificant, but not so when he stands before the Ark. Then, a deep, powerful and very remarkable voice emerges from his throat — a veritable lion's roar. And when he raises his voice, as if casually, on Friday night in the minyan, in "The voice of the Lord on many waters", it echoes through the entire brewery and expands like the rumble of thunder over the surface of the lake, gleaming darkly in its blackness beneath the open windows in front of him. But his voice also serves him as material for a rude joke: "Believe me, by the time my voice reaches Heaven it is like the fart of a day-old infant." In general there is nothing dear or sacrosanct in his eyes except the hot Sabbath loaf on Fridays over which he croons to the tune of Hallel.

When he is late coming home for lunch, one of his daughters comes to call him. He signals to her to come up to him and, holding her by the chin, he puts on a serious countenance and cracks some sort of joke, like this:

"Hurry home, Zipporele, and tell your mother I've had an accident: my appetite fell into a barrel of beer and drowned. What, did you get a fright? Go home, I'll follow you. Soon, soon."

In the past few years he has developed an increasing desire to sleep, and it sometimes happens that he stops work in the middle, stretches out on the bench, puts his fist under his head and takes a nap. When he is awakened — either by a loud bang somewhere in the brewery or by someone entering the room — half his beard is flattened, one cheek is red, and an embarrassed smile spreads over all his face like someone caught red-handed.

"A plague on it! They never let a working man catch a few winks. It is specifically stated in Ecclesiates that 'the sleep of a labouring man is sweet'."

He makes no distinction whatever between his home and the brewery. Wherever he is, he feels at home and his mood is the same everywhere and at any time. "With him it's always Purim," says the irate bailiff, who doesn't like a man to neglect his work. People too, he treats all the same, except that he is closer and warmer to strangers than to his own womenfolk, and with Vanka the drunkard who extracts the plugs from the barrels, he speaks with the same humour and candour as with Mrs. Aberdam, or even the Zaddik of Belz. "What's the difference? Their beginning and their end is the same."

More than once, they found him stretched out on the couch in Mrs. Aberdam's empty dining-room, snoring away. How did he get there? He was sitting over his accounts, moving his finger from the bottom to the top, when suddenly he came over drowsy. He lay down as usual on the bench, but from the south window a sunbeam fell on him and scorched him with its heat, and bothersome flies buzzed all over him, got into his hairy ears and tickled him. He pondered a while, crossed the yard slowly and unsteadily, his skull-cap awry, his beard pressed hard against his cheek — to the amusement of the labourers — walked into the lady's darkened apartment, lay down on the cool sofa, and there found "sweet sleep".

VIII

The Twins

A Year went by and then another, until ten years had passed — and Bracha was still childless. The first few years, the deficiency was hardly felt. Mrs. Aberdam was fully occupied with the business affairs of the brewery and her innumerable ever-pressing charity cases. Reb Naftali Zvi read his few almost unused books, put away the holy ornaments and took his regular nap in the afternoons. Reb Hirtzel Pallan worked hard to expand the various branches of his own business, investing in them new capital which he raised through brokers from Lwow; and as for Bracha, she didn't even feel that anything was lacking and still seemed to find satisfaction in polishing the furniture with a soft cloth, looking out of the window at the colourful scenery, dreaming pleasantly as she embroidered, and waiting with restrained eagerness for the return of her husband in his light trap harnessed to a glistening chestnut horse. The entire establishment, during all those years, was a kind of busy corner of life in which everything had its place, fixed and unchanging, subject to the power of some invisible ruler. of which Mrs. Aberdam was but the external manifestation.

One spring morning, at the beginning of the Passover, when the first green grass began to show at the edges of the courtyard in between the thawing snow, a niece of Mrs.

Aberdam and her husband came to the brewery from a nearby estate which they had purchased a short while previously in partnership with a Jew from those parts, and brought with them their only child, a pretty little girl of about seven, full of life and innocent wiles, the very opposite of the orphan Sosele had adopted. There was a breath of the "big world" about the child, a sort of quality that Bracha had when she first came to L. Her attire too had an aura of far-distant places. When she came, the courtyard suddenly seemed to become larger, the chestnut trees more widely spaced, and the sun played in every corner. The child ran about the grounds all day as if intoxicated, her flying golden locks tied with a large blue bow, smiling at everybody with sparkling blue eyes, flashing her white, pearly teeth and gladdening one and all with her clear young voice. All eyes were drawn to her as to a magnet.

During the Passover, when the heavy gates of the brewery were closed for nine days, it was she who enlivened the whole of the somnolent place. After lunch, the people from the brewery would go out dressed in their holiday best, the women in light-coloured dresses and embroidered pinafores, and the men in silk coats and new shoes that squeaked when they trod on hard surfaces, and they strolled about in the shade of the trees and the walls, and from time to time one of the company would break away and chase after the little girl to tickle her and lift her up a little in order to enjoy her childish protests and laughter. Especially Reb Hirtzel and Bracha. Their play arrested the sharp eye of Mrs. Aberdam more than once and set her thinking.

At the end of the holidays, the guests departed having

invited their relatives to pay them a return visit soon at their estate, which was beginning to take shape, and they were particularly pressing that Bracha and her husband should come. When the cart set out on the return journey, it was difficult for them to hold on to the child who wriggled with all her bird-like body and called to those she was leaving behind to whom she had become extremely attached. Like a sunbeam that had dropped from the skies, the memory of the child remained with them, illuminating the brewery precincts, warming the cockles of their hearts, making them yearn to see this charming little creature again, to caress and fondle her. But little by little this light also died down. The yard shrank again, the chestnut trees came closer together and cast an even bigger shadow than before. A different mood descended on the place: the sadness of the orphan child was felt more than before.

Suddenly, Mrs. Aberdam began having severe pains in her back which kept moving from place to place and even affected her chest, making her choke at nights and keep the old man awake with her moaning, to her extreme regret. The old man kept more and more to his room and was rarely to be seen outside. His legs, encased in white stockings, were swollen and there was a peculiar redness in his eyes as if his eyelids had been turned inside out. A serious theft occurred in the cellar and Israel Elia began to search for the thief secretly among the hired labourers, with the result that the atmosphere became strained and charged with suspicion, and each time he passed he would rattle his keys in stern warning. Reb Hirtzel became more and more tied up with his various business affairs and most of the week he was away travelling in the forests and villages and often went as far afield as Brod and Lwow.

And in Bracha's heart the turmoil grew. Her eyes grew larger, to such an extent as to worry those who saw her.

That same summer, one Friday, during early-afternoon prayers, Reb Hirtzel came back from his travels, alighted from his dust-covered cart, asked Brachele how she was, took a clean shirt and went, as was his wont, to the bath-house. When he returned from there, refreshed and glowing, he began to rub his wet hair before the cupboard mirror in the white bedroom. He called Bracha, showed her a few white hairs at his temples, and said with a sigh: "Do you see, dear, my hair is beginning to turn grey. I'm getting old."

"It's no wonder. You are wearing yourself out in the business," replied Bracha, a trifle querulously, the corners of her mouth beginning to quiver slightly.

"You are right, my dear. For whom do I toil?" — said Reb Hirtzel, taking a few steps towards his wife.

This time, Bracha rested her head on his broad shoulder and he put his arm around her delicate waist, and they stood like that, the two of them, gazing sadly at their full-length reflection in the mirror. They both knew, now, that they were going to be childless.

The others also knew that things were not as they should be at the brewery. The women of the town who often visited the place would whisper piously among themselves and cast pitying glances at Bracha. And the synagogue ladies, raising their eyes to heaven, would wish Mrs. Aberdam that her only daughter should conceive soon, and would urge her to try and persuade Brachele to go to some Zaddik. The old lady, being a devout follower of the Rabbi of Belz — she had no faith in the Zaddiks of other places — asked her to go there with her, but Bracha refused, saying:

"If it is so decreed in heaven, how will the Zaddik help? Look at Sosele, mother." Her outward composure did not forsake her, only her eyes grew larger and deeper and made her more beautiful still. Mrs. Aberdam also tried to appeal to her son-in-law, that he should go to some Zaddik with Brachele, but he answered:

"I have no right to demand something that is distasteful to her."

Another year went by. The appearance of the place itself hadn't changed at all, but the people in it had grown older and in all their demeanour one could discern greater caution and apprehensiveness. Also the noise of the brewery seemed to be accompanied by an undertone of hidden complaint. One day, during the summer, the Rabbi of Radichov, Reb Hirtzel's father, came to visit his distinguished merchant son, accompanied by two of the Hassids of his town, Husiatin Hassids. He stayed with his son for three days and seemed very gratified to see the prosperity and the harmony of the home. He was particularly kind to Bracha, asking a dozen times a day how she was and how she felt, to a degree that struck her as surprising and out of proportion, particularly for a rabbi. On the fourth day, he summoned his son and went out with him to talk as they strolled along the road that leads up to the distillery, along the lake. He walked with him a long time and spoke to him about "the matter", at first circumspectly and finally raising his voice in reproach, his silk coat rustling as he walked; gesticulating with his hands as he explained to him that he must divorce his wife according to the Law as ten years had passed and she was childless, God forfend!

— which was a sign that the match was not a success; and it was, of course, only a first match and there had to be a second one in consequence, and it was forbidden that a Jew should be without offspring and lose the continuity of his line, and the first thing that the Torah laid down was that a man must be fruitful and multiply and so on and so forth... Reb Hirtzel seethed inwardly but walked on in silence out of respect for his father, nibbling a leaf he picked from the hedge along the lake as he walked. When he saw that his father was adamant, he pretended to give in but said he must postpone the divorce for half a year because of a complicated and tricky business deal which called for all his concentrated attention at this time.

In this way, he went on putting it off from month to month, from year to year, until his father, the rabbi, gave up in despair.

And in the fifteenth year of her marriage, at the beginning of the year, Bracha began to feel that some change had occurred within her. As soon as the thought struck her, a sharp, strange sensation of pleasure came over her, such as she had never known in all her life. But the feeling passed immediately and a kind of hidden fear seized her which shook her whole being. She waited a few weeks to make sure, saying nothing to her husband, although she often studied him thoughtfully when she could see him without being seen. And on the heels of the fear that kept coming and going, she began to be ashamed to show herself in public, so she would confine herself to the apartment even more than before and fight the lump that kept rising in her throat. When Hirtzel was not at home, she could no longer go and sleep in her mother's bed, and used to take her mother's cook, Pearl, to sleep in the room with her. Nor did she go for her usual walks along the lake, except at times when she felt easier and even then she used to hurry back soon. She was afraid she might lose her footing and fall into the water. One day, when Reb Hirtzel got back from his travels and stood before her refreshed, sunburned and broadshouldered and well-pleased with his successes, she suddenly felt that he was getting on her nerves; and when he placed his heavy hand lightly on her shoulder, as he always used to do, a feeling of revulsion came over her and this frightened her more than anything else. From then on she tried deliberately to be nice to him and show affection, but her nausea increased from day to day, together with that other nausea, the physical nausea that racked her body until she was utterly spent. Those were days of great torture for her, particularly when Reb Hirtzel was at home. He noticed the change in her but he couldn't imagine what it was. To all his enquiries she answered reluctantly: "There's nothing the matter with me. It's just a pain and it will pass."

Mrs. Aberdam also sensed something strange in her daughter. She was very disturbed about it, but waited for Bracha to tell her. Finally, Bracha could stand it no longer and one day, as she was sitting at her window, she saw Israel Elia go by with his keys and the orphan girl, and asked him to send her mother to her. Mrs. Aberdam hastened to answer her summons. She crossed the dining-room swiftly on tiptoe and came quietly into the white room, where she found her daughter sitting slumped on the sofa, her face burning, her eyes large and wet. Smiling uncertainly in the doorway, the mother asked:

"What's the matter, Brachele?"

The tears welled in Bracha's eyes and when her mother

came up to her she clutched her hand convulsively and burst into tears:

"I don't know what's the matter with me. I hate my husband. He irritates me. He seems so cruel and clumsy. When he laughs I want to run away. I keep thinking he is making fun of me. Sometimes I feel so bad all of a sudden that I think I am going to die. My chest is bursting. Mother, I'm going out of my mind. What will happen?"

Mrs. Aberdam's heart leaped with joy. She recalled all the signs she had observed in Brachele during the past few weeks, and all this served to strengthen the great and pleasing certainty. She sat next to her daughter, took her head in both her large, warm hands as if in blessing, and said:

"Brachele, apple of my eye, you have to give thanks to the Lord for His mercy. He has listened to our prayers. You are pregnant and with the help of God you will bear your Hirtzel a son or maybe a daughter. Don't worry, my child, you don't hate him, God forbid! He doesn't deserve that. It only seems so to you. You will love him again sevenfold. There are women like that. In this respect, you take after my sister, Rivkele, may her soul rest in peace. She said the same thing. It's nature. You'll get over it, Brachele. Remember, he is your husband and you are carrying his child, to your joy and to the joy of all of us. God will bless you and your saintly father will put in a good word for you in Heaven. Don't worry, child, you have a good sponsor up there and he'll look after you faithfully. God willing, everything will go well. You must look after yourself. You are so delicate that a breadcrust can break your fingers... Don't climb on chairs any more to adjust the curtains and don't move the beds and the sofas. For

God's sake! That is forbidden, my child. You must not do any heavy work. Thank God my prayer has been answered! Have you told Hirtzel? Why, he'll dance with joy. It's a pity he isn't at home now. I'd have liked to break the good news to him. God willing, everything will be all right...Don't worry, and get those bad thoughts out of your mind..." And she wouldn't move from there until she had calmed her daughter down.

On the termination of nine difficult months of pregnancy, Bracha gave birth, one fine afternoon, to twins: two tiny but healthy baby girls, identical in every detail except that the elder one by half an hour had blue eyes, while the other one had black eyes.

The event caused a sensation in the whole compound. Reb Simha the accountant with the beautiful handwriting had prepared, even before the birth, strips of paper to hang over the windows and doors to ward off evil spirits. While Brachele was in labour, which lasted about ten hours, Sosele stood in a corner in her apartment and prayed for her, shedding tears like water, and labour pains seemed to pass through her body as if she too were giving birth. Israel Elia occupied himself with the little girl so that she shouldn't cry when she saw her "auntie" cry. Even the Gentile employees kept inquiring throughout the morning how the young lady was doing. Only Herr Lieber concentrated on his work, as on any other day.

In honour of the naming of the twins, everyone at the Brewery went to the synagogue in town on the Sabbath, where Reb Hirtzel went up to read the Law and name the twins, one after the mother's grandmother and the other after his. After prayers, the entire congregation proceeded to the brewery with their tallit-bags for kiddush.

After her difficult confinement, Bracha was weak and pale, her skin pure and almost translucent. But she felt good. There remained no trace of the horrors of the pregnancy. She submitted with pleasure to the attention with which they lovingly surrounded her from all sides. She succumbed pleasantly to her husband's caresses and was pleased to see the happiness that danced in his kindly eyes.

Although they gave her a Ruthenian woman as a wet-nurse — the wife of one of the labourers — she attended to the babies herself with the utmost devotion. She bathed them carefully, one after the other, holding the soft little body with one hand, carefully turned the child over while supporting the head, and with the other hand washed her with the warm, steamy water. After bathing them, she dressed them with great patience and made cooing sounds at them through pursed lips, occasionally even singing for them. But this thaw in her nature did not last long. After a few weeks, she gave up attending to the babies and went back to her life of seclusion and dreaming. Mrs. Aberdam and the wet-nurse took over the care of the infants and only when Hirtzel was at home did she attend to them a little to please him and to make amends for the bad feeling she had towards him during her pregnancy. For Hirtzel was very concerned for the babies' welfare and was often to be found standing between the two cradles, moving his head from one side to the other, smiling first at this one and then at that. But when he went away, she left them again in the hands of the wet-nurse, under her mother's supervision. It seemed that the many barren years had, as it were, killed in her the maternal attributes innate in every woman, and the few embers that still remained revived for a short while only after the birth, and then died down again.

The old lady, occupied as she was with her innumerable affairs, both business and charity, nevertheless found time every day for prayers (three times a day), for reading books on moral precepts in Yiddish, and for Hassidic discussions with Reb Simha, who put on an air of great attention and respect in order to please her. When the babies came into the world, she found interest in them as well. When she saw that Bracha was put out by their crying, she had the cradles transferred to her apartment, explaining apologetically to Reb Naftali Zvi:

"What can I do? Brachele takes after her late father and wasn't made for bringing up children."

He nodded with his pipe in his mouth and said nothing. As long as they were far from his room, he didn't care.

The children developed at an equal rate under the excellent supervision of Mrs. Aberdam. Soon their charming little heads were covered with soft curls: the elder one had golden curls and the little one black curls. And when they were little more than a year old, they began to toddle around the big rooms, falling and getting up again and laughing, going off separately at different angles and meeting again in an unsteady run, with arms outstretched. At this sight, Bracha would feel her heart swell and take the two of them in her arms for a moment and kiss them alternately. From then on, they never cried, either by day or night, and ate anything they could get hold of: a piece of black bread, potatoes, fruit. At first they stopped them, and extracted things from their tightly clenched fists by force, but when they saw that it didn't upset their stomachs, they let them eat to their hearts' content. Every day the wet-nurse (who stayed on as a sort of nanny to them after they were weaned) used to take them out, carrying them or leading them by the hand. They were dressed well and in good taste, and passers-by stopped to look at this charming pair, the like of which, for beauty and distinction, were not to be found in the whole town, including the daughters of Pan Yashinski, the forester.

On one occasion, Count Molodetzki, who was in town at the time and used to go every day to swing the big sledgehammer at the smithy of the estate for exercise, was passing through the market place riding his thoroughbred horse and, catching sight of the babies in the care of their nurse, he reined in the horse, leaped to the ground, took them both in his arms and kissed each one twice on the cheek. Afterwards, he enquired enthusiastically whose "chicks" these were. When she told him, he asked the nurse to convey his greetings to the father whom he knew, and as he remounted his impatient horse, he said in Polish with a click of the tongue: "Aristocratic stock."

And the bystanders nodded their heads smilingly, although they didn't understand what he was saying.

IX

The Boy Called Shalom

When the twins were one year old, Bracha became pregnant again. At the end of her pregnancy, which was infinitely easier than the first one, she gave birth to a son and they called him Shalom, after her father.

The joy in the brewery compound was indescribable and spread from there through the whole town. At the circumcision three distinguished-looking old men, dressed in satin and sable, sat at the head table: the Rabbi of the town, the Rabbi of Radichov, Hirtzel's father, and Reb Naftali Zvi, all chewing over sweetmeats and religious verses with their toothless gums. Mrs Aberdam supervised the refreshments in the women's section and also among the men. She handed things around herself and got her helpers, Sosele in particular, to hand round the rest of the good things that had been prepared for the celebration. The host himself, feeling good from a mixture of wine and beer prepared by Reb Simha, and beaming all over with happiness, twisted his body this way and that as he danced and danced again, alone and with others. First, he danced on the floor; afterwards he climbed on a bench and danced there; and eventually even climbed on to the table. He scattered copper and silver coins to the poor and pressed his guests to keep on drinking, and in a voice that was clear at first and finally hoarse he sang all kinds of songs and ditties, commencing with *Shoshanat Ya'akov* and ending with a Polish or Ruthenian song with rather risqué words. His hat was pushed back off his large forehead and his capote was open and swinging. Everyone declared they had never seen him like that before. If anyone else had let himself go like that, they might have taken a stern view of it, but Reb Hirtzel — that's different. Even the Rabbis nodded their heads as if to say, let his happiness be his expiation.

Not so the mother. She sat in the white bed in the adjoining bedroom, dressed in her wide mantle, and wearing the glittering earrings in her ears that Hirtzel had bought her, indifferent and sad. She looked at the red face and hairy skull of the newborn child, which moved its lips all the time as if sucking, and she could not understand how she had given birth to this. Through the door she could see the revelry and the uproar and the hot tumult came to her like a tormenting noise which only added to her wonderment and made her eyes even larger. The women bent over, passed soft fingers over the swaddled mite lying on a long pillow and gave the mother the traditional blessing that she be privileged to bring him up to the Torah, the marriage canopy and good deeds. But she looked at them, smiled with her pale lips in bewilderment and understood nothing of what they were saying to her. Only when she recalled that the boy was called Shalom after her late father was her heart moved and she bent over and kissed him on his soft cheek.

In a few weeks it became evident that the child was outstandingly beautiful, exactly like his mother. The same whiteness of face and the same big black wondering eyes; only the blackness of his unusually long hair aroused a peculiar feeling in the beholder. But, it transpired that he was as naughty as he was handsome; a cry-baby and a cross-patch he was, and it was impossible to see him in all his beauty except when he was asleep, because when he was awake his face was generally contorted, covered with tears and perspiration and frequently blue from the effort of crying. When he cut his first two teeth a little before their time, he used to bite the nipples of his wet-nurse's breast — she was the wife of another employee and she pinched him when nobody was looking, calling him a "cursed wolf-cub!"

This time too, the same performance was repeated as after the birth of the twins. For the first few weeks, Bracha's maternal feelings were alive and overflowing, but little by little her heart quietened down and she began to languish, eventually handing the baby over to her mother as before. This is exactly what Mrs. Aberdam had been waiting for all the time. From the day the child was born, she seemed to grow young again. She became erect once more and her eyes regained their former sparkle. The backaches vanished like magic and she paid more attention to the broad band of her matron's wig, making sure that it was straight and properly adjusted. Sometimes she would sing an almost forgotten song from her girlhood days in a voice a little cracked and quavery with age. Because of Shalom, she left the affairs of the brewery in the hands of the bailiff and the accountant, and even most of her charitable work she turned over to them. In particular, she asked Sosele to attend to the guests and to the poor, and maybe as a reward etcetera etcetera... For she (Sosele) realised by now that God was not going to work any miracles for her, and she was to be found most of the day in Mrs. Aberdam's apartment, for she loved the babies very much and even roped in the orphan girl whom she brought with her, to help attend to them. The old lady's attention was also diverted somewhat from Reb Naftali Zvi and she did not take care of him the way she used to at the beginning. But he was entirely unaware of it. He sat in his room, browsing over a book entitled *Kahal Hassidim* and slept a lot. He had given up his carving altogether because his hands shook, and once he cut his finger and caught fright when he saw the blood. Luckily Reb Israel Elia happened to come by and bandaged the cut for him with cobwebs and the bleeding stopped.

Shalom was born between Purim and Pesah, and when the hot fragrant summer days came around, the old lady would pick him up in her arms and walk with him for hours in the courtyard and show him to all the workers on the place and the guests, and talk to him about the different jobs that were being done and the people, as if he were big enough to understand.

On one occasion, the old lady wasn't paying attention — the wet-nurse had gone to her native village for the day to attend her mother's funeral — took the wrong container and gave the boy the previous day's milk to drink by mistake. The child suddenly fell ill and hovered between life and death. Bracha was surprised to discover that the child's illness didn't upset her as it should, and although she bestirred herself to attend to him and felt that her face expressed motherly concern, her heart was almost mute. The sight of the child's suffering face annoyed her more than it moved her. The old Jewish doctor of the town and also the specialist, Reb Aron Shoub, almost gave him up. The boy vomited practically the whole of his insides. His head drooped on his chest or on his shoulder and he couldn't open his eyes whose lids were stuck together because of the fever. His skin burned like a furnace and his dry, cracked lips trembled without stopping. His soft moans were pitiful to hear. Twice, he had convulsions that continued for more than an hour, and they were waiting for a last seizure. Reb Hirtzel sat grieving on the sofa in the room, and Bracha sat on a chair opposite him as if turned to stone, watching him with sad, steady, unblinking eyes.

Only Mrs. Aberdam, who did not move away from the big cradle, attended to him all the time, straightening his body, wetting his lips with cold milk diluted with water and sugar, and fanning him with her apron. It seemed as if she had forgotten everything far and near, and her entire world centred on the baby's cradle. The third seizure did not come and the baby remained alive, to the joy of Mrs. Aberdam, Reb Hirtzel and everybody there — except Reb Naftali Zvi and Bracha. But from then on, all kinds of sicknesses attacked him one after another. A few months later they noticed that his belly was swelling and turning blue, until it was as taut as a drum, while his legs grew thinner and weaker. The old lady said: it's nothing — water in the stomach; lots of children get it. Nevertheless she consulted a doctor and various knowledgeable people of her own accord, but they were unable to find a remedy. They washed him in bran-water, in different kinds of fragrant herbs which the employees gathered from the sediment on the threshing floor, mint flowers, tree bark and the like, but nothing helped. Until Fanny Shachnovska, the old Polish midwife came and said that they must get half a log of centipedes from a damp place, fry them in fresh butter and smear the child's belly with the ointment for seven consecutive days, three times a day, and it would return to normal. Which they did. Vanka, the drunkard, brought the worms in his red kerchief which he placed inside his holiday fur hat. He found masses of them crawling among the roots of a rotten tree behind the brewery on the lake side, and scooped them into the kerchief with his hands. The old lady herself fried them in a pan, smeared them over the baby's belly, with a whispered blessing on her lips as she did so. When Bracha learnt of this she could not touch the child or his clothes. And indeed, after a week or ten days, the belly began to subside and turn white again until it went back to normal.

From then on, the old lady was inseparably bound to the child. For to all her feeling for him was added a feeling of guilt, that she had made him sick.

When he began to walk, at the age of a year and a half, he suddenly came down with a bad case of pox, which broke out all over his body, even on his face. The child scratched himself with his nails, wounding himself until he bled, so the old woman trussed his hands with soft napkins and he lay like that, writhing and screaming for several days until his skin healed. From lying so long his body was weakened to such an extent that he was unable to walk. His arms and legs had grown thin and bent and his ribs stuck out through his fine, transparent skin and they began to fear that he had rickets. Then began the fattening process. How many stone jars of cod-liver oil they brought him from Brod! How many raw eggs they crammed into him! How many little meatballs of pigeon in boiling soup did they feed him! And that's how it went on, sickness and recovery and sickness again, until he turned three. It seemed as if hidden forces were conniving to bring him down but the old woman protected him like an iron wall. And when he turned three he emerged from all his illnesses clean and soft and lovely like a snake emerging from its skin, and began to walk and run and romp about. His physique improved and his face grew more and more beautiful, more radiant, and his limpid eyes reflected a keen intelligence.

X

The Good Neighbour *Pan Yashinski*

At that time, the Count's forester, Pan Yashinski, came to live opposite the brewery, in the fine wooden house with the painted, ornamental porch entwined with flowering convolvulus and surrounded by a garden with flowers always in bloom.

Pan Yashinski was a Pole of good family, whose beard, a Franz Josef beard, and thick short mustache were as white as snow, but his face was young, ruddy and clear, his smooth chin soft and round, and in his eyes — the fire of youth. His wife, Pani Yuzia, looked very young, almost like a girl with her fine figure and delicate face, resembling Bracha in build but more emotional and active than her and devoted heart and soul to the running of her home and to bringing up her children. She had three daughters — living dolls that walked around on legs as slender as narcissus stems.

Very soon, the children of the brewery got to know the little girls of the Yashinski place and began to play with them every day. The Pallan children spoke Polish, for their nurse spoke to them in that language. Even their father and the old lady used to speak the language to them partly out of snobbishness and partly just for the fun of it. Anyway, certainly not out of any intention to bring them up in a foreign language. It was clear to everyone that eventually they would speak Yiddish, as behoves the children of good Jews. But not Bracha. She of all people spoke only Yiddish to them although she knew Polish better than all the rest of the family, having brought the language with her from West Galicia when she was still a child. She hated any form of affectation, whether open or disguised, but she did not object to their speaking a foreign language and took it as a matter of course when she heard their pleasant chatter, for actually it was not she who had to bring up the children. Perhaps just because of that the children were very attached to her. They were quiet and subdued when they were with her, treating her with great consideration, and any rare sign of warmth on her part would make them very happy. Just as if they were dealing with a pleasant stranger for whom they had to show respect and regard.

The children of Pan Yashinski sometimes used to come to the brewery and play with their friends in the garden, but they were wary and a little afraid of the gloomy, noisy buildings. Mostly, the Pallan children used to go to them, at first with the nurse and afterwards alone. In the clean, well-kept grounds, full of greenery and moist sandy paths, which they used to enter through a small gate in the high stone fence, there were many dogs: hunting dogs and domestic dogs large and small, long-legged and thin, short-legged and clumsy, smooth and hairy and curly-haired — and the children used to play with them without any fear, even when they growled and bared their teeth and opened their cavernous mouths. A multitude of cages, big and small, some of wire, some of wood, were suspended outside on a wall of the house, and the twittering and chirping of all the winged creatures confined in them filled the air of the courtyard; in particular, the voice of a starling that knew how to say two short words. If a cat came and cast a covetous look at the cages, a dog would immediately straighten up, thrust its head towards the intruder and put him to flight with one bark.

Pani Yuzia was very friendly to the Jewish children out of a liking for strangers, which was stronger than the traditional hatred for Jews. She looked after them as if they were her own children, and was always most solicitous to return them to their parents safe and sound. She took particular note of Mrs. Aberdam's injunction (she had a great respect for this old lady) not to let them taste any of her food "which is forbidden to us by the laws of the Israelites", and the woman took great care to carry out the old lady's orders. Only fruit would she hand out to them in generous quantities, and that too only after innocently asking Mrs. Aberdam if there was any prohibition about eating fruit as well.

The twins are all over the good neighbour's place, running about between the flower beds and in the finely-gravelled courtyard, stumbling and falling and getting up again; suffering scratches and pinches from the squire's daughters without complaint, with tearful eyes and laughing faces; pulling the dogs by their tails and their ears and putting their tiny hands fearlessly between their teeth and getting them wet with their spittle; breaking into a children's dance, lifting their dresses with one hand in graceful poses, until Pan Yashinski, his hands on his hips, throws back his handsome head in a resounding roar of laughter while Pani Yuzia replies with her own brief, tinkling laugh, raising the corner of her white apron to wipe away a happy tear.

Shalom alone, the only boy amongst the girls, created trouble for this charming little group. He had a habit of worrying the dogs, teasing them until they got into a rage and bared their teeth at him with a threatening snarl; he damaged the plants in the garden and pulled them out to see if they had long roots, climbed up tender trees or hung from them and broke their branches; snatched food from the hands of one of the girls, his sister or one of the neighbour's daughters, and threw it over the high wall. The girls would get cross and call Pani Yuzia and she would come pattering along in her embroidered slippers and start solemnly preaching to him, just like a priest preaching to his flock from the pulpit. And Shalom stood listening attentively, eyes downcast and cheeks puffed, but when she finished what she had to say he gazed at her with his large, penetrating eyes, pursed his lips, adjusted his hunting cap on his head and went out of the yard without a word. Then Pani Yuzia ran after him, caught him under the armpits and tried to placate him and pleaded with him to stay with the girls and go on playing, but he pulled himself free and went off even more angry than before. Only several days later, after many entreaties on the part of Pani Yuzia who went to the old lady and to Bracha consumed with regret and sorrow, and appealed to them to persuade the boy to come back and play with the girls "for how can they play without a boy" — did he go back with manifest pride to his games and his pranks.

But he did not remain interested in the Yashinski place for long. His attitude to the "fair sex" began to take a negative form — as is usual at this age. All the girls, including his sisters, seemed silly to him, just chatterboxes and gigglers, although most of them were older than he was, and he even took a dislike to Pani Yuzia, if you don't mind *(her and her sentimentality, her and her sweetness, her and her moralizing!).* Sometimes he forgot himself and mimicked her sing-song way of speaking, pulling a face and producing a funny sort of whistling sound. This hurt Pani Yuzia and her eyes would fill with tears, but after a moment she'd grab hold of him and kiss him firmly on the lips to his great mortification, his outraged heart palpitating furiously all the time.

But when Pani Yuzia sat in the room and played the piano and the sounds — pleasant sounds, thundering sounds, stirring sounds — wafted through the open window, he'd stand outside and listen, holding on to the trunk of a tree with both hands, one leg planted as if frozen on a stump in the flower-bed. The sounds flooded into his soul like impetuous waves, filling it with sweet anxieties tinged with a profound sadness. Once he asked Mrs. Aberdam if Jews were allowed to play the piano, so weird and wonderful did her playing seem to him.

Pan Yashinski he liked very much, but he was rarely at home except on holidays, when his friends, the few squires in the town, used to come and visit him: the postmaster, the school principal, the Canon, sometimes the Jewish apothecary as well who was like a squire to all intents and purposes. Then Shalom would take himself off because the roisterers behaved coarsely in their cups, laughing wildly all the time, and ignored the boy entirely. He'd slink away to the brewery (only the twins remaining behind) and prowl restlessly in the silent courtyard, picking up bits of gravel and broken glass which he'd hurl over the roof in the direction of the lake with all his might, and stand, one leg up, leaning against the picket fence, watching the hens pecking in the vegetable garden, whistling quietly to himself. Or he'd go into the somnolent brewery where the door is always wide open and the atmosphere is cold and stark and heavy with the smell of dampness, and take a few steps to bring him under the cooling basin. But when he sees the vats gleaming balefully in their black-mirrored waters, a slight uneasiness comes over him and he begins to retreat until he comes into the sunlight again. He has a feeling that the hobgoblin that the old lady talks about is going to pop up out of some dark corner...

"Silly fools!" he growls to himself, meaning all five girls. But actually, he has a grievance only against Pan Yashinski's guests who don't know how to behave.

XI

Vanka the Extractor

T ogether with the less admirable qualities that manifested themselves in Shalom — obstinacy, quarrel-
someness and intractability — there were other qualities
which were not properly understood by the brewery
people but, without their being aware of it, made them
very affectionate and tender in their attitude to the boy.
First of all, his unusual beauty — the amazing whiteness
of his face in contrast to the blackness of his large eyes,
his clear forehead and his thick black curls — immediately
won the hearts of everyone who saw him. So too his
rather peculiar ways: his excessive taciturnity, unusual
in a child his age, particularly struck those who heard
his clear and well-developed speech. When he wanted
to express some idea, out of his mouth would come the
concise, pithy sentence of a grown-up person, spoken with
quiet composure and without the grimaces and cockiness
of someone trying to be smart. Occasionally, he would
suddenly be seized with a compassion not usual for him,
which would wipe out in one fell swoop all his maddening
pranks. Just as he molested the cats, the dogs, and the
plants, viciously pulled out the hairs of Reb Simha the
accountant's beard, scratched Reb Israel Elia and made him
bleed, and even pulled Reb Naftali Zvi by his coat — so
would he dole out beer to the poor, fondly watching their

Adam's apple move up and down as they drank, run errands for the old workmen, and take his portion of meat or milk to the woodshed where the cat had given birth to kittens in the straw.

His magnanimous and gentle soul would show itself in particular when he was interested in something. He used to look on in silence and with complete absorption. He used to look intently at every activity, every implement in the brewery and the ice-house, in the building where they made the malt and in the mill, he would inspect the vats and taste the brew to see if it had fermented sufficiently, separate the leaves of the hops, examine and smell their yellow pollen — pick up every vessel and implement in his small hand, turn it over and scrutinize it until he worked out for himself what it was and what it was used for. Only when something was too complicated for him did he turn to someone with an abrupt query: "What's this for?" The person addressed would begin to explain with lengthy preambles and at great length, as grown-ups have a habit of doing when they explain something to a child. Having grasped the matter after the first few words, he never waited for the end of the explanation but turned and went away.

He couldn't stand Reb Simha because of his perpetual smile and his smugness, but when Reb Simha managed to catch him between his knees he liked to stand there for a few minutes and pull the hairs out of his beard one by one, getting particular enjoyment from the way the thick-bearded Jew flinched and closed his eyes at each pull and jerked his mouth back like a dog. He had a specially big grudge against Reb Israel Elia the bailiff, because of his strictness with the workers and the way he took everyone to task, as if they were trespassing: and the bailiff was the one who was always trying to make approaches to him: he would hold out his closed fist to him as if there was something in it for him and open it to show it was empty; he would steal up behind him and swing him into the air by the armpits. The boy doesn't cry out; he just kicks his legs back and waves his arms, in an attempt to hurt the man in the stomach and catch hold of his beard, until he is forced to let him go, with a smile of discomfort. He used to put his tongue out at both these men whenever he came across them and screw his face into all kinds of grimaces as he imitated their way of speaking, which made his beautiful face quite ugly. They, of course, were never angry with him. A broad smile would spread over Reb Simha's shining face, and the bailiff would content himself with shaking his bunch of keys at him and calling him sharply: "Little hater of Israel."

"What did you say, Israel?" — said Mrs. Aberdam, who passed by at that moment.

"I said he was a hater of Israel, hee-hee!"

"As long as he doesn't hate all Israel, God forbid!"

"Ai, how clever he is!" cried Reb Israel in wonder, nodding his head with delight.

On the other hand, the boy was very much attached to Vanka the drunkard, whose occupation it was to draw the bungs out of the empty barrels with a small instrument every day of the week, and drink all day in the village pub on Sundays, and stagger through the streets when evening came, accompanied by a crowd of Jewish and Gentile children, singing at the top of his hoarse voice. Sometimes he makes clever speeches, or cries like a spanked baby; sometimes he laughs, sometimes he spits. And Reb Simha says of him, in the words of the sages: "Just a braying goy."

Throughout the week, the face of this Vanka (he was an old bachelor, short and very thin, and it was impossible to estimate his age as he had neither beard nor mustache and even the hair on his head was the colour of flax) was calm and serious, and a small iron crucifix swung on his bare smooth chest as he worked in silence, all his attention concentrated on his work. Only when he sees an injustice being done on the premises to someone, whether from inside or from outside, he flares up, raises his voice in a violent curse, throws down his instrument, rams his cap on his head and runs home; he can't work in such a place! And it takes a lot of pleading and coaxing and pats on the back to get him to return to work.

That's how he is on weekdays, but on Sundays he turns into something entirely different.

All his life, he wanted to rise to the position of stoker. It was his big dream. He would go to Mrs. Hanna, prostrate himself before her, kiss the hem of her skirt, her shoes, the floor, entreat her with tears running down his face: "Gracious Pani, make me a stoker and I'll get rid of this accursed machine." She always promised that in half a year's time, after Pesach or Succoth, they would put him on to stoking. She even mentioned it to Reb Israel Elia several times, but the bailiff always laughed and promised and promised and laughed, and had no intention of doing anything about it because there were always arguments between himself and Vanka and they used to needle one another with a relish. And in general, what's one thing got to do with the other? How can anyone think of separating

Vanka from his machine for pulling out plugs?... That's how the matter continued for several years. But eventually the place of the assistant stoker fell vacant and Vanka succeeded in achieving the honour he so much desired. On the Sunday after his appointment he drank more than twice his usual amount, but his mind stayed lucid out of sheer excitement. Towards evening, he arrived at the courtyard with his usual escort, climbed on to a wood-pile and sat down, without his cap, his blond hair sticking to his forehead and his temples, and screwing up his face and beating with his fists on his bare chest, he called out to the escorting mob who had now been joined by the local people:

"You see, I've been made a stoker at last, blast him! I'm sure I'll be a stoker in hell as well. Yes, in hell! And then, good people, this is what I'll do, 'pon my life: when His Worship the Devil orders me to boil the big pot in which our Pani Hanna will be cooked, I'll pull out firebrand after firebrand from the furnace, secretly. By God I will! All His Worship's watchfulness won't help him any. But when they cook Srael, blast his guts! I'll add another log of wood and then another, 'pon my life I will. So!... So!... So! Cook, roast, burn, you son of Satan! Blast him, a stoker I am and a stoker I shall be!"

The whole crowd roared with laughter, and even Reb Israel Elia, who was also present with his bunch of keys, laughed into his beard but said to himself: "Just you wait, you son of a bitch. I'll get my own back."

Actually, he found the business about hell very amusing and couldn't resist telling Sosele about it but she, instead of laughing, grew frightened and spat several times to ward off the Devil: "*Tfoo*, the babblings of a drunken

goy... Everything I dreamed — on him and on his head!
Tfoo!"

This entertaining goy was a special favourite with Shalom.
From the time he became a stoker he would often sit before
him in the alcove of the giant furnace, facing the light of
the flames, on a stump of wood or an upturned cask, chin
in hand, and listen to the stories the little old man serenely
told. Vanka's stories were a veritable treasure trove: tales
of demons with tails and ghosts wrapped in white sheets,
one-toothed sorcerers and witches riding on broom-
sticks, red-bearded robbers and wicked beasts that lurk
in ambush. And as he told his stories everything seemed
to come to life and his words were interspersed with
witticisms and peasant idioms as sharp as sickle and scythe.
While he talked he was mostly bent over the wood and
the furnace, but when he turned his face to the listening
boy, his eyes were burning, from the heat of the furnace
as well as from his own enthusiasm. Shalom's eyes too
burned with imagination.

Vanka would accept a gift from no living creature; only
from Shalom did he occasionally accept a piece of cake
or the remainder of a Sabbath loaf. He would take it with
great politeness and thank him very nicely, but he didn't
eat it himself. He'd wrap it up carefully in a piece of paper
and put it in his coat pocket and take it for the children
of the brother with whom he had been living for thirty
years, in a hut next to the stables. When he received the
gift he was always a little upset and slightly offended,
but he didn't have the heart to refuse "the little master".

Whenever Shalom saw his beloved Vanka misbehaving
on a Sunday it grieved him very much, and as it wasn't
within his power to snatch him away from his large escort,

he would dash in shame to the far end of the yard or into the house and lie there in torment. And next day, when Vanka came to work, his face pale and more wrinkled than usual, his hair combed down on his thin neck, and in his eyes the pained calm after the storm, Shalom would take pity on him, press close to him and squeeze his hand, his little heart contracting and expanding all the time.

XII

A Fight and its Consequences

Besides Vanka, there were two other people that Shalom was very fond of: Mende the deaf-mute and Reb Reuvele the pedlar. The former was a permanent resident of the brewery but never appeared outside. For a number of years, he worked under the supervision of the brewer at malting the barley, that is to say — moistening the grain to make it germinate and drying it in order to make the malt from which the beer is brewed. The latter, a pedlar from the neighbouring town of T., was just a guest who used to spend a night or two at the brewery with his pedlar's sack and then proceed on his way to the country villages and fairs, to gather the crumbs of a livelihood for himself and his poverty-stricken family.

Mende the deaf-mute had been a dashing fellow of striking appearance before he came to work at the brewery. His shiny crop of black hair, his even white teeth, his hat jauntily tilted to one side like a cocky "sheigetz" — gave him a particular charm in the eyes of Gentile girls in the town. Even the poorer Jewish girls, the tradesmen's daughters, were attracted by his gallant appearance and would whisper terrible stories about him. He had no real trade, although he was deft at anything he tried, because of his quick temper and impatience, which made the craftsmen to whom he was apprenticed drive him out. But eventually the family married him off — his parents had both died of typhus within one week — to the crippled daughter of a beggar from their vicinity, who used to go begging with her father through the countryside and saved up a sum of money for a dowry. At the beginning of the "honeymoon" he was happy. In front of all his acquaintances, both Jewish and Gentile, he would describe his wife's charming figure by putting his hands on his hips and nodding his head; and passing his right hand across his outstretched left arm like a fiddler and clicking his tongue, he described all the magnificence of the wedding. And with a wicked wink, he would hint at all sorts of intimate pleasures. The little money his wife possessed served to support them and set up a home. But it didn't take long before the woman grew tired of the monotony of home life; a roving life, from door to door, drew her with invisible ties, and she began to tempt him too in the sign language that she had learnt from him, to go out with her. The two of them, with their cleverness, their quickness and especially with their disabilities, could have picked up money like dirt. But he refused point blank because he was a proud man and hated hand-outs. If he thought anything was wrong, he would raise his eyes to heaven and pass his outstretched finger across his throat, meaning: *God slaughter me for such a thing.* She wrangled with him for several months, they even exchanged blows, but when he refused to give in to her she linked up with her father again and the two of them went off and left the deaf-mute destitute. Afterwards, there were rumours that she had taken up with another beggar and borne him a child, but Mende never saw her again because she never returned to that town. Then he came to work at the brewery as a day labourer, and gradually acquired the art of making the malt. When the man who was the expert at it left, he was put in charge of that work.

Although his wife left him, to his sorrow and speechless wrath, his jollity and his joking did not forsake him, and during work — he worked like a devil! — he would dance around, emitting peculiar sounds from his defective throat which he called (by placing the palm of his hand against his cheek and opening his mouth wide) singing, although he had never heard any in his life. As for those 'with the bumps on their chests' — meaning women — he wanted nothing more to do with them. If any of the Gentile girls working on the premises made eyes at him, he'd snatch up a fistful of stones or anything else that came to hand and throw it at them, blushing to the roots of his hair and shaking all over with fury. Because of that they used to infuriate him by touching a finger to their foreheads to say that he was not right in his head.

Shalom loved to come to Mende, to the chill, murky malt-house with its high vault supported by thick, stone pillars, where — on the slightly-sloping stone floor — the golden barley was laid out flat and steeped in water, sprouting pale long stalks like grey, curly hair. He'd sit there on an empty cask, patiently watching the deaf-mute at work. When he stopped to take a break, leaning against one of the pillars, his hairy legs bare and wet, both hands resting on the top of the large broom, Shalom would ask him for a cigarette in sign language and the deaf-mute would give it to him with pleasure, glancing quickly this way and that to make sure nobody saw, with a warning finger on his lips. Shalom would take one or two puffs, screw up his face, throw the cigarette in the water, and listen for the sizzle as it went out. After that, they would "converse" — about the fawning accountant and the strict bailiff, and the deaf-mute would curse the two of them with a horizontal movement of both hands in the air, saying: May a grave be dug for them shortly, in our day. Shalom would laugh uproariously, drumming his legs on the cask with delight.

The deaf-mute lived in one of the cubby-holes on the top storey of the brewery where, in addition to a few utensils he had brought with him from the house that his wife had left behind, he had all kinds of tools, big ones and small ones, for whittling; and in his leisure time he would sit, bent diligently over his carving, and produce all kinds of wooden figures and toys and bring them afterwards, his face aglow, and offer them humbly to the "slender lady", Bracha, as a gift. She would thank him with a pleasant nod of the head and put them in a prominent place to please him. He made things for Shalom and the twins too: carts, flutes, dolls, slings, spinning tops and the rest, thereby endearing himself to them more and more, until calamity struck out of the blue and put him to bed for the rest of his life.

The awful thing happened on one of those freezing winter mornings, when the lake beside the brewery lay imprisoned in a greenish sheet of ice and the fine, crisp snow gleamed white and fluffy on the rooftops. The frost pressed with arms of steel, and at night the wooden boards sprung loose from the nails in the rafters with an explosive sound like shots from a rifle. The dung froze under the cows. For three days now, there had been no brewing for the boiler had sprung a leak. They examined it and found a crack in it. They brought the boiler-maker to repair it and he had been working at it with his two assistants for the past three days. The echo of the blows from the big sledgehammers deafened the whole town. The cellars and the empty barrels in the yard answered each others' echoes. The labourers used to come each day to see if the repair was finished so that they could return to work, because there was no other work to be found in the winter — only a few were engaged in breaking ice on the lake — and the work in the warm, sweet, satisfying smell of the brewery is most pleasant then. That morning they also came. They lit a small fire in the furnace and stood in the big alcove warming their rough hands, blue with cold, drinking beer from a large jar which they rounded off with roast potatoes, chatting and joking with the boiler-maker and his assistants who were busy on the job. Amongst them was a new employee who had arrived not long ago from some distant village that nobody knew of, a man of giant stature. This "giant" used to boast about his great strength and told all sorts of wonderful stories about his taking on several farmers at the same time in a fight, and encounters with wolves and bears — while his small, grey eyes flashed beneath the small forehead, almost like a forest boar. But none of the labourers had tried wrestling with him yet so they didn't know whether his strength lay in his loins or in his mouth. On this occasion, too, the talk turned to deeds of heroism, and the giant again began to expatiate on his own exploits. Whereupon one of the young labourers came up with a suggestion: "You know what? Let's get the mute to try his strength against this smarty... Hell break this fellow's bones."

The workers agreed delightedly. The giant, who had suddenly fallen silent, nodded his consent. They sent

someone to call Mende from his warm attic. He appeared
a few minutes later, wearing a short, winter coat, bare-
headed, his hair falling over his face which was blue from
the sudden cold. His hands were thrust into his trouser
pockets and he stood there slightly hunched as if shrinking
from the cold. The labourers welcomed him with a wild
ovation, and indicated by means of various signs that they
wanted him to fight the giant. The mute, who at first
couldn't make out why he had been summoned here, spat
in their faces and turned to go back to his attic and to the
tools that he was busy with at the time, but one of the
labourers indicated to him, by shrinking back with his
hands over his face as if defending himself — that he was
a coward. Then the eyes of the deaf-mute began to flash.
He went up to the man, caught him by the neck and pushed
him down hard until he fell to the ground with a moan.
The labourers slapped him on the back and roared: "There's
a champ for you! A fellow like that deserves a treat."
They offered him a sip from the jar that had been refilled.
He downed a big draught, took a potato, split it open,
crushed it between his fingers, crammed the white pulp
into his mouth, and let out a wail as he burnt his tongue.
All this time, the giant sat at the side, his head drooping
as if he were dozing, chewing on a straw between his
teeth, as if it was all the same to him if the deaf-mute
agreed to fight or not. Mende did not look across to where
he was sitting. He began to wave his hands about, asking when the repair of the boiler would be completed,
but the labourers kept pulling him the way they wanted,
to make him try his strength and teach the stupid giant a
lesson. He still tried to refuse with an embarrassed smile
and a deprecating wave of the hand, and took a step

towards the door. But the way the giant was sitting there, unperturbed and making as if he was asleep, began to annoy him considerably. A sort of nameless fear rose from the bottom of his mute soul and enveloped his brain, but he overcame it, and signalled with his hand and with a desperate attempt at a throaty whistle: "Good, I agree. Stand around in a circle." The labourers made way for him and woke the sleeping giant. He drew himself up slowly and held his hands out to the fire, with a slight yawn, as if to say: "What do you want of me?" After that, he looked the deaf-mute up and down, from head to foot, smiled, and signalled him to come on. Mende pushed his hair from his eyes, which glimmered like a pair of Havdalah candles, shifted from one foot to the other a couple of times, the sinews in his neck swelling and nostrils dilated. He made a swift leap, seized the giant by the neck, and, digging his toes into the ground, tried to throw him in one move. But the giant planted his legs on the ground like two iron poles and didn't budge from his place. Then the deaf-mute tried a trick. He stuck a leg between the giant's legs and hooked it around one of them, and while he was shaking the giant's long neck with all his might he suddenly gave a pull with his leg. The giant staggered about half a yard to one side and almost fell to the ground with his attacker.

The labourers fell back and shouted: "Bravo, Mende!" But the giant didn't fall; he rallied, straightened up angrily, and broke himself free, hurling the deaf-mute away from him. Mende hopped several times on one foot and fell, but as he fell he twisted around and sat down. The labourers stared at the giant in amazement, as he stood there in the middle, legs astride, with an ominous glint in his small grey eyes, the eyes of a forest boar.

Mende got to his feet, pale and trembling with rage, his eyes filmed with reddish tears. He was aware of nothing around him, seeing only a large formless creature, a sort of mountain, standing before him; and he had to throw this mountain down, uproot it, overturn it. He rubbed the sore place, stepped a few paces back and charged with full force, head down, straight for the giant's stomach. The giant was jolted from his place by the force of the impact and hit the wall with his back. Then the deaf-mute quickly sprang on him again, grabbed him by the neck and began to shake him in nervous fury, but the giant managed to rally again and stood there without budging, feet astride, as if to say: "Go on, try and move me!"

Meanwhile, a number of other people had congregated there: the bailiff with his keys, wearing thick woollen mittens; the two ice-breakers, their mustaches covered with frost and glistening icicles; the red-haired servant girls with buckets of dripping water in their freezing hands; the boiler-maker and his assistants — all of them crowding round to watch the performance. When the deaf-mute saw he couldn't get the better of his opponent, anger began to burn in him and, in sheer desperation, he fell upon the giant again and sank his teeth into his neck. A savage roar, like the bellowing of a bull when it smells the blood of the slaughter-house, petrified the whole brewery; the boiler, the cooling basin, the tubs, the vats and the open cellar answering in a long-drawn echo. The blood of the onlookers congealed in their veins. The giant seized hold of the deaf-mute's hands and detached them by force from his wounded neck; caught him by the waist, lifted him above his head and hurled him with terrific force towards the furnace. Tr–r–r–ach! They heard the sound of breaking bones and a shocking, blood-curdling scream that split the air for an instant and stopped. Everyone dashed up to the fallen man but there wasn't much they could do for him. He lay there with the whites of his eyes turned up, one leg stretched out and the other bent towards his stomach, his soft, repeated groans smothered in the blood that oozed from his mouth on to the floor. His spine and two of his ribs were broken. the labourers carried him to his attic, alerted Mrs. Aberdam who sent first for the "experts" and after that for the doctor as well. The doctor cracked jokes, felt him over, and bandaged half the wretched man's body. For about two months, he lay hovering between life and death, screaming strange sounds that frightened everyone out of their wits, but in the end he pulled through. He was bed-ridden for the rest of his life.

He remained lying in his room in the attic, getting his food from the old lady's house (his relatives in the village had disowned him and refused to take him in) and the Ruthenian maid-servant used to come in each morning to tidy the room and make his bed, doing her work with bent head and infinite compassion. At the beginning Mrs. Aberdam and Bracha used to come to visit him in his room and encourage him, assuring him that with God's help he would still recover, but as the days went by and his condition continued unchanged, their attentions stopped and he remained lying there alone and abandoned. Only Shalom did not let his friend down. From the day the accident happened, he became even more attached to the deaf-mute and used to come to him every day and whenever he was free. He brought him delicacies that he received from his mother and his grandmother; he handed him his tools in bed, watched him and tried to help in every way he could. Shalom himself began to try to use the tools, and when he succeeded in making some toy or other, the eyes of the deaf-mute would shine with pleasure. He'd take the little head of the child in his two hands and gaze into his eyes affectionately, with the devotion of a sick dog.

After a year or so, the deaf-mute made himself a sort of wheel-chair and if there was someone to carry him downstairs and put him in it, he would propel himself to various parts of the premises where work was going on and sit there and supervise, scold and threaten, just so as not to be a parasite and eat without working.

XIII

Reb Reuvele the Pelder

S halom was almost as fond of Reb Reuvele the pedlar
as the was of the deaf-mute. He was a little man with
straight, wide side-locks, a small dark beard greying so
that it looked as if it had been sprinkled with flour, and a
mustache beneath the blocked nostrils stained brown from
too much snuff-taking. He was dressed in rags and his
eyes were always watery — but he was a good-hearted
man by nature, always jolly and full of jokes. When he
appeared from the neighbouring town, two or three days
before the Fair, after having made the rounds of the villages
and the estates, weighed down with his heavy sack full
of rabbit- and hareskins, strands of flax, pigs' bristles,
horses' tails and so on and so forth, all the employees
would lay down their work and wait for him to come
trotting along, stooping and grimy and full of dust up to
his sash into which the ends of his long capote had been
tucked; or filthy with mire up to the knees, depending
on the season. When he reaches the brewery door, he puts
his sack on the ground and sinks down on to it with a
groan as if he's going to faint. "Ah, a taste of Paradise!
In the shade of the generous Countess' right hand! Ah,
it's good here!" From his bosom he takes out the box made
of horn, opens it, holds it to his nose and takes a deep
sniff from it. Then he takes a large pinch and sticks it up

111

his nostrils, twisting his whole face first to the right, then to the left and thereupon shakes the whole yard with his sneezes. When they hear the sneezes, all those who are eager for a good sniff of snuff go up to him, wipe two fingers clean on their trousers, and help themselves from the box which he holds out with one hand, using the other to slap them on the hand if they take too much. After resting on the sack for a few minutes, he'd get up, drag the heavy sack along the ground as far as the passage and enter the house of the "Countess" — as he called Mrs. Aberdam. First he conveys dozens of greetings from his missus, declaring that since the last time he was here she hasn't grown a single tooth and can't chew any hard food, except sour milk. Mrs. Aberdam stands there, laughing and sighing at the same time. "Hoi, hoi, Reb Reuvele. How long are you going to go on clowning? You'd better wash your hands and sit down at the table. Pearl, bring bread. Reb Reuvele must be hungry."

The dark-skinned, untidy-looking cook whose tight bodice is shiny with age and fat in the parts that protrude, pulls a face as Reb Reuvele goes into the kitchen, searches in the pots like someone thoroughly at home, and would also go sailing into the next room but the old lady stops him with a warning finger: "Don't go in, Reb Reuvele. Reb Naftali is reading."

"Ah well, I'm not particularly keen on seeing Reb Naftali anyway. 'Strewth, I prefer a gravy stew... And how is the pair of cucumbers (meaning the plump little twins), and the little ethrog (meaning Shalom, splendid and reserved)? And how is the 'thirty-two' (meaning Brachele, silent and withdrawn)? Ai, folks! if we had just the crumbs from your table in my home, my jokers would be dancing on the walls...Ai, the life of a beggar!"

When the twins, who were at the Yashinskis, and Shalom, who was with the deaf-mute, heard that Reb Reuvele was there, they came running: Shalom carrying a hammer and tongs, and the twins dragging the squire's little girl after them. They surrounded him and pulled him by the capote, the ends of which had already come out of the sash and were hanging down to his feet. He evades them, patters into the passage and comes straight back waving over his head a cloth bag full of small, three-cornered nuts which he calls "shickernusslech" (he explains the name: they have been proved effective for dispelling drunkenness. That is to say, if a drunk man eats a fistful of them, one by one with long intervals in between, he can rest assured that his drunkeness will pass over), and gives a little to the twins who have grown taller and already stand as high as his ears. They take them and divide them between them without quarrelling, putting some as well in the little hand of the neighbour's daughter whom they have in tow, and go skipping gaily off to continue their game. And Shalom, who also gets a share, stays a while with Reuvele, hangs around him affectionately, and enquires after Manele.

Reb Reuvele had a son at home whom he sired late in life, a hunchbacked sickly boy; he loved this boy with more than ordinary intensity, and was always speaking of him and his health. Shalom also loved this boy. Although he had never set eyes on him, he used to think of him for hours on the days when Reb Reuvele stayed with them and kept begging the old pedlar to bring him with him next time. Shalom pictured Manele as a pale, weakly, silent boy with light, sad eyes, gazing at the world with a serene, level look that penetrated to the heart of everyone who saw him; his desire to know the boy and to spend some time with him grew stronger and stronger. "Never mind, to me he'll talk," he suddenly said out aloud to himself during the meal.

"What did you say?" asked the old lady who was always watching his slightest move, dining serenely at Reb Naftali Zvi's right. — "I thought you said something."

"I didn't say anything," said Shalom, blushing.

But Reb Reuvele never brought the boy.

"You understand," he explained to Shalom, "I always go on foot and he's very weak, he couldn't walk with me. I go from village to village, from estate to estate — how can he go after me with his weak legs? Perhaps in another year or two, when the good Lord makes him stronger..." And this same Reb Reuvele who always had a smile on his face, suddenly grew sad and tender when he spoke of his son, Manele. Then the tears sprang into Shalom's eyes too, and his longing for the boy increased even more.

During the summer, Reb Reuvele refused to stay in the guest room, preferring to sleep in the hay-loft because of the "perfume" that pervaded it. Some of the guests used to follow his example and go and sleep there with him, in the soft, fresh, fragrant hay, for he would entertain them until midnight with funny tales and frightening stories from the villages and the forests, from the estates and the graveyards. The stars peeped through the cracks in the high wooden empty roof, and the hay tickled their skin while the stories tickled the imagination and kept sleep away. (It was hard to sleep, anyway, those bright summer nights.) Sometimes Reb Israel Elia would slip in and sit there unobtrusively listening to the pedlar's tales.

114

Reb Reuvele told far more stories in the winter. Then, he would sit in Mrs. Aberdam's kitchen with the rest of the guests that happened to be staying at the time, joined by the bailiff, Sosele, the orphan, and the cook. If it was not too late, Mrs. Aberdam herself would also come, wearing her wide pinafore, leading Shalom by the hand, and sit down on the upholstered chair which Reb Israel Elia brought in for her. Sometimes, when Reb Hirtzel was not at home, Bracha would also come from the wing. Only Reb Naftali Zvi and Reb Simha the accountant never came. The former preferred to pore over one of the chapters of *Talpiot* which he had recently acquired, or prepare new "sheviti" for the minyan on the brewery premises; and the latter kept himself aloof from the rabble and those common Jews, and if he did not go home he would drop his head on his ledger and snore away.

The kitchen is beautifully warm and pleasant. The smell of the food that has just been consumed still pervades the room. Pearl rests her thick, dirty arms on the table, drops her kerchiefed head down on them, and after listening to the beginning of the story for a few minutes, falls asleep. The pots stand scrubbed and drying on the stove, an occasional drip producing a long, sizzling sound. Outside, the wind is blowing and plasters soft snowflakes to the window-panes. Shalom, wide-awake, is propped up between the old lady's knees and she keeps stroking his neck as far as his skull-cap with warm, soft fingers, ever so delicately. Everyone there has one red cheek, the one turned towards the stove. And Reb Reuvele sits at the head of the table, his face relaxed, rosy and soft, his gentle eyes shining, and empties his treasure trove in which old people find delight.

XIV

The Story of the Witch

All eyes are fixed on his pale lips. He takes a good pinch of snuff and then begins:

Outside, there was a snowstorm that mixed heaven and earth into one white jumble. I'd never seen such a storm in my life. You couldn't see a house, a tree, a bush — nothing. The roads were buried under snow. It was impossible to proceed because you couldn't draw breath and also for fear of being buried beneath the snowdrifts that the good Lord had sent us. He had unpicked all the pillows and the featherbeds in heaven, and shaken them into the air! This time I was not alone, as I usually am, but in the company of another beggar, a pedlar like myself, who had foisted himself on me on the way. Perhaps you knew him — Reb Berl, may he rest in peace. When I saw Satan dancing before us, I said to myself: "Ai, Reb Reuven, do you want to live to see your missus and your family? Don't be a smarty: just pick up your feet and turn about and go back to the village you came from half an hour ago." I told my travelling companion what I was thinking and as he's always scared and has a tendency to entrust his precious bones to whoever happens to be a bigger hero than he is just so as not to be responsible for them himself, he agreed with alacrity and we went back. What shall I tell you? It was just a miracle that we reached the last house of the village, which became the first for us on our return, as is usual, and to our joy we could still see a little light in the small window hidden in a thick wall of straw and rotten leaves. I, the hero if you please, knocked on the door with my stick once, twice, and after a few moments it opened and the head of an old Gentile woman was framed in it, a head unnaturally large and distended tied with a black coif. Her face was covered with long warts, all of them hairy, and she kept shaking her head without stopping, "No–no–no–no!" My eyes lit up. I knew her. A few years back I had bought a cow from her with its tail chopped off, and although I lost money on the deal I wasn't going to tax her with it now. I addressed her in words as soft as butter:

"Have pity, dear grandmother, and save us. Take compassion on us and let us into your house, to sleep this night. You can see, white dove, what the Lord Blessed be He has brought upon us. The world is coming to an end. There is no road, no path, and the snow sticks the eyelids together. It can kill you! You must remember I bought a cow from you with a lopped-off tail, with good money, not counterfeit, God forbid. I wish you had cows like that to sell every year and not just to me... Also to others, I don't begrudge them at all. Let them also profit..."

The woman growled something or other with her toothless mouth. She let us into the room and gave us, out of a large, black earthenware bowl, some hot milk to drink with a rubbery consistency and the sort of smell that turns your insides. "I'm afraid she's giving us cat's milk to drink," I whispered to my companion who was just beginning to get his wits back. But he didn't get excited about it and drank up all the milk, licking and smacking his lips. He must have been very hungry and thirsty. Afterwards, the old woman went to the cellar-storeroom on the other side of the passage and stayed there for about an hour. Berl and I began to pace up and down the rough, mud floor, from the icons swallowed up in the gloom on the wall to the smoking hearth and back. I wandered into a corner and my foot encountered something soft, and alive. Something mooed and a very long black calf arched itself up, first on its hind legs and then on its front legs, its long tangled hair standing up like the wool of a ram, and began to sneeze just like a human being, pardon the comparison. A–tshoo, A–tshoo!

"What's there?" my companion asked in a frightened voice, not daring to come one step nearer.

"Nothing, Berl, a devil in the form of a calf. Can't you see? Can't you hear?"

I made a joke of it but I felt as if a swarm of ants was crawling over my back under my shirt. I went up to the hearth and began to warm myself at the dying fire because I'd become very cold. Two or three dying embers flickered with a bluish flame. The calf scratched its swollen belly with a hind leg, lay down again with a human groan, lay its head on its shoulder with its eye open, gazing at us, at me and Berl. Afterwards, the woman brought in a pile of rags and offered us a bed on the ground. Berl promptly lay down in his wet coat and heavy top-boots and covered himself over the head with the rags, although the room was as hot as a Turkish bath. I too stuck my face into the rags at my head, but I peeped out with one eye half-open and observed all the movements of the accursed old dame. She pottered around in the room for a while, clattering pots and scraping with a scoop, and went to the storeroom several

119

times and back, whispering mysteriously all the while and shaking her head: *No–no*. Eventually she extinguished the fire in the hearth. The black cat crouching near her took fright at the sizzling sound, leaped over the stove and shot away, passing like a devil over me and my neighbour and disappeared with a loud bang under the bed. The old woman undressed in the dark, bent down under the bed and fished out the cat which was moaning in the weirdest way, calling it by all kinds of endearing names like "black thief", "gorgeous bastard" and "cursed devil"... pushing it down in the bed as you have to do with a recalcitrant child. Then she also lay down, with it. Silence reigned in the room. The storm increased in intensity outside and the wailing of the wind, as it swept through the chimney, made the ice-particles dance and set the lids a-clattering, and frrrrrr... as the soot spilled over the quenched fire.

"What's there?" Berl asked me, stealthily sticking his head out of its fetters.

"Nothing. The Angel of Death came down the chimney." I answered lightly, but my heart was right down in my boots. My neighbour turned over several times, groaned, murmured names that were strange to me, and finally went to sleep, snoring like a beheaded calf. But I didn't sleep a wink. I peered around in the dark to see the room and what was in it, but everything was blurred and confused. The snow seemed to make the inside of the room lighter, but in fact nothing could be seen in it clearly. In the end I got all mixed up and didn't know where I was. I seemed to be lying with my head on the threshold, the black calf lying on my right and the cat lying on my chest, oppressing me, its green eyes fixed on me. I tried to move a limb but I couldn't. In this state I lay and suffered for several hours, it seemed to me. Suddenly the cock crowed midnight and the room was illuminated with a weak, cold light. I couldn't see where the light was coming from. I opened both eyes, raised my head slightly and there I saw the old woman, half naked, getting out of bed, tresses of white hair on her head instead of the black headband. She bent over the cat, stroked it, tickled it, tucked it in and kissed it, and then came up to us to see if we were asleep. I shut my eyes and opened my mouth and lay there breathing heavily as if fast asleep. As soon as she went away I peered again through narrowed eyelids. I saw her go to the hearth, take out of the niche beneath it a bit of broken earthenware, dip her little finger into it and rub it on her forehead, shaking her head no–no. When she had finished smearing, she put the dish back in place, and whoosh! — she rose into the air like the wind and was swallowed up inside the chimney. The fear of God fell upon me and a cold sweat broke out all over me. I drew myself up and sat there with my eyes wide open, but again — a gleaming darkness and nothing more. I sat like that for a few minutes, shocked, petrified with fear. Suddenly I heard the calf straightening up with a peculiar mooing sound. It sneezed, ground its teeth, and began to walk about the room breathing loudly and sniffing. Eventually it reached the niche, stuck its head in, sniffed at it and sniffed again — and whoosh again! It too rose into the air and was swallowed up in the chimney. That was too much for me. I grabbed my sleeping neighbour by the shoulder and shook him hard:

"Reb Yid, Reb Berl, Reb Gimpel, Reb Zerach, wake up! The river is on fire!" He awoke reluctantly and mumbled sleepily with a heavy tongue and gnashing his teeth: "Wh—a—t? Where? Wh—a—a t?"

I was sorry for him and said to myself: If I'm lost, I'm lost... but why should I frighten him too, poor fellow? Better he should sleep and not know anything. But as a person who has been awakened can't asleep again, he tossed from side to side and began to pester me with questions: What was the time now? Was it far to the village of Lashkiv?... I answered something just for form's sake and in my heart I prayed that he'd fall asleep again so he shouldn't see the sorcery. After a while the cock crowed again. You're in for it, brother! And indeed, there came the same rushing sound through the chimney — and the old hag was standing in the middle of the room. A moment later, again that rushing sound and the calf arrived and stood beside her. I managed to lie down quickly and cover my face with the rags, peeking out only through my eyelashes. The old hag moved herself from side to side as if inspecting the room. Then she climbed into her bed, and began to kiss and tickle the cat. The calf scratched itself again with its hind leg as earlier in the evening, and lay down with a very human groan. I turned to my neighbour beside me and found him sleeping like a dead man, blowing bubbles with his lips.

Why draw it out? The night lasted about a year for me and when the window began to pale as the dawn began to rise, I got up. My companion also got up. It was terribly cold in the room. Our teeth chattered without stopping. The calf lay in the corner, its head on its shoulder, eye open, and the cat was already up and about and rubbed itself against our legs. I asked Berl how he passed the night.

"V—v—very well," he answered, his teeth chattering.

122

"Is that all?" — I asked, surprised.

"What more can a Jew want?" He also answered me with a question, scratching himself all over. "As for those things that bite, to tell you the truth I've stopped being aware of them. Hoi, hoi! It's just a matter of getting used to it, like everything else."

I saw he knew nothing of all that had happened and I had no desire to tell him. The more he knew the more scared he'd be. I picked up my sack and he his, and we crept out stealthily...

"What a yarn!" — Reb Chaimel couldn't contain himself. He was always sceptical about Reb Reuvele's stories, but the rest of his listeners were all under the spell of the story and sat gazing at him with affection in their eyes.

"You understand about stories like you understand about those animals that you buy and sell," said Gad the glazier (he was also there for the night) sarcastically to Reb Chaimel.

"And I tell you," wheezed a skinny Jew with the remnants of a green scarf round his neck and a black goatee that seemed to have been stuck on to his chin — "and I tell you that there *are* witches, God help us! My brother-in-law Tzalel once quarrelled with his Gentile neighbour, old-man Kyril with the gammy leg, and Kyril said to him in anger: 'Tzali, in half a year's time your right hand will wither.' You all know my brother-in-law Tzalel with the withered hand. It's eighteen years already and he can't move his hand. A trifle, eighteen years! There *are* witches, God protect us!"

"In our place," another man breaks in, a heavy fellow, a country villager to judge by his appearance, "there was a Gentile woman, a terrible witch who used to take on the shape of a cat and come every day and take milk from our cow, until they began to notice it. My late mother was a toughie and nothing could daunt her. She was no woman, just a 'cossack'. And once when she went to milk the cow she took with her a meat-chopper that had just been sharpened. She'd just sat down on the stool when the cat arrived as usual, stretched itself out between the cow's legs, looking up at the udder and mewing as if asking for a drop of milk. What did my mother, may she rest in peace, do? She took good aim with the chopper, and trach! the cat's paw remained lying in the muck. And guess what? the witch wasn't around for several months and when she emerged at last her foot had been lopped off and bandaged in rags. I saw her myself with a bandaged leg. I swear, there are witches."

XV

The Story of the Hobgoblin

Pearl, who'd been sleeping on the bench, suddenly stirred, mumbled something cross and unintelligible and fell soundly asleep again. A thought crossed Shalom's mind: *Maybe she's a witch?* But when he saw that no-one was taking any notice of her, he also lost interest. The audience sat silent for a moment, gazing at the good warmth that emanated from the stove.

"Granny,"—Shalom suddenly shook free from Mrs. Aberdam's caresses—"Granny, I'd rather you told us the story about the hobgoblin. It's better than Reb Reuvele's story. It's not so frightening."

Everyone began to press the good lady to tell the story of the hobgoblin. Actually, they've heard it before but they've "forgotten the details," so never mind, let her tell it again. She's blessed with the gift of being a good story-teller. Ai, that one about the burning bed... Let her tell the story of the hobgoblin! Her stories are true ones!

At first, Mrs. Aberdam refuses, excusing herself on the grounds that she can't tell a story like Reb Reuvele does. But eventually, when the long silence begins to irk, she places Shlomke on her knee, pats her lips with two fingers, an affectation permissible only in her, smoothes her matron's wig which was tidy anyway, shakes the long agate earrings she is wearing, and begins, in her unhurried, even tone of voice:

When several years had gone by after the death of my first husband, may he rest in peace, I married Reb Naftali Zvi, may he live to a ripe old age. I was about thirty-two then, or maybe a little more than that, but I was full of youthful energy — much more than the young girls of these days — and itching to get started and do something. For I was used to being active from the day my poor father died and the burden of earning a living fell on my shoulders. My brothers-in-law had pulled out and gone off to businesses of their own. And the needs were many: I had to give to charity and to public causes, and generally prepare myself for the world to come. When I came here I had only my daughter Brachele with me, my elder daughter, Judith, having died of the croup, Heaven protect us! Reb Naftali Zvi's shop, I'm ashamed to say, was nothing to speak of. And Reb Naftali himself was a bit ineffectual, an idler if you'll pardon my saying so — a stay-at-home who liked everything to be handed to him on a platter. I'd brought a little money with me but I didn't know what to do with it. So I journeyed to see the Rabbi of Belz, who is related to us on my mother's side, and poured my heart out to him with tears and supplications. Believe me, my heart was full. He seemed not to bat an eyelid. All he said was (in that peremptory way he has with me): "Go home. When you get back, go straight to the Squire and lease the brewery from him. God willing, there will be a blessing on you and all your work." I ventured, very gingerly of course, to raise difficulties: "And if, Rabbi, the brewery is already leased to someone else?" but he didn't let me finish and ordered the gabbai to "remove this woman" from the room. As you can well understand, I hurried home, went straight to the agent, Pan Grabinsky — I could still speak Polish from home — and leased the brewery for five years. The previous lessee had left that very week, before the expiry of his lease, because he had lost a lot of money on it. I set to work and I saw immediately, within the first few weeks, that every corner of this house had indeed been specially blessed for me. I found a good brewer, our Herr Lieber. For half the success of a brewery lies in the brewer. The barrels filled up with beer and the beer, thank God, is good and always in great demand. The big 'prosperity' had begun... They began to come in coaches from the villages and the towns, from far and near, to buy for cash. I took on more people to help me run the business — Reb Simha and you, Reb Israel Elia — and forbade Reb Naftali Zvi to lift a little finger. "I want", I said, "a division of labour between us: I'll handle the life in this world and earn a living for us, and you will make provision for the next world." That was the condition I laid down before I took over the brewery and he accepted with pleasure. A year, two years, three years went by without a hitch. Every year I travel to Belz and offer my thanksgiving with a generous hand. It's worth it, don't you think?

One winter morning, in our fourth year here, three of our employees came to me and told the following tale: The previous evening, having stayed on after the big brew to clean the boiler, as they were sitting in the alcove near the fire roasting potatoes and chatting in the dim light while they waited for the water to boil, all of a sudden a podgy, nimble figure popped out of the cellar and clambered on to the broad leather belt that carried him along until he was squeezed between the wheels and the tubs; but he emerged unharmed and walked towards them with a measured tread, a sly, ingratiating smile on his face. He was

127

dressed in a short, red coat and black trousers, bare-headed like someone thoroughly at home, with a small pipe dangling from his mouth over a goatee beard. Going up to them, he made a sign with his finger that they should light his pipe, which had gone out. The terrified Gentiles obeyed — and he burst out laughing in the voice of a one-year-old infant, turned about and went away again, through the tubs and the wheels, and vanished into the cellar as if he had never been. When I heard this story I thought they were trying to pull my leg, and I made a pretence of setting their minds at rest by laughing it off. But I kept the matter in mind. Barely a couple of days later Pearl, who was then a young girl, all milk and roses though no great beauty, burst out of the milk-cellar, frightened out of her wits, her eyes bulging and her face as white as chalk. After we'd managed to bring her to herself, she reported that she had already been on the steps on her way out when a wind suddenly arose and blew out the candle in her hand. Then somebody small but very strong hugged her until her bones felt crushed to pieces and kissed her hard on the mouth. All she could do was scream and when she did the "fellow" promptly disappeared, laughing with the voice of an infant aged one. One night, a short while after that, I heard a noise in the storeroom and the faint sound of breaking. Trach! trach! trach! — as if someone were throwing eggs on the floor. I remembered I had bought several hundred eggs that same day and placed them in a big basket in the storeroom. I wrapped a light robe round me, lit a candle, and with a whispered "Shema Yisrael" I went to see what was going on there. I went in and I saw: all the eggs were arranged in concentric circles in the middle of the floor, like precious stones. I bent down and picked one up, then

a second, then a third. They were all whole and intact.
I put the eggs back in their place and went back to bed.
I didn't close my eyes all night...

I didn't tell anybody what I'd seen. Next morning,
I threw a few things into a bag and left for Belz. No one
knew what for. When I walked in — the door was always
open to me — the Zaddik said with an angelic smile:

"So? the mannikin is causing an uproar at your place?
There's nothing in it. It's worth your while to put up with
him a little. He'll come off the loser in the end. And you,
Hanna, go home in peace, and don't forget to double
your contribution. It's not your money that you're giving...
Efraim! remove the woman!"

I went home and spoke no more about the matter. And
when they came running to me with his latest pranks I used
to tell them off, laughing to myself all the time.

Hanukka came round. Some two dozen large waddling
geese had been fattened up in the coop, to make dripping
from for Pesach. I had bought the geese from the Squire
and they were the big kind that you don't see today. The
ritual slaughterer came and killed them and cut away the
fat, and we filled every vessel in the house with it. On the
second night of Hanukka I made the kitchen kosher and
cleaned the stove in accordance with the ritual laws, and
I was all set to melt down the fat that would be kept for
Pesach. On the stove, I placed five pots and two small
saucepans of solid fat cut into pieces. The pot had barely
managed to heat up when the fat began to bubble and
splutter noisily and run over the sides on to the stove,
making it smoke like a chimney. I brought in more of the
Pesach dishes that stood packed in the attic and went on
filling container after container. My heart pounded like

a blacksmith's sledgehammer while I worked. I recalled
the wife of the prophet who cried out to Elisha and he put
a blessing on the oil and it never ran out. And like her,
I kept carrying away one full jar after another and didn't
feel the heat of the stove at all, or the steam that rose from
the fat and literally scorched my face. Brachele, who was
then a child of about eight, stood by silently watching me
work, her eyes alight with interest. She was small and very
thin. I had almost forgotten she was there, so absorbed
was I in thinking about the miracle," when suddenly the
child called out:

"Mummy, Mummy! Look, a little hand in the chimney
asking for bits of crisp fat; give it, Mummy. It must be a
hungry boy. How thin his hand is!"

I looked inside the chimney and there, just as she said,
was a tiny hand extended with its fingers curled inwards,
as if asking for alms. I don't know what possessed me.
I gave the little girl an angry push:

"Get away from there, stupid! there's nothing there!
Why do you poke your nose into everything?"

But the hand kept coming nearer and nearer although
it didn't get any bigger, until it was suspended over the
dish in front of my very eyes. It was so thin, the fingers
so pale and delicate that I simply couldn't help myself:
I took a few of the crisply-fried pieces of fat which had
managed to cool off in the dish and held them out, but at
that moment something in me rebelled. *Don't give, you'll
spoil everything*... I couldn't decide whether to give or not,
and when I was almost touching the diminutive palm,
I suddenly lowered my hand and dropped the pieces of
fat back into the dish. At that moment the hand disappeared
and at the same time everything stopped. The fat came to a

standstill in the pots and the noisy bubbling stopped. You understand: as the "secret" was out, the unending flow stopped. Perhaps I was just being tested: I should have given the pieces of fat. Actually, the fat sufficed for the whole of the winter and at Pesach time I distributed generous quantities of it to the poor in the town, without giving up any of my own. And it took us right through till after Succoth — and the taste of it was heaven! It was granulated and orangey in colour and none the worse for standing. In all my life I had never known such excellent goose-fat... The Zaddik of Belz knew what he was talking about. He always knows...

When the old lady ended her story there was a smile of approval all round. Only Reb Reuvele's mind was withdrawn. In his imagination, he was gazing far into the distance, way over the heads of the gathering. He had no doubt gone back to his miserable home and was seeing in his mind's eye his poor Manele putting out his hand to ask for food...

Bracha sits without speaking, her cheeks aglow, her eyes shining moist and warm. As she has heard the story of the blessing of the fat many times she fully believes every detail of it (although she doesn't remember the incident concerning herself), and in her imagination she relives the scene which carries her back to her childhood and makes her heart swell with sweet nostalgia. Little Shalom slides to the floor, lays his head on the old lady's knee and closes his weary eyes.

"The child's asleep. It's time to go to bed!" — Mrs Aberdam breaks the silence. Shalom opens his eyes, turns a loving look on the old lady, smiles and says in a perfectly clear voice:

"I'm not asleep. Tell us again about the burning bed. I want to hear it."

But at this moment, the heavy, warning strokes of the big clock in the dining-room fill the air. Each sits counting to himself and at the end of the twelfth stroke Mrs. Aberdam gets up from her chair, the rest following suit, and all disperse to their sleeping quarters.

XVI

The Desecration of the Scroll of the Law

Reb Naftali Zvi's health was deteriorating rapidly. His face was full, his whole body round and fat, and his paunch pushed his ritual fringes further and further away from his knees; but there was a permanent pallor on his face, his eyes grew redder and redder (the lower lids looked as if they had been turned inside out), his lower lip hung down always wet from the spittle that ran from his slightly open mouth, and his greying hair grew sparse and stringy. His speech too became burdened and faltering and when he began a verse from the scriptures it was difficult for him to finish it, and he'd keep going over the same thing and mixing it all up and what he said didn't make much sense. Mrs. Aberdam expressed concern to the people on the place about his sudden decline and attended to him with solicitous devotion, thereby only making him fatter, his face paler and his tongue even heavier. What is more, he began to display a peculiar irascibility which he had not had before and would sometimes suddenly get worked up over nothing at all and behave (pardon the expression) like a youngster or a boor. That too made Mrs. Aberdam unhappy and she kept thinking of her first husband, his gentleness and his charm, although she always tried to drive away these pleasant memories out of pity for Reb Naftali Zvi. She summoned the old Jewish doctor, who looked him over, kidding him as he always did, and pronouncing that this was only "premature old-age." What does it mean? Old age that has come before its time. And what is the treatment? — There *is* no treatment: just less to eat and less to drink... Nevertheless, he prescribed some kind of drops to be taken twice a day, and they didn't help at all.

They were up to "Noah" in the weekly portion of the Law. Ice and snow had not yet come to the land; just a cold, heavy downpour day and night; even the smell of the *menthe* on brewing days was swallowed up in the perpetual wetness and the fog. It was impossible to go outside because of the mud and the chill that penetrated to the very bones. Whoever came into the house brought in cakes of black mud with his shoes or top-boots. Brachele closed the flat and didn't let the children in, although there was an iron grid before the door. Everyone on the premises was bad-tempered. Herr Lieber's nose was like a waterskin full of greenish blood and his mustaches hung down dejectedly, with the water dripping from them. The children hadn't been to the Yashinski place for two weeks now, and if Pani Yuzia hadn't come several times a week to enquire after the children, they wouldn't have known whether they were alive or dead, God forbid. They did their lessons in the old lady's apartment and in their free time they read, or played quietly, or occupied themselves with some game or other. The deaf-mute in the attic lay groaning and grinding his teeth with the pain in his broken back, but no one took any notice of his groans just as he himself didn't hear them; and even Shalom, who went to see him several times, couldn't ease his suffering.

On Sabbath morning, the minyan assembled in the

well-heated prayer-room. In spite of everybody's efforts
to wipe their shoes, the floor was covered with muddy
footprints within a few minutes, and the people tried to avoid
looking down at them. They prayed slowly and without
much enthusiasm. The Reader attempted a hoarse trill as if
in protest against the drizzling of the water outside. The
noise of the rain and the high waters spilling into the lake,
rose and fell as if in accompaniment to the prayers and the
singing. Then they came to the reading of the Law. The
officiants stood around the Reader's table. They began to
call people up. Reb Simha hadn't come this time, so the
reading was given to Reb Zusia the Melamed, who came
to pray in the minyan on rainy days as he didn't live far
from the brewery. Because of his shortsightedness he half
lay on the open Scroll of the Law, and he read in a tearful
voice and with considerable effort. His way of reading
irritated Reb Naftali Zvi this time, and he began to shuffle
his swollen feet under the stand and hitch up his prayer-
shawl which kept slipping off his shoulders. He was called
up third, and stumbled badly over the Blessings, and when
Reb Zusia pointed to the portion of the Law to be read, he
pushed his finger away angrily. After him others came up,
until the last two portions, *Acharon* and *Maftir*, had been
read. Now they had to lift the Scroll of the Law into the
air. The process of lifting it on those Saturdays at the
beginning of the winter is difficult and dangerous, because
the weight is on one side, on the left, making it difficult
to balance. That is why some people roll up the Scroll a
little before they raise it, and that's what they wanted to
do this time as well. But Reb Naftali Zvi, who was still
standing at the table, pushed aside the man who was going
to lift the Scroll, seized the handles, straining with both

arms, pressed the wooden rods down on the edge of the table until the Scroll was almost upright, bent his knees, and with one sweeping movement lifted the Scroll into the air and turned to show it to all the congregation. The bystanders stepped aside, astonished and a little alarmed. At that moment the accident occurred: the old man's left arm suddenly went weak and the heavy side of the Scroll began to wobble in the air. The man standing next to him made a dive to catch it but only caught hold of the parchment and half the Scroll unravelled, turned a somersault in the air, and went plunging to the ground. The fear of God fell upon the whole minyan and cries of *Woe, woe!* filled the air. When they lifted the Scroll from the floor a moment later, the handle was broken as if some heavy boot had stepped on it, and the parchment was all crumpled and dirty in one place. Mrs. Aberdam came running in from the women's section with a cry of distress. She thought Reb Naftali had had a heart attack and fallen. But when she saw what had really happened, she felt no better. On the contrary, she stood there speechless, her mouth open, her arms hanging loosely down her sides, unable to utter a syllable.

The grief of the congregation was so great that it was almost unbearable. They rolled up the Scroll, tied it, and put on its mantle, handling it as they would a sick person. They placed it carefully in the Ark, but could not work up the courage to begin with Mussaf, the latter part of the service. Reb Naftali Zvi sat in his place as white as a sheet. His lips moved but no sound came out of them. Israel Elia sat fanning himself with his tallit. Mrs. Aberdam, who was still with the men, kept repeating that she would go early next morning to see the new Rabbi of Belz (the old one had passed away in the meantime and his son, Reb Issachar Ber now occupied his seat). The men tried to pacify her and in a mixed clamour of voices suggested all kinds of amends: the whole congregation would fast for one day; they'd fast every Monday and Thursday for a certain time; they'd donate something to charity; they'd buy a new curtain for the Ark; they'd write another Scroll of the Law; they'd set three Jews studying chapters of the Mishnah. Sosele, who was also there, swallowing hard and jerking her head each time she did so, also kept at the old lady like an importunate child, stroking the strands of the silk shawl on her shoulders and entreating her in a tearful voice to go back to the women's section. She, Sosele, would think of something. Leave it to her. She'd give all Reb Israel Elia's salary for half a year to charity. The old man isn't to blame at all, he's a weak sick man. Why did they let him lift such a big Scroll? You need the strength of a goy for that...

Eventually, the congregation calmed down a little and recited the Mussaf service in a low voice with a broken heart. Then each one went off to his home and table. They didn't drink Kiddush; they didn't eat kichel. The wind outside lashed the cold slanting rain in their faces. The water even penetrated their shirts, right through to the skin. They shivered from head to foot from the cold within them and without.

The day after Sabbath, work resumed as usual. A heavy shadow seemed to hang over the whole brewery. Mrs. Aberdam did not go to Belz because she was afraid to leave Reb Naftali Zvi alone. From the time he came home from prayers, he lay in his bed unable to move hand or foot, as if he'd become paralyzed, God forbid! He only moved his head from side to side on the pillow, moaning, *Oh my heart, my heart!* No one came to visit him. They were all ashamed and depressed, each wrapped in his own grief and disgrace while he worked, and even more so during the break-hour. So the entire burden of Reb Naftali Zvi's illness fell on Mrs. Aberdam. Only Sosele would slip in two or three times an hour on the tips of her toes and ask in a whisper how the old man was. Bracha shut herself up in her apartment and waited fearfully for the return of her husband who was away travelling, and every hour he delayed was a tortured eternity for her. The children did their religious and secular lessons with their tutors in sad silence, and when they were dismissed they sat quietly in the room: the twins busied themselves with their embroidery and Shalom buried himself in a book to the exclusion of all else.

It the evening, Reb Hirtzel returned home. He had already heard what had happened. As he was passing through the town, he stopped in to see the broker about something and it was he who told him about the accident in the minyan at the brewery on Saturday.

When he came into the house, he found Brachele sitting at the end of the sofa, leaning back with her eyes closed. He went up to her quietly, and passed his hand lightly over her head. She shuddered, opened her enormous eyes, looked at him for a moment and burst into a flood of tears.

"Calm down, darling. Things like that happen and no one is to blame for them. He is a weak old man."

"It's an omen. Terrible things are going to happen here. Oh, Hirtzel, Hirtzel. I want you to swear that you won't go away any more. Don't leave me here alone. You daren't leave me alone. You don't know what you're doing."

138

He was at once frightened and elated. What suffering, and what dependence on him! He sat down beside her, rested his cheek ever so lightly on her shoulder so as not to hurt her. He thought she would quieten down, but instead she began to shake with subdued, strangling sobs which positively rent his heart. At a loss, not knowing what to do for her, he got up and began to pace up and down the room, listening to her weeping that seemed to go on for hours, that seemed interminable. He wanted to say something encouraging, soothing, but for the life of him he could find no words.

About an hour later, Bracha stood up and said in a weak voice, though a little calmer, that she was very tired and wanted to lie down but before doing so she would give him his meal. The children, as usual, were with her mother. They only came to Bracha in the mornings. She didn't see them all day, because of the rainy weather.

After she had set the table for him and put his whole meal in front of him at once, she went into the bedroom to lie down.

When he had finished eating, Reb Hirtzel went quietly into the room and found Bracha asleep, so he went across to his mother-in-law. The children, who were still awake after having eaten, were happy to see him, clamoured around him and pressed against him lovingly. The girls asked him to stay at home for a few days. Grandpa's ill, mother's irritable, and they're just generally scared. Everyone is scowling and the rain doesn't stop and the wind moans all night in the chimneys and raps on the window panes... There were tears in their eyes. Each supplemented what the other said. He did his best to set their minds at rest, and promised to remain at home all week. Until after Shabbat.

Mrs. Aberdam came in. She had already managed to recover and was in full control of herself. She asks after Bracha: good that she's gone to sleep. Reb Naftali feels a bit easier. No, she won't be going to Belz until her husband is well again. He is extremely weak. His legs are swollen like barrels, Heaven help us! and he is complaining about his heart. Reb Hirtzel has undoubtedly heard already about the catastrophe that occurred last Shabbat. She herself fasts all day: Israel Elia is also fasting and so is Sosele; and Pearl; even Herr Lieber, they say, has only eaten once, although he doesn't come to prayers. Bracha isn't allowed to fast. She isn't strong enough. On Yom Kippur too, her fasting gives them a very anxious day... She has also sent money to the study-house for them to recite psalms and learn chapters of the Mishnah. And she has ordered new handles for the Scroll of the Law, from Brod. God willing, when Reb Naftali Zvi gets better, she will make the journey to Belz and ask the Rabbi for an 'intercession' on their behalf. He, Hirtzel, must just keep a good eye on Bracha who is in a terrible state, and let us hope that this business will not affect her delicate heart....

Reb Hirtzel went in to see the sick man and wish him well. Afterwards, he called the three children, wrapped them up in capes and mufflers and took them home. Perhaps under their father's wing, they will sleep without being afraid.

XVII

Two Old People

G raf Molodetzki's agent, Pan Grabinski, was a man well on in years, cultured, courtly and well-liked by others, but completely overshadowed by the horde of women that always surrounded him. He had been living in the manor in L. for almost forty years and it was from him that Mrs. Aberdam leased the brewery at the time. Apart from his wife and three grown daughters, none of whom was married, there were also — as mentioned previously — several sisters, sisters-in-law and distant relatives, some of them widows, some old maids, some living there permanently and others who came and went — so that the manor was a kind of women's house and the Jews in the town jokingly called him Shaashgaz (the name given to the keeper of the harem, in the Book of Esther).

Pan Grabinski was noted for his chivalry, particularly towards "the ladies", and he liked and admired Mrs. Aberdam no less than he did the noble ladies of his own people and class. When she came there three times a year to pay the lease (she paid a third at a time), Pan Grabinsky would invite his wife and the other ladies into his study, which was full of antiques, heavy, valuable pictures, animal skins and antlers, guns and similar objects, and present her to them — all over again each time — enumerating the virtues of "the most gracious Mrs. Aberdam" and.

complimenting her on her excellent Polish. The ladies — most of them dressed in black, with crucifixes on their breasts — would nod their heads to her as to a genuine aristocrat. She was a little put out by this performance, but afterwards, she always left there full of exhilaration and thanksgiving to the Lord and to the Rabbi of Belz. And sometimes the memory of the late Reb Shlomke would rise before her, flicker, and disappear again.

Mrs. Aberdam saw Pan Grabinski just those three times a year. The rest of the year he was completely taken up with the women who surrounded him. He never came to the brewery. He relied completely on Mrs. Aberdam and believed everything she reported when she came to pay the rent. Pan Grabinski often went riding in the town in the company of his ladies on thoroughbred horses, and all eyes followed the lady riders with the white hair and closely-fitting dresses, the finely-tooled riding boots and the little caps perched on top of their coiffured heads. And in the winter he was also to be seen with them, skating for an hour or two over the ice on the lake opposite the brewery. He was very good at it, gliding over the ice with the skill of a glazier drawing a diamond across glass. Then too, many people stood at the fence and watched the magnificent sight. But Mrs. Aberdam had no time for such things, so she never saw him except when she went to pay, although she remembered him with kindness and if anyone referred to him in her hearing by the name of Pan Shaashgaz she would correct him in all seriousness, saying: "Pardon me, Pan Grabinski is his name. If there were more well-bred people like him among the goyim, it wouldn't be a bad thing for the children of Israel."

For their New Year, in the season of the snows and the

ice, Mrs. Aberdam always sent one of the hired hands with a greeting and a gift to the house of Pan Grabinski (she didn't forget Pan Yashinski either), and every Purim, Pan Grabinski sent a greeting and a gift to "the gracious Pani Aberdam". They carried on like this for more than thirty years until one day, at the end of the winter in which the Scroll of the Law was desecrated, Pan Grabinski's rule came to an end.

Graf Molodetzki, having squandered most of his possessions in Paris, was heavily in debt, what with all the interest and the compound interest that he had to pay, so he was forced to seek ways of increasing his income in order to ward off bankruptcy. So he began to demand of his agents that they double his income at all costs. And wherever an agent failed to show results within a short time, he changed him for someone else, someone more forceful. So came the ruin of the gentle Pan Grabinski.

When Mrs. Aberdam was at his place the last time, dressed in her holiday finery as was usual on these visits, and was raising her silk dress above the underskirt of satin yellow as a leaf of gold in order to take out her long, cloth purse, she caught a brief glance of his face and saw that it had changed for the worse. The colour had drained from it and his courtly joviality was gone. Nor did he summon his wife and relatives this time as he always did, but accepted the proffered money with a faint sigh and invited Mrs. Aberdam to be seated while he wrote out the receipt. But the writing of the receipt dragged out endlessly this time. Several times he began to write and stopped, crumpled up the paper and threw it angrily into the basket. Eventually he turned to Mrs. Aberdam with a poor attempt at a smile:

143

"It's difficult, the devil take it! Mrs. Aberdam. This is, apparently, the last receipt that I'll be entitled to write for you. That's how it is. After you've served your masters loyally for nearly forty years — you are dismissed just like that, and without proper compensation either. Nor do you have much prospect of finding another position, most gracious Pani Aberdam. But to hell with the compensation, to hell with the job! That's not what this old heart will grieve for. This place, to which I have become attached with the very roots of my being, to which I devoted all my love, my youth, my strength — how will I leave it, gracious lady? How?"

His old, kindly eyes grew moist and he continued with a bitter laugh: "His Excellency ordered me to increase his income. I have never been able to skin people, so how will I do such a thing in my old age? Raise the rents? Work the employees harder? Let out part of the Palace? Sell most of the horses? Dismiss some of the loyal staff? No, no! Pan Grabinski will have no hand in this! I suggested to His Excellency that he reduce my salary by half. Never mind, I'll manage with less, I'll cut down my household expenses to a minimum. The gentle ladies will do without things... But His Excellency, instead of accepting my sacrifice, wounded me deeply. He wrote me a letter full of sarcasm about my genuine and generous offer. He called me a silly old man and described my sacrifice as the 'alms of a beggar'. I have nothing to answer. The letter of dismissal is there, on the cabinet. So who knows if we will ever see each other again, gracious lady. We have both aged very much and I am departing with my family for my forgotten fatherland in the Pozna region. Shortly, my successor will arrive. I feel very sorry indeed for the gracious Pani Aberdam. The new agent will press and press, for that is what His Excellency the Graf wanted: to press and press and increase his income. *So!*"

Mrs. Aberdam was sick at heart. The pain of Pan Grabinski was added to her dread of the new agent and her worry about her future in the brewery, the lease being due to expire at the end of the coming winter. She wanted to say some word of encouragement to him, but she didn't know what to say to give heart to this honest, noble old man. So she sat there dejectedly, her fingers falling away from the purse, her wordless sympathy showing in her wise old eyes.

Pan Grabinski suddenly pulled himself together, dipped the quill firmly in the ink, and began to write the few lines in large, shaky, uneven letters. This time he succeeded. As he courteously handed the receipt to Mrs. Aberdam, their trembling fingers met.

"God will not forsake us, Pani Aberdam."

"God goes with the righteous, Pan Grabinski."

She saw nothing on the way home. In her apartment, she took off her best clothes and hung them up one by one in the big cupboard, put on her house-coat and went into the room of Reb Naftali Zvi who was feeling a little better and sat all day on the sofa, his swollen legs in woollen felt slippers sticking out straight in front of him like foreign bodies. Beside the sofa stood a table with his books (he had long given up making sacred ornaments). First she asked how he felt and whether they had given him his glass of hot milk. Then she told him she had just come from Pan Grabinski. Reb Naftali Zvi looked at her blankly.

"I paid the second third of the lease. The Graf has

F

dismissed him from his post, poor thing. Soon, a new agent will come. My heart is full of foreboding."

"My stomach hurts," replied Reb Naftali Zvi with trembling lips, his eyes beseeching like the eyes of an infant.

"Perhaps you'll have a glass of hot tea with blackberry juice? You know it always helps you..."

"Take me outside," the old man mumbled, tears gathering in his eyes.

A feeling of dark horror came over Mrs. Aberdam. *Why, he's gone altogether infantile!* A cruel longing entered her mind. She was seized with a desire to take hold of her cheeks and scratch them with all her might, but she conquered it and went up to her husband, and put her devoted hand on his skull-cap:

"What's happened, Reb Naftali Zvi? Did something frighten you?"

"I want some honey-cake," he smiled, his face turned up to her. Black spots began to flutter before Mrs. Aberdam's eyes. *Woe is me! The old man has really grown infantile! He is lost!* A frightening thought kept nagging at her. The incident of the desecrated Scroll stood vividly before her eyes and she recalled with dread that she had not yet made the journey to Belz to put it right, and this was the result.

"Where should I take you," she asked, getting a hold on herself with difficulty.

"I want honey-cake!"

She went into the dining-room, took a slice of honey-cake out of the sideboard, left over from Shabbat, and handed it to the old man with a hand that trembled. He snatched the cake from her and began to gobble it ravenously, gathering up the crumbs that fell on his coat with his swollen fingers.

From then on, with all Mrs. Aberdam's efforts to hide it, the whole courtyard knew about it, and from the courtyard the news went out to all the town that Reb Naftali Zvi had turned senile, the good Lord preserve us! and was not in his right mind. Everyone on the premises sympathised with her but didn't dare express it to her face, because of her silence.

The work of the brewery went on as usual, but there was not a smile to be seen any more on the face of anyone in the compound.

Mrs. Aberdam made preparations to go to Belz. Although she had not yet seen the new Zaddik, she was confident that he would help her.

The Death of Reb Naftali Zvi

Mrs. Aberdam came back from Belz in very low spirits. The new Zaddik, whom she had seen several times before but not from near, was even sterner and crosser than his father of blessed memory. The first day she came he wouldn't let her in, and the gabbai who always used to run in front of her to clear the way for her, hinted by means of peculiar grimaces that he couldn't do anything for her, to his regret. It was the Zaddik's wish. And when she went in next day, tired and cross herself, the Zaddik read her "chit" with a short growl into his thick beard and mustache, glanced at her once under bushy eyebrows with a look of anger and reproof, and when he finished reading and she prepared to add a few words verbally, as she usually did, he silenced her with a wave of his large hand. He sighed, blessed her coldly and ordered the gabbai to "remove the woman".

For her bad luck with the Rabbi she naturally put the blame on herself and not on the Rabbi. He must certainly have found her wanting in some respect. Who knows what it was, or if it was remediable. All the way back in the waggon (two and a half days she travelled, although it was spring and the roads were dry, for she had to change waggons three times on the way) she took moral stock of herself, coming always to the bitter conclusion that she shouldn't have married again after the death of her first husband, the pious Reb Shlomke. All her troubles pointed to that, and who knew what was in store for her when the new agent came. Perhaps he was a bad man and hated Jews.

Might she not be left destitute and have to wander from her nest with her old and helpless husband? Was it possible that in her old age she would have to be beholden to someone? For she was not very well off. She had known that all the time. Only two people knew: Reb Simha the accountant and herself. But he didn't know that she knew...

But when she got home and saw how dazed Reb Naftali Zvi was, and the oppressive mood that pervaded every corner of the place, and Brachele who could face no-one and almost never left her apartment, and the children who had become adults to all intents and purposes, setting about their duties quietly and gravely, fully aware of the situation — she determined to overcome her bad luck and apply herself even more to the business of the brewery and charitable deeds. "For who knows what the morrow will bring," she said to herself, in the words of the Proverbs. She must make money for both worlds. If the Zaddik doesn't help her, she has no alternative but to do it all herself, and God will not forsake her for her intentions are of the best. Maybe the Godfearing Reb Shlomke up there in heaven will intercede for her. Why, even when she was with Reb Naftali Zvi she never forgot him. Especially when she looks at Brachele, she seems to see his shadow over her face.

So she began to spur on the workers to pay more attention and try harder. Her eye drilled into every corner, twice as much as in previous years: no forgetting, no negligence, no waste! Reb Simha the accountant began to fear her, possibly because he felt he was losing his grip. He now saw that she really understood accounts — and he thought all those years that she knew nothing about it and allowed himself to get a little lax with his work! She warned Reb Israel Elia a number of times to keep a sharper eye on the Gentiles who came to the place so they shouldn't take anything, from a barrel to a husk of grain which is good for animal fodder. On Saturdays, she used to lead Reb Naftali Zvi by the hand to the minyan and place him carefully in his chair, and help him into his capacious prayer-shawl with the heavy silver-ornamented band. He obeyed her in everything like an infant, and when she went out to the next room, the women's section, all the worshippers would look at him pityingly, sometimes with a faint smile of derision. Only Herr Lieber gave her no cause for complaint. He did his work faithfully and didn't change in any way. He didn't even stop curling his mustache which was already getting grey, and went on cooking the *cholent* on Shabbat on the window sill, and would accost the boy, Shlomke, with his one and only joke: "So, what is beer?" And when the boy gave him the answer he wanted: "Beer is only liquid bread", his happiness knew no bounds. *"That's it! Not everyone knows that!"*

Mrs. Aberdam informed Reb Simha firmly that she wanted to know the exact state of her finances and she was giving him a month to bring her a clear, exact statement of account, so that she could know how to plan her actions for the future. *"For who knows what the morrow will bring. It is also for the good of all of you, Reb Simha. How do they say in the Proverbs?: He also that is slothful in his work..."* "*...is brother to him that is a great drinker,*"

Reb Simha rounded off the quotation, hastily correcting himself: "I mean to say — *a great waster.*"

It was a late spring with a plenitude of warm rain and pleasant storms. For two or three days a week the sun shone brightly; for the rest, heavy clouds hung in the lowering skies, while lightning crackled and thunder rolled and the lake was full to overflowing and the labourers ran barefoot in the yard, their heads covered with folded sacks, and vegetables sprouted in the beds, covering the black earth with large, fresh green leaves. Heaps of barrels lay about heavily as if swollen by the rain, and the steam was swallowed up in the accumulated waters of the rain the moment it was ejected from the brewery. But when the rain stopped, the sun emerged, freshly washed and pure, high up in a sky of deep crystal blue, and on the ground the well-trodden paths dried in a twinkling and it was pleasant to walk about outside on the soft earth and breathe the fragrant air and feast the eye on glistening strips of foliage of every type and listen to the chorus of the birds as they flitted about and chirruped in a sort of ecstatic intoxication as if they had just come out of the Garden of Eden. It seemed as if the spring would never end: the sadness had rosy cheeks.

The festival of Shavuot was drawing near. The children of the town were already to be seen walking about in the side streets, studying the trees and assessing with expert eye which were nice enough to provide "greenery for Shavuot". The chestnut trees had a profusion of pinkish blossoms in their thick, heavy foliage. Even the acacia with its light leaves was still in bud because of the cold and the moisture in the air, that spring; so too the azederac, all purple and white. The entire estate was a mass of leaves and flowers.

On days when the sun shone bright, the windows of Bracha's house were wide open, and with her handkerchief she'd shoo out the flies that gathered there during the rainy weather. Shalom would stroll around the yard and its environs, an acacia branch in his hand, taking in everything around him. He'd even stop and discuss the greenery for the festival with the boys of the town, whether he knew them or not, giving them good advice and promising to help them when the time came to go searching around the brewery. He even said he would prepare a long stick for them, with a cleft at the top so they could lop off the tender branches without having to climb up the tree, an art which Mende the deaf-mute had taught him. He learned that three of the boys were getting together to decorate the Husiarinic study-house and would be starting work in a day or two. This partnership in a mitzvah pleased him considerably and he promised them masses of flowers and branches from the brewery grounds and willows from the edge of the lake.

It was a fine morning. The twins were again at Pani Yuzia's place. (Shalom didn't go there any more. From the day he read the two books, *The Tribe of Judah* and *Yossiphon*, and knew what the Gentiles had done to the people of Israel, he hated them and the landed gentry in particular and kept away from them. He also had a grudge against his sisters for associating with them and liking them.) While he was walking about outside, he suddenly saw his grandmother come out of the yard all dressed up. He walked up to her to find out where she was going. Seeing him, she said:

"Shlomke darling, I'm going to the Rebbetzin. The two of us are going out to collect money for a poor bride.

I may not be back before evening. Keep an eye on Grandpa from time to time, son, You know he can't do anything for himself. If he wants something give it to him. D'you promise?''

"Yes, I promise."

"And I rely on you. I know you'll keep your promise."

And she set off down the street, a fine, elegant, stately figure of a woman. He stood gazing fondly after her for a few moments.

The fine air, the brightness of everything and all nature in bloom captivated his little heart, and he wandered around outside for about an hour. He passed the hedge alongside the lake and cut a few willow twigs just to try out his pen-knife and see if it was sharp. Then he went into the vegetable garden, cut off a large pumpkin-leaf with his knife, pared it down to the hollow centre-stalk, being very careful not to perforate the head. Then he split the top with his knife and put the stalk in his mouth and blew into it, producing a sort of wheezing note like a hoarse trumpet. When this musical instrument wilted, he took a thin grass stem, placed it between both thumbs, and bringing it up to his lips produced all kinds of noises, the most successful being the crowing of a cock, sometimes an old one, sometimes a young one depending on the distance between his thumbs. These sounds attracted a number of children, amongst them his sisters and the neighbour's daughters, who stood on the other side of the fence and looked on enviously and asked him to give them the ''whistle'' he had in his hand, but he didn't even deign to answer them... He pulled himself up with a start, suddenly remembering what his grandmother had asked of him. He threw everything down among the vegetables, hurried out of the garden and went to the old lady's house to see how the invalid was faring.

In the yard, the new plug-drawer was banging with his machine. All the usual noises were issuing from the brewery. Herr Lieber was striding diagonally across the yard to get to the malt-house, and when he caught sight of Shalom he beckoned to him to stop and began: "So beer...." but this time the boy took no notice of him as he hastened towards his grandmother's apartment. In the open doorway of the wood-shed, Israel Elia stood shaking his keys threateningly in someone's face as the boy went by and it infuriated him as usual. Shalom ran up the steps and entered the long hall. He went through the big diningroom and carefully opened the bedroom door. There was a vast silence and a peculiar atmosphere in the rooms. Without doing so consciously, he began to walk on tip-toe, until he reached Reb Naftali Zvi's room. Hesitatingly, he pushed the handle down and even more hesitantly he opened the door slightly and put his head in. A heavy odour, hot and stifling, enveloped his face. His eyes widened as he saw Reb Naftali Zvi lying on the sofa with his body in an unusual position. The start he gave opened the door further, so he went into the room. His eyes popping with fright, he looked at the body of the man lying there. His legs, which were badly swollen over the felt slippers, were stiffly extended, with the feet straight up in the air as if tied together; one arm hung down the side of the sofa, reaching to the floor, the hand very yellow and the fingers splayed and swollen, like stumps of wax-candles at the end of Yom Kippur. They almost stood upright on the floor. But most frightening of all was the face. The head had fallen to one side, the eyes wide and staring, mouth open, and hair so pale on the parchment of his face that it looked like nothing more than faint smudges. Flies moved quietly on his gown, but not a single one on his face, which was horrifyingly smooth and waxen and glistening with cold sweat.

He's dead! the terrible thought flashed through the badly shaken boy's mind. For a moment he stood petrified, then he began to back away slowly, unaware that he had his own mouth open, just like the man lying there. The door, which was only slightly ajar, pushed against his back and almost closed behind him. Terror invaded his limbs, but he couldn't turn his face away. He stretched his hand out behind him, felt all around until he succeeded in catching hold of the edge of the door and opening it, and crossed the threshold backwards. He closed the door, stood there in the bedroom for a moment and then suddenly swung round and dashed terrified into the dining-room, from there into the hall and out. He jumped down the steps and ran as if pursued into the middle of the yard. There he stopped. He wanted to shout but he had lost his voice. He looked frantically from side to side and didn't know what to do. His heart was thumping so hard it shook his whole body. As he stood there stunned and bewildered and shaken to the depths of his little soul, Mrs. Aberdam came hurrying from the gate, coat flying, her face flushed and her eyes fearful, her hands moving as if trying to catch something. When she saw Shalom standing in the middle of the yard, the way he was standing and the look on his face, she cried out:

"Woe is me! My heart told me... What's going on at home? What's happened!"

The boy didn't answer. He just kept looking at her, a

thin film of tears in his eyes. The old woman grabbed her cheeks and pinched them hard and then began striking herself on the top of the head with both hands, until her shawl slipped off her shoulders. Then she spread her arms out like the wings of a bird and made a frantic dash for the house with total disregard for her age. A moment later Pearl, the cook, burst out of there with a terrible wail. The brewery noises seemed to halt in mid-air. Bracha's head stuck out of the window of her apartment for a moment and disappeared again, leaving the window blank and ominous. From way inside the brewery, Herr Lieber came running, bare-headed, hair dishevelled. Behind him ran Israel Elia, caftan open, and after him Vanka the stoker, his fur hat in his hand, all ready to cross himself. The cook's wailing filled the air and silenced the noise of the brewery. The two Gentiles working in the garden stuck their spades into the loose ground and, resting on them with their bare arms, looked on with surprise and amusement.

In a flash, everyone knew: The old man had departed this life.

His death was an event that absorbed Shalom to the exclusion of all else. That night, after going to bed in his mother's apartment with his sisters, he did not close an eyelid because he couldn't tear his thoughts away from the dead man. He kept seeing him over and over again as he lay there on the sofa. Although he didn't actually see what they did to him, he knew they took him off the sofa and laid him on some straw on the ground, feet to the door, and covered him with a black cloth and placed a lighted candle at his head and the beadle of the prayer-house sat and watched over the body. The waxen face of the dead man, smooth and cold, was constantly before his eyes, and no matter how hard he closed them, or how much he turned over and covered his head with the burning blanket, he couldn't drive away the terrible image that plagued him ceaselessly. The twins, annoyingly, slept a deep, untroubled sleep. Only his mother tossed and turned all night, without uttering a sound — and that increased his dread even more because in his imagination he could see her open eyes staring unseeingly in the dark. He prayed silently for morning to come quickly, and the moment dawn broke he dressed with chattering teeth and went outside without washing his hands. He walked a little while in the silent yard (an order had been given the previous evening not to work in the brewery on that day and the gates were closed as on Shabbat), and kept looking in the direction where the old lady lived, where the dead man lay. Then he went out into the street and stood in the middle of the road, looking to see if his father was coming in his horse and trap. He was certain he would come. It was impossible that he shouldn't. And indeed, at eight o'clock, Reb Hirtzel came driving along in his dusty carriage. The horse was sweating, and its chest was quivering with the effort. Reb Hirtzel already knew what had happened, and when he saw his son standing in the road waiting for him, he pulled up and enquired after his mother with great concern.

"She's in bed," the boy replied.

"Did she cry?"

"No. She's quiet. Hasn't said a word."

Shalom clambered on to the back of the cart and the horse entered the yard at a leisurely pace, nodding its head up and down. At the same time, two men arrived from the Chevra Kadisha, the Burial Society. One of them was carrying a bundle of shrouds under his arm. The two of them went up to Mrs. Aberdam's apartment, backs bent, their beards still a little wet after washing. The wood-shed was open, and inside the Jewish carpenter from the village was sawing wood to make the coffin. It occurred to the boy that he ought to see how the purification was done and although the sight of the dead man still filled him with horror, he made up his mind to steal into the bedroom and see what they were doing from there. He must see it. He'd get under one of the beds and peep.

A few at a time, the townspeople began to gather in the courtyard, to pay their last respects to the deceased. Soon there were several score of them, men, women and children.

Shalom lay under the bed and watched through the aperture what the two men were doing. The taller of the two recited a lengthy prayer over the dead man from a small, thin book. Then they brought hot water in a big jug, undressed the dead man who was stiff and hairy and yellow all over, placed him on a broad plank resting on a couple of chairs and washed the body lightly, taking care not to turn it over on its face, by turning it first to one side and then to the other. They rubbed it well, cleaned between the fingers and the toes and in the ears, and cut the fingernails and toenails with a knife. After that, they placed the dead man on some straw and emptied the jug over his head, the water running copiously over the floor. They took an egg, broke it into a basin, poured in a little wine, mixed it all together and washed his head, then washed and combed his hair. While this was being done, the dead man's cheeks wobbled like empty pouches and his whole body rocked with the motion. Then they

propped him up and in standing position dressed him in
a shroud, trousers and girdle (which they fastened without
tying), kittel, white robe and hat; they put on his fine
prayer-shawl and cancelled one of the ritual fringes.
Then they put him down on a different spot (not where
they did the purification) facing the door. They washed
their hands in water and salt, talking quietly to each other.
Finally, they brought the coffin in, picked the body up
off the ground, placed it in the coffin, pressed it down
well and covered it with a black cloth. Then began great
activity in the house. Shalom slid out from under the bed
and mingled with the people going out. His heart was
hammering as if it was going to burst, his head spinning.

At ten o'clock the coffin was taken out of the house and
down the steps, to the accompaniment of the chanting of
the Chevra Kadisha. The crowd that had assembled at the
steps parted to make way for the pallbearers. The beadle
flitted in and out of the crowd, rattling a collection box,
repeating in a nasal, lugubrious voice: *Charity will save
you from death! Charity will save you from death!* Many
people put money in the box. The coffin-bearers seemed
to be in a hurry and positively ran along with the burden
on their shoulders, the crowd on their right and on their
left and behind them, with sad faces and glistening,
frightened eyes. The old lady walked behind the coffin,
escorted by several worthy ladies of the community, and
crying quietly into a handkerchief. Bracha walked beside
her husband with a stony face, moving like an automaton.
After them came the twins, also crying quietly though
with a barely perceptible undertone of indignation as if
some wrong had been done them. Behind them walked
Shalom. He only bit his lips, with a bewildered look in his

eyes. Pearl, the cook, kept up her piercing, sing-song lamentations all the while.

When they reached the gate, Mrs. Aberdam turned round and asked her daughter to go back home. She is not strong enough for this and the cemetery is far. She herself and Hirtzel will, of course, go on to the cemetery...

The children remained behind with Bracha. They stood at the gate, following with their eyes the rapidly disappearing funeral procession. The crowd churned up the dust with their feet as they hurried along, the stragglers puffing and panting to keep up and stumbling over obstacles on the way. Then Bracha and the children turned back and went slowly into the courtyard, weighed down by an oppressive feeling as if they had been robbed and left destitute.

XIX

The Weeping of Bracha

During Shiva, the seven days of mourning, prayers were held in Mrs. Aberdam's apartment. And when it was over, Mrs. Aberdam got up from the low stool and went back to her work in the brewery, head high and with an even greater willingness than before. Everything she was required to do in honour of and for the soul of Reb Naftali Zvi, she did and more. As he left no son, she engaged a pious Jew to say Kaddish in the morning and the evening and study a chapter of the Mishnah every day. She also put on her glasses and wrote in her own handwriting on the fly-leaf of the prayer-book the exact date of his death, so as to observe the day each year. She distributed his clothes among the poor (except his best tallit which he was buried with), and took out his bed and had it placed in his own room, where it could stand and not be touched by anybody. His books she divided into three: part she gave to Reb Hirtzel, part to the synagogue, and a few for herself — books on ethics which she could read although they were written in Hebrew. The two pairs of phylacteries she kept at home — maybe they would be needed for the rapidly growing grandson, for Shlomke, grandson of the one who is already a veteran up there in heaven.

There were signs of new and renewed vigour in her, as

if her life-force had been doubled. As for the worrying business of the change of agent, she simply put it off and refused to delve into it too deeply. There was plenty of time for that and no doubt the Lord would not forsake her. She was confident that she now had two advocates in heaven: Reb Shlomke and Reb Naftali Zvi, for she had treated them both very well and they must surely remember her kindly. The sting from her last visit to the Zaddik would not allow her to place any reliance on him or seek any support from him; whenever she called him to mind it hurt, so she tried not to think about him. It was like having a grudge against an estranged relative. Never mind, the Lord would save her. Salvation from that quarter, so to speak, was sweeter and surer.

The work in the brewery went on apace. Latterly, business had been improving. New customers came from a number of distant villages, the price of barley was low and the hops, too, were not expensive, the brew came out well and Herr Lieber's face glowed with satisfaction. He too seemed to have doubled his energy. Someone came from the big Halperin brewery in Brod, tasted the beer and praised it highly. Also the "beggars" came from far and near to solicit money from her: and Mrs. Aberdam gave more generously than ever before.

Only from her daughter did she derive no satisfaction. None at all. Reb Hirtzel was complaining that his various businesses had become more than he could cope with. They were draining him dry mentally. Those bloodsuckers in Lwow knew no mercy. But on the other hand it wasn't possible without them because the squires always demanded payment in cash. Oh dear! No matter how hard he calculated he never seemed to see the end of it... But although his business affairs involved enormous sums of money — that wasn't the main trouble. The main worry was Bracha's condition.

The death of Reb Naftali Zvi affected her very badly. He was, it is true, just a stepfather, but even more than at the beginning, she isolated herself in her apartment, her large eyes always fixed in a long, alien stare. She even cut herself off completely from her children now, as if they were strangers to her, as if she didn't feel that they existed. And worst of all, she began to get violent fits of sobbing that would attack her quite often. Nobody had ever heard anything like it: first, it would start quietly and then get fiercer and fiercer until it pierced the eardrums, and from the ear it penetrated the heart, terrifying, shattering, filling the listener with immeasurable pain. Sitting alone in her bedroom behind the window-screen, she would go on crying for hours on end, sometimes in the daytime but mostly in the evening and at night. It was a sharp, quivering of sobbing that gave one's heart a wrench. She would be seized with a crying fit at any time, whether Reb Hirtzel was at home or not. At first, Reb Hirtzel would sit beside her and talk or keep silent to calm her. Mrs. Aberdam also used to come in, and Sosele (ai! she was herself the unhappiest of women since the day when a relative of the little orphan girl came and took her away to his home, against her will and against theirs), and they pondered the matter and sent the children to her; perhaps they would have a good influence on her. But to no avail. Brachele went on crying. Even the labourers in the yard used to listen to the soft sound of her weeping, which went straight to their hearts. At first they tried to give advice, afterwards they only shook their heads, and finally they gave her up altogether and left her to cry to her heart's content; perhaps she'd cry until the source of her tears dried up and then she'd stop.

When she stopped crying, she would fall silent but even in her silence the echo of it seemed to linger. Sometimes she would appear outside afterwards, with her soft, young, slender figure and her fine, delicate face, and it was almost undetectable in her that she had cried so much and shed so many tears. And then whoever saw her felt an urge to do something for her, to give her something, to run errands for her, to revive her, to pay homage as it were. All eyes hung on every movement of her lips and every twitch of her eyebrow.

Various Jewish ladies who were normally never seen on the brewery premises, began to call on Mrs. Aberdam, sigh for her, turn up their eyes and offer advice about treatments tried and proven in similar cases. Just like the time when Brachele was childless. But Mrs. Aberdam's face was closed now and her mind seemed to be on other things. What advice could mere mortals give her?

Shavuot was over. The summer days followed bright and hot and people began to come from the town to bathe in the lake. The squires came with their families, all dressed in summer clothes. They'd cross the little wooden bridge that leads to the pretty bathing pavilion built on piles in the middle of the lake, chattering and laughing loudly, the children carrying baskets full of sweetmeats and flowers that they picked as they came. The Jewish children stood watching them enviously from a distance. Next to the pavilion there was also a part fenced off for swimming but Jews were not allowed in there. The fish flashed through the green waters like darts and slivers of silver and gold, swimming into sight and out and in again with a slash and a swish, splashing a drop of freshness into the hearts of the beholders.

One day that summer (Graf Molodetzki was coming to hunt with his entourage) there was some big fishing in the lake, by order of the agent. They opened the sluices of the canal on the slope and in the course of a few hours drained all the water out of the lake. One could see the mud at the bottom and the springs from which strong streams of fresh water gushed gurgling forth. The entire floor of the lake, extending over a vast area, lay exposed and gleaming in the sunlight. The large, well-nurtured fish could be seen struggling and thrashing about in the cold mud and tensing to leap into the air. The palace servants moved about in their short smocks and bare, dirty feet, gathering the slippery fish in their hands and slapping them into big pails filled with water. All along the hedge around the lake stood crowds of people from the town and farmers and peasants from the environs, watching the entertaining spectacle. Everyone in the town knew that in almost every Jewish house that evening there would be a savoury, well-spiced meal of carp or perch or bream or, at least, a few of those small fish that are good to fry in butter. It's just a pity that today is only Tuesday and it's impossible, in the heat of the summer, to put some of it aside for the Sabbath. The whole town was excited and agog over the event, each one waiting impatiently for what the fishermen would bring him either from the leftovers or from what they took away. Reb Hirtzel's children were also among the spectators. The twins with Pan Yashinski's daughters and Shalom on his own, a little distance away from them. Shalom was impatient for them to get done with the fishing and close the sluice-gate so that he could see the lake fill up again to revive the floundering fish before they expired. He felt very keenly for them in their agony, as if they were human children like himself. The sun began to go down and a cold wind rose over the naked lake. The pails were already full and the men carried them away two at a time, backs bent under the weight. Then they blocked the opening of the canal and the spring water began to gather in the lake, levelling out the bottom and little by little covering the rest of the fish. The fishermen emerged slowly from the lake and gathered together at a spot near the pavilion. Setting the pails down on the edge of the lake, they formed a circle around them and burst into song. Even the lowing of the herd returning from pasture did not disturb their singing, as it rose fresh and clear from the throats of tough and hardy workmen.

Only in the yard of the brewery, where work had stopped by now and the labourers and their haversacks had gone, could the sobbing of "the poor young lady" be heard.

The moon rose full and large and red in the east horizon and made for the highest point of the heavens. The singing of the fishermen died down slowly and the subdued weeping of Bracha grew louder and louder until the sound of it spread to all the courtyard and beyond.

XX

Reb Hirschele "Merubeh"

T he day before the Shabbat after Tish'a Be'Av, at
eleven o'clock in the morning, a small farmer's cart
harnessed to a rustic horse pulled up at the gate of the
brewery and a Jew descended from it carefully. He was
short, broad and paunchy, with a copious beard down to
his navel, his whole face pink and smiling in a forest of
hair. In one hand he carried an old woollen scarf and in
the other a rubbed and crumpled leather bag. His clothes
were also crumpled and he walked with his legs wide
apart because of his big hernia, which made him look
as if he were trying to catch a chicken. He was sweating
profusely from the heat and dragged his feet as he went
through the yard, raising a cloud of dust with his large top-
boots. He lifted his burning face, eyes blinking in the
blazing sun, sniffed the air with considerable pleasure and
looked to all sides as if expecting someone. Eventually,
his little eyes came to rest on the steps leading to the
apartment of Mrs. Aberdam, mistress of the brewery. He
nodded to himself and made for them.

Just as he reached the top step Mrs. Aberdam emerged
from the lobby and when she saw who was there she was
a bit nonplussed for a moment and then cried out:

"Why, Reb Hirschele! We had almost given you up.
Welcome! Come inside."

Whereupon he let out a ripple of laughter, nodding his head and making eyes at her, and said in a pleasant voice:

"God preserve you, Mrs. Aberdam, God preserve you. I'm late this year. After Pesach I was sick (may you be spared a similar fate) for about three weeks. He–he! My (excuse me) hernia was playing up. I lay in bed at home (may you be spared) and was delayed till now. And how is Reb Naftali Zvi? In good health, I trust?"

Mrs. Aberdam is not ruffled by the question, but answers with a sigh:

"Haven't you heard, Reb Hirschel? Naftali Zvi, may he rest in peace, passed away about two and a half months ago..."

"Ai — Ai — Ai!" cried the guest, shaking his head, "and I heard nothing about it. Ai — ai — ai! Two and a half months ago? That is to say before Shavuot? Ai — ai — ai, such a dear person! Why, he was still in his prime, may he rest in peace! In his full vigour. Last year still — he was in the best of health. How could it be, all of a sudden?... Ai — ai — ai!"

"Come in, please, Reb Hirschel. It was sudden and not so sudden. A sort of heart attack, the Lord preserve us. I went out in the morning to collect for a poor bride with the Rabbi's wife, and we had just been to two or three houses and my heart said to me: *Hanna, hurry home. Something bad has happened there.* I made my excuses to the Rabbi's wife and ran home as fast as could. I came in the gate and there was my grandson Shlomke standing in the middle of the yard as if transported, so help me God. I knew at once that this was final. Lying there on the sofa he had breathed his last.... without confession. Who knows, perhaps he just went like that, without having time... There was no one to close his eyes and they remained open..."

They went in to the cool dining-room. There sat Reb Simha the accountant who had brought his ledgers to work on there because of the intense heat, and next to him, leaning against the table, stood Shalom, watching Reb Simha work and enjoying the jokes he kept cracking as he added and subtracted. Reb Simha held out his hand in greeting to the advancing guest, without raising his eyes from his ledger. Shalom did likewise, as was the custom.

"Reb Hirschele has come!" Mrs. Aberdam announced, seeming pleased to have him.

He placed his bag and his scarf on the sofa and said:

"You no doubt thought that Hirschele 'Merubeh' wouldn't be coming any more this year. Eh, how could you think such a silly thing, if you'll pardon my saying so? Hirschel Merubeh is not one to forgo Mrs. Aberdam's roast! Believe me, the taste of it doesn't leave my mouth all year; and actually, my dear Mrs. Hanna, I'm practically on an empty stomach. I prayed this morning in the village of Zavitch and apart from a small glass of brandy and a biscuit I haven't eaten a thing. If I am not mistaken we are on the eve of Shabbat and it is almost midday and I can already smell the thing....Ah! A pleasure!"

Being inside the house, it was better that he shouldn't say anything more about the deceased as it might affect his appetite for the roast in the evening. But Reb Simha who couldn't stand the expansiveness of the Husiatinic collector and wanted to needle him a bit, said, without lifting his eyes from the ledger:

"Indeed, Reb Hirschel, we were saying that you

must have drowned, if not in brandy, at least in borscht."

"I'm surprised at you, Reb Simha," replied Reb Hirschel pleasantly," it's just the reverse! Everyone knows that all the brandy and borscht usually drown in me, not I in them, he–he! Not so, Shlomke? Ai–ai! Since last year you've grown two handbreadths, praise the Lord! You can be sure, Mrs. Aberdam's grandson has also grown in Torah and good deeds. Which tractate of the Talmud are you learning?"

And he settled down in one of the armchairs and smoothed his beard in pleasurable anticipation like a man testing his son on a Sabbath afternoon.

"*Baba Kama*," replied the boy, his eyes glued to Reb Simha's accounts.

"Chapter?"

"*Merubeh*."

Reb Hirschel was convinced that the boy was making fun of him and even suspected that Reb Simha had prompted him. He answered:

"Ah, so! And I said you are learning *Drech Eretz*" (punning on the name of the chapter, which means "respect").

The boy didn't catch the sly dig, just as he didn't know in his innocence that he had offended Reb Hirschel, for he was really up to that chapter.

The nickname of "Merubeh" by which Reb Hirschel, collector of donations for the Zaddik of the Husiatinic Hassidim was known, could be interpreted in various ways. Some people took it to refer to his shape, the word meaning "square"; others — and they were the majority — spelling the word slightly differently to mean "much", called him Merubeh because he ate a lot, drank a lot, slept a lot, demanded a lot, and so on. He himself couldn't care less, and wore his nickname like a jewel.

Mrs. Aberdam, who had gone into the kitchen in the meantime to tell Pearl to set the table for Reb Hirschel and give him a first course of gravy-roast, came back and informed her guest that he was going to get his wish right away. She also asked him to excuse her as she had to go somewhere on a charitable mission and would be back soon. Reb Hirschel would spend the Sabbath here and would no doubt wish to take part in the reading of the Torah. The whole minyan would be pleased to see him.

Reb Hirschel, who was busy at the open bag on the sofa, nodded his head and made some sort of noise in his nose, but his mind was preoccupied with one disturbing question: *If Reb Naftali Zvi is dead, who will I get the donation from?*

When he heard about the gravy-roast, and especially when the kitchen door opened and the enticing smell assailed his nostrils, Reb Simha could no longer sit quietly at his accounts. His mouth began to water and the figures seemed to bubble before his eyes like drops of fat. What did he do? He closed the ledgers, stuck them under his arm and went to the office to put them away so that he could go home. Shalom made to go with him but Reb Hirschel detained him:

"Sit with me, Shlomke. What do you say to a little chat about Hassidism? After all, you are the grandson of a lady who is a great Hassid, although her Zaddik is only the Rabbi of Belz..." The boy wasn't a bit keen on discussing Hassidism, but he stayed because of the novelty of it.

"Will we meet at the mikveh, Reb Hirschel?" asked Reb Simha, in the doorway.

173

"God willing, if the steam is not too thick, He–he!"

Pearl came in, spread a cloth over half the table and set a place. On the table she put salt and horseradish made with red beets and a whole round chala of fine flour baked just that morning. Reb Hirschel took a gown out of the bag, rolled it down to the ground like a kittel and examined the rents in it.

"Perele," he said in a wheedling voice, without looking at her, "I next to the patches you put on last year, there are new tears.. Come and see."

"Leave it on the sofa. When I'm finished I'll mend it."

"Don't forget, Perele, it is the eve of Shabbat today and I haven't got any other gown for the bath-house."

"Don't worry. Until you're ready to go, I'll have it fixed."

Reb Hirschel looked at her with half an eye and cried out gaily:

"Ai, Pearl, if only I were a bachelor, or a divorcee, or at least a widower...!"

"Shame on you, in front of the boy!"

She went out and came back a moment later with a deep plate, and in it the slice of roast in a sea of brown gravy. The hot, fragrant steam filled the air and Reb Hirschel began to blink hard and dilate his nostrils. He put down the bag, took off his velour hat and adjusted his skull-cap, went into the passage to wash his hands, came in again holding them up in the air, wiped them on a towel hanging on a nail in the wall, and gabbled off the relevant benediction with eyes piously turned up. Then he sat down at the table with a good feeling, passed the knife over the whole loaf and said the blessing loudly; then he broke the bread in the middle, cut off a piece, dipped it in salt and tasted it;

next he turned his attention to the roast, inhaling its aroma, studying it from all sides. His beard was dishevelled and sweaty, his lips pursed together as if sucking, his face glistening from the steam. He took one half of the chala, stuck four fingers deep into it and pulled out the inside in one piece. This he dipped into the gravy, pressing it a little and letting go and then repeating the process until most of the gravy was soaked up into the soft bread. He tried to lift it with his fingers but it fell to pieces because of the weight so that he succeeded in getting only part of it into his mouth, wet crumbs falling on his beard, on the tablecloth and on his clothes. He ate greedily, his eyes partly closed in order to savour it to the full.

Shalom did not take his eyes off him. After a few mouthfuls, Reb Hirschel murmured to himself:

"Ah–ah–ah! Moshe Rabenu, if you'll pardon me for saying so, was a batlan. An utter batlan. You hear, Shlomke? Moses wasn't smart enough, believe me!"

The boy fixed his wide-open eyes on him, waiting for some wisecrack.

"You tell me, why did he have to go to the bother of dividing the sea? He could have dried it up naturally. All he had to do was ask the Children of Israel for their chala, take out the soft insides and put them in the Red Sea, and before you could say Reb Zorach it would have dried up. He just wasn't smart, if you'll pardon my saying so."

He stuffed his mouth up with chala and a piece of meat which he picked up with a fork and dipped in the red horseradish.

Shalom chuckled inwardly at the old man's words but he didn't want to give him the satisfaction, so he didn't react to his joke.

"What do *you* say?" Reb Hirschel stopped chewing and turned his eyes on the boy.

"The Children of Israel didn't have chala, because the dough didn't manage to rise..."

"Aren't you smart!.. Go, Shlomke, bring me a jug of beer from the ice-house. But for goodness' sake, only the stuff that Herr Lieber drinks. D'you hear?"

The boy went and brought the cold beer. Reb Hirschel grabbed the sweating jug with both hands and took a long draught from it. He pulled out his dripping whiskers and went on eating the roast, humming to himself all the while. And the more he ate the more absorbed he got until he forgot all about the boy, who sat there drawing with a pencil on a piece of paper.

In the meantime, Mrs. Aberdam returned. With both hands in the pockets of her wide apron, she stood before Reb Hirschel who was sucking a delicious bone.

"Would you like something more to eat?" she said. "Actually, I wanted to give you some beetroot soup and some dessert as well, but they aren't ready yet. We'll be eating in an hour's time."

"Never mind, Mistress Hanna, never mind. Eating meat sort of gives you an appetite. Especially if you have it with sharp horseradish. God willing, in an hour's time I shall do full justice to the meal." (And as he spoke, he thought to himself: I shall ask her for one of her old silk dresses for my missus.) "And how is your son-in-law, Reb Hirtzel? How's he doing? The Rabbi, may he live a good long life, asked me when he's coming to see him... Ai–ai–ai!" He gave a deep sigh, a fine man like Reb Naftali Zvi... How many like him will you find? He was a Hassid through and through. Who could ever have thought such a thing!

I can imagine how sorry the Rabbi (may he be blessed with a good long life) will be. Ai–ai–ai!"

As if reading his thoughts, Mrs. Aberdam replied:

"The one thing has nothing to do with the other. As long as the Lord keeps me alive and I can afford it, I shall go on paying the donation, even if I personally go to Belz. Reb Naftali's portion has been entrusted to me and I have to handle it as if he were alive."

Reb Hirschel rejoiced inwardly but made as if he didn't understand.

"What, does the minyan take place as before? Ha? If you'd like me to read a portion of the Law tomorrow, I shall have to go over it after bathing... But with fish, Mrs. Aberdam."

"With very nice fish. From our lake."

"Shlomke, be so kind as to bring me water for the finger-bowl before I say Grace. Thank God, I've satisfied the needs of my mortal flesh for the time being. Na!"

XXI

Two Jews Came from Afar

Graf Molodetzki's roisterous hunting-party came to an end. The grand company that had been merrymaking in the town, mainly in the environs of the palace, disappeared, as if they had been a dream. The Graf departed (Mrs. Aberdam and Reb Hirtzel tried to see him about the brewery but couldn't get to him), with all the noblemen after him. Next day, Pan Grabinski also departed, with his women, and the new agent, Pan Lasoti, moved into the monor. He was a young bachelor, tall, with a short red beard, who always wore leather gaiters and carried a plaited whip in his hand and was accompanied by three streaked hunting hounds, sometimes on a leash sometimes without. There was something Mephistophelian about this man. Immediately after he took over, he was to be found in every place, on horseback or on foot — in the fields, on the roads, in the forest, at the distilleries, in the drying-house; and he even visited the brewery twice in the first week after his arrival, looked into every nook and cranny and every branch of the work, nodded his head, blinked, but didn't say a word.

Mrs. Aberdam invited him to her house, put food and refreshments and some fine old liquor before him, presented her three grandchildren to him, told him about her being a widow and mentioned her daughter and son-in-law. On the subject of her son-in-law she dwelt a little longer, describing how he got on with the gentry, even with grafs. Here, Lasoti spoke freely, his eyes darting everywhere and taking in everything. His voice was very hearty, but not natural, as if some malevolent thought was hidden behind it. He drank to her health, praised the food, tickled the children under the armpits with the end of his whip, and kept smoothing his thin mustache and red whiskers with a small brush all the time. Then he went away with his swift, youthful stride, the dogs running before and after him. As for the renewal of the brewery lease — there's still time for that. He hopes he will find a suitable opportunity to speak with the gracious lady. Yes, he understands their concern but — he is new here. He has to familiarise himself with things first.

"What do you think, Shlomke: is the new agent kindly disposed towards us or not?" Mrs. Aberdam asked her grandson, whose intelligence she prized.

"He's a bad man," the boy replied without hesitation. "While he was tickling us with the whip his eyes were not looking at us. His voice doesn't come from the heart."

"Oh my God, what's going to happen to us!"

Mrs. Aberdam decided that if she couldn't reach an understanding with Pan Lasoti she'd go to Belz again and wouldn't budge from the Rabbi's room until he promised her that everything would turn out all right. "I shall speak to him about Brachele and her crying too," she said to herself. "Never mind, he's a Zaddik and a relative of ours and he has to know everything. And if he can help — let him do so!" she added defiantly.

Several weeks went by. The Jew who recited Kaddish and the students of the Mishnah came every Thursday to get their pay and invariably carried away with them a jug of beer as well — something to drink for the Sabbath. Everything went on as usual. Even Brachele's crying was something they'd grown used to, and the old woman, although it broke her heart to hear the doleful wailing of her only daughter, reconciled herself to it for want of an alternative and transferred all her love and attention to the boy, Shalom. She was always telling his lay and religious tutors to pay particular attention to the boy because he had a good head on his shoulders. The boy really had an alert mind and a penchant for the Torah and religious teachings. He knew the "lesson" after going over it the first time. He would learn a verse from the Bible with the commentaries and know the Onkelos translation to every verse in the Pentateuch and remember the tonal accents. His handwriting was exceedingly good. He spoke Polish and German. He had a flair for figures, as Reb Simha could testify, and pored over his father's books to which the books of the deceased had been added. He was particularly fond of books about the Talmudic sages and spent hours reading *Sefer HaBrith* which he found among his father's books. Whoever came there derived considerable pleasure from him and would try to argue points with him so as to hear his adult and appropriate replies. The girls too grew bigger, learned well, excelled at handicrafts and were most meticulous about orderliness and cleanliness, but there was nothing exceptional about them. They were both kind and charming, and prepared their lessons for school (the old lady had in the meantime put them into the primary school in the town, where the Principal was an elderly Polish spinster by the name of Panya Kruzuvna), and the two of them would bring home the same marks and the same prizes for tidiness and "excelling in their studies".

The Principal simply adored the two of them and on one occasion she could not restrain herself and went to Mrs. Aberdam's house to sing their praises. She wanted to go to the girls' mother as well, but Bracha was having one of her depressions (luckily she wasn't heard crying at the moment) and the old lady made her excuses to the teacher with great tact and graciousness and thanked her a thousand times for having taken the trouble and so on... And when she left, Mrs. Aberdam escorted her as far as the gate.

It was a summer of plenty. The crop was good and everything was cheap. The hops, too, in the hop-gardens of the Jews (at that time the Gentiles did not yet go in for growing it) were successful in those parts and they were already busy with the picking. But the hops had failed in Bohemia and Moravia, so that merchants from there were showing up already and the Jewish brokers went from one holding to the other, from one estate-owner to another, offering incredibly high prices. Mrs. Aberdam, having ensured for herself the quantity needed for the brewery for a whole year, was worried about one thing only — the renewal of the contract with the new agent. She had even decided to make a lease for ten years at least this time, for this was not Pan Grabinski and his successor was not to be relied on. She also saw to it that she had a large sum of money handy in cash, against the time when she would need it, in case she was asked for a big advance payment.

While she was occupied with one thing and another, one day there came to the brewery two Jewish guests from a distant place and asked for the lady of the house. They made straight for her place as if they had been there before. They said they had heard of her charity and good works and her great hospitality, and as they were passing and had still a long way to go, they had come to her house to rest for a day or two, if the lady has no objection, and afterwards they will continue on their way. They are forest merchants from the other end of West Galicia, beyond Kraka, from the town of Oszpiechin, Ozwieczim in Polish, forest merchants and sons of forest merchants for generations. They have been touring Graf Molodetzki's forests for about a week, and got as far as Brod; and now that all the accounts and assessments are lying ready in their travelling-bags, they are on their way home and from there they will continue the negotiations with the landowners over the price of the forests. Fine forests! Possibly, when they buy the forests, they will have to build a steam saw-mill here, and perhaps even a small railway-line in order to transport the rafters and sleepers to the nearby station which will be erected shortly. In short, wealthy people and big merchants and at the same time evidently pious Jews, Hassidim, and men who get things done, to boot. They were dressed in long coats and their side-locks were curled down right into their long beards and their clean yarmulkas stuck out under the velour hats on the back of their necks. They gave their names: the one was called Akiva Holtzhendler and the other, Gedalia Nussenbaum (most appropriate for wood merchants) and addressed each other affectionately as Reb Akiva and Reb Gedalia.

In the whole little town of L. such fine Jews as these could not be found. They spoke with a Polish lilt and some of their words were strange and not commonly used in these parts. Their inflexion made them sound perpetually surprised at something, and everything they said sounded like a question. They immediately opened their handsome leather bags and took out some holy books, and volumes of the Mishnah, and asked for water to wash their hands and sat down to study in a soft chant — a veritable pleasure to listen to!

To Mrs. Aberdam, Jews of this kind were familiar still from the good old days in her father's house in West Galicia, although these two were of an even superior type. Their appearance, their manners, their speech, and their good breeding gave her great pleasure, and her honest heart failed to give her warning.

Naturally, she received them with great honour and gave orders to have a fine room prepared for them with good beds. And she gave Pearl instructions to prepare special meals and not be sparing of anything. *Such wonderful Jews — such great merchants!* When Shalom came in, she put her hand on his head and presented him to the important guests, praising him a little to his face and making him blush. She also praised her son-in-law: he too is an important merchant, but he is mainly in the produce line. He has a special storeroom here at the brewery, and he also supplies the barley they need for the beer. The crop has been good this year, but the prices will be low and that is a pity because he bought a lot of new produce as last year was a lean year and the prices went up. In the course of this it came out that one of them, the taller of the two, Reb Gedalia Nussenbaum, had known Reb Elhanan Bardash, may he rest in peace, and had had business dealings with him on a few occasions. Alas! there aren't people like that today... He was a man of his word, and his piety was like a smouldering fire in his bones. Mrs. Aberdam fervently hoped that one of them would mention her first husband, the saintly Reb Shlomke, but as no one did she turned the conversation to the subject of her second husband, Reb Naftali Zvi, may he rest in peace, and praised him and lamented his absence. But in her heart of hearts she meant Reb Shlomke, and as she spoke she pressed the boy's head to her with infinite love.

The men stayed at the brewery for another day, and another two days. They took an interest in everything and asked innocent questions. Although there were some big, famous breweries where they came from too, one couldn't see the wood for the trees. That is to say, being so preoccupied with their timber business they didn't have a chance to see this industry. They also went into the town and walked about with serious mien. In the morning, they went with their tallit and tefilin bags to the prayer-house (they themselves were followers of the Viznitz Rabbi) and their names were promptly taken up from one end of the town to the other and all sorts of exaggerated reports got around about their wealth and piety. They gave to the synagogue generously and even donated a substantial sum for the purchase of a new set of six volumes of the Mishnah; they gave for the sick and for the cleaning of the ritual bath. Then all kinds of people began to call on them in Mrs. Aberdam's house. The Rabbi himself invited them to his house and they had a discussion about the Torah: and thereupon the word went out that they were highly learned men. The Rabbi gave his blessing for the success of their business and expressed the hope that they would come and live there in connection with it. In short, the town had found something to keep it occupied.

Reb Simha, the accountant, was also very taken with them, though out of a certain self-disparagement, as he could see from their questions how well-versed they were in accountancy and bookkeeping according to the latest methods. Anyone working for experts like these could learn a great deal from them!

When Reb Hirtzel returned home, Mrs. Aberdam told him about the two big merchants from Oszpiechin and their learning and wealth, and after spending about an hour in his apartment speaking to his depressed wife and trying to soothe and console her, and after seeing the children and petting them a little and giving them their presents, Reb Hirtzel went to his mother-in-law's apartment and greeted the guests who returned his greeting. They chatted for a while and when they saw that they were dealing here with a man of the world and a gentleman, who also knew Polish well — they too opened up and began to display their knowledge and talked with him enthusiastically about business and markets and companies and advertising methods and competition and credits and so on and so forth. Reb Hirtzel enjoyed the conversation very much. It transpired that they often went to Germany, and one of them (Holtzhendler) had also been to Holland and even as far as England and was familiar with all the new business methods; he was also *au fait* with what was going on in the world, for he took the paper, *Neue Freie Presse*, every day without fail, and knew the inner workings of the Stock Exchange. Nussenbaum, the taller one, was rather quiet: evidently, he was the more learned of the two in Torah but not in worldly affairs.

At their request, Reb Hirtzel took them on a tour of the surroundings in his carriage, and Shalom went with them. On the way, the merchants, with disarming frankness, told him (though somewhat vaguely) about the forests they were contemplating buying and asked for his opinion and advice. Incidentally, they also asked about other businesses, and enquired — if they may, of course — about his own and that of Mrs. Aberdam. What was the nature of the business? They had never had anything to do with a business of that kind, although there was a flourishing beer industry not far from their place — Pilsen — but they themselves knew nothing about it. *You can't see the wood etcetera etcetera...*

What is more, they had no idea at all that Jews worked in the beer industry. They were sure that this was a Gentile occupation only. Brandy — yes, but not beer. Actually, when they were in Brod, they heard that there was a big brewery "Halperin's, I think, ha?" but they didn't get round to seeing it. Perhaps when they're there again, they'll go and see it. They also plan to visit Kapelush's, the famous manufacturer of liqueurs. As they are going to establish themselves here, God willing, they have to acquaint themselves with the various local enterprises, for business is a sort of wheel within a wheel.

Warmed by their deference, Reb Hirtzel was most gracious and obliging and explained to them everything he knew. And they, careful not to offend against good taste by seeming unduly curious, casually threw in a question here and there on one point or another, and he let them into the innermost secrets of the businesses. After all, he was only giving measure for measure: they hid nothing from him, so he hid nothing from them. The conversation came around to Graf Molodetzki's estates and the shakiness of his position. Incidentally, they've heard that he has a new agent here. They say he's a veritable Haman. Pity, pity! Noe they'll have to negotiate with that one about the forest, and the previous one was a decent fellow, they heard. What's the name of the new one? Pan Lasoti. Yes, Pan Lasoti. They have a card for him from the Graf. Before they leave, they may go and call on him. Perhaps Reb Hirtzel would like to come too? On second thoughts, maybe he's right: local people don't always have the right effect. In that case, they'd have to rely on Our Father in Heaven for support, isn't that so?

Shalom, with all his aloofness, liked being in their company, because of the novelty and the aura of the big world that they had about them. They became friendly with the clever little boy and amused themselves by talking to him about the Torah and worldly matters. They asked him tricky questions and gave him riddles and arithmetical problems to solve, always deriving great pleasure from his answers even when they weren't correct. The very first day, the younger of the two, Holtzhendler, asked him for a piece of paper and wrote on it, in Latin characters, four large, clear letters, like this: G.m.b.H., with a full-stop after each letter, and said that these stood for four German words and anyone who knew anything about business must know what these letters signify. Shalom took the piece of paper and studied it from all angles. His little brain grew weary but he couldn't work out the meaning. The visitors looked on delightedly.

"Well, do this, son: go and ask the people on the premises, the accountant, the bailiff, the brewer, and maybe your father too. And if they can't solve the riddle for you — we will. But better men first."

And Reb Akiva and Reb Gedalia exchanged fond looks.

Shalom shot out of the room like an arrow, ran around with the note and asked whoever he came across, without result. He saw his father returning in his trap, but he had qualms about asking him. Perhaps he wouldn't know either, and then he'd be doubly sorry. But after a little while he couldn't contain himself and handed the note to his father. Reb Hirtzel looked at it for a minute, two minutes. He said he'd seen that abbreviation a number of times and it seemed to him that he knew the answer, but it escaped him for the moment. The boy was relieved. He went back to Reb Akiva and gave back the undeciphered note. Reb Akiva seemed to derive a strange enjoyment out of the situation. He stroked the boy's cheek, looked at his companion fondly, and asked:

"Well, Reb Gedalia, what do you think? Should I tell him?"

"I think that was the condition, Reb Akiva."

"Well then, I would have you know that those are the initial letters of 'Gesellschaft mit beschränkter Haftung,' that is to say — a limited liability company. And A.G. — do you know what that is?"

"G. I know: Gesellschaft."

"You're sharp one, son! A. is Aktien. That is, a stock company." Reb Akiva talked a lot but he didn't actually explain the business of a stock company or a limited liability company, and the boy didn't insist this time because he found the mere sound of the words wonderfully stimulating and contented himself with that.

In short, the two important guests, the big forest merchants, Reb Akiva and Reb Gedalia, slept at the brewery three nights and enjoyed good food and generous hospitality. At his mother-in-law's request, Reb Hirtzel took them right through the brewery and showed them everything, carefully explaining what each object was used for and how it worked. They showed no more than a casual

189

interest, as might be expected from strangers and laymen. In Reb Simha's office they glanced at the account books, just to see the system, and threw out some casual questions and comments. When they passed the deaf-mute's room and heard what had happened to him, they were shocked and kept coming back to the story, always extolling the liberality of Mrs. Aberdam. "A great lady," said Reb Gedalia.

They had called on the agent, Pan Lasoti, twice already and each time they came back they cursed him vehemently and commiserated with Mrs. Aberdam for also having need of this Haman. And in the evening of the third day, they hired a good cart and on the fourth day, early in the morning, they took leave of Mrs. Aberdam and Reb Hirtzel, who was still at home, and the children who got up early, whom they gave a small gift of money, and asked them to convey their regards to their mother, wishing her a complete recovery. After that, they parted graciously from the rest of the people there who were already at work. They shook hands with Herr Lieber and spoke to him in fluent German. Then they climbed into the cart with their elegant suitcases, courteously giving way to each other with a great show of mutual regard, and eventually sat down side by side, covering their knees with a kind of hairy blanket. When the cart began to move, they turned up their hairy, shiny faces and blessed those they left behind and the cart moved out of the gate of the brewery yard.

XXII

A Visit to Pan Yashinski's House

During the time that Reb Hirtzel was at home, Mrs. Aberdam had a talk with him and suggested that he ought perhaps to withdraw gradually from his various businesses, which were evidently not going too well, and begin to get into the brewery business. To tell the truth, that was what she had wanted right from the beginning, immediately after his marriage, but as he wanted to be his own master she didn't want to force him into anything. This man's wishes must be respected. But now that she was widowed and getting older from day to day, as was natural, and had no children besides Brachele, it was only right and logical to her that he, her son-in-law, should come into the business which she had kept going for so many years. Also, the lease is about to terminate and has to be renewed shortly, and — as he knows — the agent has been changed in the meantime and who knows whether they will not need to be on their guard and fight with all their might, and she — an old woman broken on the wheel of life (she hopes he won't think she is uttering anything sinful) — what influence can she have with an overlord who hardly knows her? They say he is a hard, cruel man. The merchants from Oszpiechin who were at his place also testified to that. He, Hirtzel, knows how to speak to people and how to deal with squires. He knows their ways and has a command of their language, and would certainly succeed, with God's help, in renewing the lease for the following ten years, or even more. It was her wish that after a hundred and twenty years he, her son-in-law, should remain in the brewery which, thank God, is a nice business, and if he wishes she is prepared to make a partnership agreement with him until the time when she will pass over into the next world and everything will pass into his possession.

Reb Hirtzel thanked his mother-in-law for her kind offer, saying that he would consider the matter, although he was quite satisfied his mother-in-law should remain the owner of the business as she was up to now without limiting her in any way. As for the matter of renewing the lease, he was perfectly willing, naturally, to help her to the best of his ability. Of course he'd go to Pan Lasoti and try to speak to him. He hopes that the agent will respect her right of preemption which the squires themselves are most particular about, and will not lease the brewery to anyone else without first trying to come to agreement with her. It's possible that she may have to pay something more, but as the business is going well there's no harm in raising the rent a little. But it would be advisable, before going to the agent, for him to have a word with their good neighbour, Pan Yashinski, and find out from him how to set about negotiating with the agent, for Pan Yashinski has certainly managed by now to get some idea of the man over him.

So Reb Hirtzel Pallan went to the house of the forester, Pan Yashinski, straight after the evening meal. Pani Yuzia, who received him in a flutter of delight, hurried away to inform her husband that Pan Pallan had come to the house, and then showed him in. Before he went in, Reb Hirtzel took off his hat, put on his small silk skull-cap and smoothed his greying beard and mustache. He was all charm and courtesy. Pan Yashinski rose to his feet and came forward to meet him. Taking him by the hand, he led him to a chair next to the table covered with a white, lacy, embroidered cloth with fringes. The sitting-room was as clean as a new pin. In the corner stood a piano covered with a white cloth runner, delicately embroidered. On the table burned a lamp with a green woven lampshade, embroidered with red flowers. Some potted plants completed the picture. There was an air of happy domesticity about the room. Reb Hirtzel asked after the lady of the house and the dear little girls. Pan Yashinski offered his guest a thick cigar with a fine aroma, which be took out of a locked drawer, and asked about business and political affairs. He hasn't been reading newspapers at all lately. When he didn't renew his subscription, they went on sending the paper for a few more weeks and then stopped. Until now, he'd been getting his papers a day or two late from the postmaster, but he hasn't been bringing them for about a fortnight now. So he has no idea what's going on in the world.

Reb Hirtzel answered all the questions amiably and composedly, smiling sometimes to Pani Yuzia who sat a little way away from them, fidgeting all the time in an attempt to pull the narrow sleeves of her blouse down to her wrists, sometimes to Pan Yashinski who lounged completely relaxed in his chair, his magnificent white head uncovered. Pani Yuzia enquired most tactfully and sympathetically after Pani Pallan (she always listened to her crying with the anxiety of one woman for another and wanted to know if she was feeling any better), and the little ladies and the sweet little gentleman. Ah, once the Panitch used to come every day to play with the girls; now he is apparently occupied with his studies. Israelite children study so much! They're still babies and they're already absorbed in a book!

Reb Hirtzel answered politely and put some questions of his own. Pani Yuzia regretted that Jews are not allowed to eat with Catholics. She would very much have liked to give him some refreshments: a little wine with butter biscuits. Reb Hirtzel half rose from his chair and thanked her courteously. Then Pan Yashinski, with a youthful laugh, suggested that she should give him some nuts, the kind he brought from the forest. And when the nuts were put out on a glass tray with a nickel-silver nutcracker, Pan Yashinski said that he found these nuts in a squirrel's nest, so they were all full and healthy, because those shrewd little creatures knew how to select the best. They weigh them in their paws, put down the light ones and take the heavy ones. This summer, he found four such nests, and now they had a small sack full of choice nuts which would suffice for the whole winter — "if Pani Yuzia won't make so many nut cakes...."

"Well! I don't bake so much. Not even half of what the postmaster's wife bakes."

And so they chatted until they got on to the subject of Pan Lasoti. At the mention of the new agent's name, Pan Yashinski's face darkened. Reb Hirtzel intercepted a look he threw Pani Yuzia, and indeed the good woman got up from her place, excused herself and went behind the screen into the next room.

Pan Yashinski drew his chair closer and said:

"There are hard times ahead of us, good neighbour. Pan Lasoti, although a Catholic, is a bad-hearted man. He is a threat to me and the rest of His Excellency Graf Molodetzki's employees, as well as to the lessees of the distillery and the flour mill and the brewery and the small estates. This gentleman's whip is not going to rest."

"Pardon me, my good Pan Yashinski, if I ask you frankly: Do you have any facts?" asked Reb Hirtzel uneasily.

"I don't have any actual facts, but from a number of casual conversations I have had the privilege of having with Pan Lasoti, I have gathered that his intentions are not good. What is worse, His Excellency has given him carte blanche and he can do just what he likes with the property, without having to account to anyone. You understand, good neighbour? Carte blanche is a dangerous sword in a heartless man's hand."

"Pardon me again, worthy Pan Yashinski: isn't it possible that Pan Lasoti has created a storm because he's new here and young and, maybe, impetuous — whereas his intentions are not really bad. I've known people like that among the gentry and believe me, Pan Yashinski, they're not always bad. You just have to know how to deal with them."

"If only that were so," said Pan Yashinski smiling under his mustache as he straightened up in his chair, "but I, to my regret, have seen several unmistakable signs. After all, I'm a hunter by profession, as my good neighbour knows, and I can smell a dangerous beast on the prowl a long way off. Oh, oh, dear neighbour, to my regret my sense of smell doesn't usually deceive me."

"Perhaps we should try to get around him. Every man

has his little weaknesses: some like honour, some attention, some a nice word, some a gift. Even wild animals — to use my good neighbour's apt simile — can be made docile, and some of them can even be trained to be useful."

Pan Yashinski twirled his mustache, and said with laughter in his eyes:

"I see my dear neighbour understands people But Pan Lasoti is a sly fox and won't fall into any trap. I am prepared to give you my hand on it. This man has a lust for power which we can't satisfy. Besides, he's all for changes. I've got his measure. He'll no doubt want to change his staff. As I see it, there isn't a single one among the people in his Excellency's service who will find favour in the eyes of Pan Lasoti. He always looks for a pretext. What is worse, he doesn't say much and what he does say — is open to various interpretations. You never know what he thinks of your work. His smile undulates on his lips like a thin serpent. Such a smile is liable to bite."

Suddenly his tone changed:

"If evil befalls a dear and noble person like Pan Grabinski, and in his old age he is deposed and left virtually destitute — he and the ladies dependent on him — that is a wrong that has at least been done by His Excellency and the disgrace is not so great. But we are liable to be driven out by this rogue and petty tyrant — how will we bear the wrong and the shame? I tell you, dear neighbour, if something bad should happen, I don't know if I'll be responsible for my actions, if I won't put a bullet from my rifle into someone..."

Reb Hirtzel, seeing how excited Pan Yashinski was, tried to calm him down.

"Let us hope, Pan Yashinski, that nothing of the kind

will happen, but one should be on guard. As they say in the Proverbs, *Happy is the man that feareth always*. I am pleased to have had the opportunity to discuss with you a matter so important and vital for you, and also for me though not directly, for my mother-in-law's contract for the brewery terminates in the spring, and it is better to know with whom we are dealing. With that, I think, we have exhausted that part of the subject for the time being, and can go on to more general, pleasanter topics."

Pan Yashinski excused himself for a moment, got up and went to the door. He moved away the screen and whispered his wife's name. She appeared right away with a smile on her face, touched her hair lightly, stretched herself and apologized:

"I was sitting over some work and almost dozed off. What do I see? Pan Pallan hasn't even touched the nuts yet. You offend me..."

Reb Hirtzel gave a half bow from the waist and thanked her gracefully. He sat down again and took a nut between his first finger and thumb and the shiny nutcracker in the other hand. The conversation that followed was refined, well-mannered and bright, tinged with humour and the lightest of light gossip, laughter and pleasantries. They smoked some of the good cigarettes which their guest offered in a silver case, Pani Yuzia smoking with particular refinement, until Reb Hirtzel took his watch out of his pocket and cried out in surprise:

"Sir, it's already ten o'clock!" and with that he rose to his feet and look leave of his good neighbours.

XXIII

Days of Uncertainty

In order to find some sort of balm for Brachele's afflicted spirit, her husband occasionally asked her to go with him in his carriage to the places where he worked. She agreed at the beginning with equanimity. The sight of the fields, the meadows and the woods; the air shimmering in the light of the late afternoon sun; the singing of the birds and the chirping of myriads of unseen insects; soft clouds floating idly in the sky and the smoke of distant chimneys; the galloping of the horse and the rhythm of the wheels — all these might have had a salutary effect on Bracha's mind if it weren't for the physical discomfort she suffered from the actual journey. Each time she set out, she was at first shaken out of her lethargy and filled with wonder at the sights. Her eyes came alive and the wind brought colour into her cheeks. But after travelling for half an hour or so, she suddenly faded. Her face fell and shadows filled the hollows in her cheeks. The light in her eyes was extinguished and her body seemed to crumple up. She began to groan quietly, and groan again with the effort of trying to suppress her groans. She was simply not strong enough for all this travelling. Several times, Reb Hirtzel consulted doctors in Brod and in Lwow and they gave him all kinds of advice and medicines for her, but nothing helped. It was even worse when she went by train. Once she travelled by rail to Lwow with Reb Hirtzel, and on the journey they actually feared for her life. She didn't stop vomiting and fainting. Reb Hirtzel supported her precious head all the way, sometimes on his shoulder, sometimes on his knee. Their fellow passengers sympathised with them and gave her some kind of drops and brought her water to drink — but they could not alleviate her suffering. The two days they were in Lwow, she enjoyed herself reasonably well. She visited a number of places with him and even enjoyed the theatre and the panoramic depiction of *The Battle at Raclawice* by Matejko. But all the time, she kept remembering that she still had to travel back and the mere thought of it made her feel faint. They returned in a hired carriage, but this journey too was difficult, although not like a train journey.

After a few such journeys, she didn't want to go travelling any more; nor did Reb Hirtzel suggest it any more. Instead, he sometimes took the twins with him, or his only son, Shalom. He enjoyed having the boy with him most, as he could talk to him about his affairs like a grown-up person.

About two weeks after the departure of the Jews from Oszpiechin Reb Hirtzel came home from one of his business trips and, finding everything in order, he went into his apartment with an almost happy feeling. Bracha actually came out to meet him, without the usual expression of suffering on her face. He saw, what is more, that she seemed to have come alive. He put his hand on her head in greeting, as he usually did, and asked her how she felt.

"Thank you, not bad. I've been waiting for you, Hirtzel. I have something to tell you." Hirtzel's heart leaped. What's this — something new? Aloud he said:

"Right away, darling. I'll just put my case away and take off my overcoat."

When he came back from the lobby, he smoothed his clothes and looked at her questioningly.

"You know, I've been thinking all the time about the two Jews who were here. I didn't like them. You'll see, they came here to lease the brewery."

Her words hit the honest merchant like a blow. Such a suspicion was so far from his own mind and reasoning that it could only be a figment of his sick wife's imagination. He was very careful how he answered her:

"On what grounds, Brachele, do you suspect them?"

"Why do you need grounds? Investigate, and you'll find out," she replied gravely, almost sternly.

"But they're just wood merchants and came to see forests in the neighbourhood. I am afraid, darling, you are suspecting really genuine people."

"I told mother and she also rebuked me. I'm surprised at the two of you for being so blind. Look, I told it to Shalom and he agrees with me," she cried, with a rising note of anger in her voice.

Reb Hirtzel was somewhat put out, but he laughed to himself: She's found backing in a baby! And aloud he added:

"And how, in your opinion, can we investigate the matter?"

"That's your affair."

He had never seen her so sure of herself in all the time he knew her. That same day he spoke to his mother-in-law about Bracha's suspicion, and they both rejected it as something completely untenable. Only, in order not to upset their loved one in her excited state, they agreed

201

to look into the matter although they had no idea how they would set about it.

It was already the month of Elul. The cold winds came and whipped through the trees. The leaves were already turning yellow and some had begun to fall. The face of the lake was wrinkled with the sadness of approaching winter. Pan Lasoti had forbidden the Jews to bathe in it, but even of the gentry very few came to bathe there, and then only in the middle of the day. The Days of Penitence were approaching.

Mrs. Aberdam had become accustomed to her widowhood by now and was managing her affairs with a masterly hand. Reb Simha's "balance-sheet" which was finished at last, was not at all clear as it should have been. But one thing in it was very clear: Mrs. Aberdam had hardly any actual property and if, God forbid! she were to leave the brewery and realise everything in order to pay her debts — she *might* be left with enough to buy a small house. But this knowledge did not stop her from carrying on with her numerous charities and good works. On the contrary, she became even more convinced that no one in the world could remove her from the brewery, which had been in her possession for dozens of years already. And if Pan Lasoti wanted to lease it to someone else, he wouldn't be able to find a Jew who would be prepared to trespass on her domain. A Jew wouldn't do such a thing to another Jew. And if such a criminal were to be found — there was still justice in the world. She'd insist firmly that the Rabbi of Belz take the matter in hand seriously. After all, he had a certain responsibility towards her, for his late father was the one who told her to lease the brewery. Such an offender could be excommunicated, he could be arraigned before

202

the religious court, his beer could be boycotted. Jews, thank God! are not like that. She judged the world by her own standards.

The more she thought about it the more confident she grew about her position. And — as if to prove to herself how strong she was — she ordered a Scroll of the Law from the scribe in Radichov, in memory of Reb Naftali Zvi, whose partnership in the brewery had lapsed.

Reb Hirtzel, who now stayed at home for days on end because his business was slack, tried several times to talk to Pan Lasoti, but the latter would dismiss him with a joke or a casual word on other matters, and finally told him off rudely, saying he didn't like pesky Jews. The brewery is the property of His Excellency Graf Molodetzki and he, Pan Lasoti, has been authorized to act for him and he will do whatever he thinks best. Until Mrs. Aberdam has paid the last third of the money, there is nothing to discuss about any future lease.

Reb Hirtzel, who wasn't used to such behaviour or such language, especially from the Polish gentry, was most offended, but he managed to restrain himself from answering back, because he remembered what he owed to his mother-in-law. He left the agent with the intention of never coming to talk to him again. When he got home, he reported the conversation to Mrs. Aberdam. She was not surprised. All she said was: "We have a God stronger than all the agents in the world."

As if by agreement, they stopped talking about the matter and waited patiently for the time when they would have to pay the last third, which wasn't far off: namely, at the beginning of the calendar year. They tried writing to the Graf in Paris and received a polite reply in which his secretary begged to inform the gracious lady in his name that, to his regret, everything has been placed in the hands of Pan Lasoti. The lady may rest assured that Pan Lasoti would not do any harm... As for the two Jews from Oszpiechin they forgot them entirely. Nor did Bracha mention them again.

Reb Hirtzel was now at home regularly. He was still very attached to his wife, although she seemed to have withdrawn again. She hardly ever spoke to him and if she said a few words in the course of a day, they were irritable and snappy as if they were intented to hurt him. Every word like this from her would astonish and distress him, but he always controlled his seething emotions and answered gently or not at all. Her crying rang perpetually in his ears and filled him with fear. He turned more and more to the children, enquiring about their studies and their work. The twins required no special attention or notice. They did their lessons at home, sewed, embroidered, read, danced and helped their mother and the old lady willingly without a murmur. They bloomed by themselves, like flowers in the meadow or in the woods.

Not so Shalom. His character was complex and unusual. With all his quickness, integrity and ability, he showed a number of traits that aroused concern. He insisted fiercely on his independence and wouldn't listen to anyone if he didn't want to at that particular moment. He would disappear from the house for hours on end, passing the time alone by the lake or in the environs of the brewery, and when asked where he had been, he'd answer with an abstracted look and a faint smile: "Oh, just somewhere..."

He was already eleven years old and his father began to worry seriously about his education. It was no longer possible to meet his educational requirements here, in the small town, especially in the sciences and practical subjects. Reb Hirtzel wanted to send him to Brod, to put him into the high-school, and also place him in the hands of a good, well-educated tutor to teach him the Bible and Hebrew. He even tried to discuss the subject with Bracha, but she took it amiss that he should be asking her advice about something which was his responsibility and about which he alone had to decide. She had no right, she said, to express an opinion on his education up to now. He must be guided by her mother, Mrs. Aberdam, who was like a mother to the child... She grew agitated as she spoke and her eyes filled with tears. A few minutes later, her long-drawn weeping could be heard.

When Reb Hirtzel spoke to his mother-in-law about it, she objected with all her might. It was not fitting, she said, for her or for the Rabbi of Radichov, for the memory of Bracha's late father for whom the boy was named, that their grandson should be educated by Gentiles, God Forbid! After all, he can learn Torah here too. And if the religious tutors are inadequate, they can give him to the Rabbi for a few hours. The son of the rich man, Adler, was also learning with the Rabbi. As for his lay education — when, God willing, the matter of the brewery is settled, she will take it upon herself to bring a teacher from Brod, like Kardimon, the lessee of the neighbouring estate, does. Then the girls would also benefit and learn German language and literature from him.

Reb Hirtzel could not hold out for what he wanted because his will-power had weakened over recent years. Partly because of his wife's condition, which caused him great distress, whether he was at home or on the road, and partly because of his business, which was going downhill all the time. Also, the matter of the brewery and Pan Lasoti, which was still in the air, unsettled him more than it did Mrs. Aberdam, who was the person directly concerned. So he went around as if in a fog, bewildered by a host of problems that seemed to have no solution. He suffered worst on the days he spent at home. He began to lean on Shalom more and more, gradually finding in him the only prop for his bewildered, perplexed soul. He would spend hours with him: talking, studying, strolling in the grounds of the brewery and its environs, and learn from him all about the work and the various tools and implements. Through him, he came closer to the people who worked on the place, as well. He began to respect, almost to love, Herr Lieber, although he had never spoken more than ten words with him and then only in connection with his work. A number of things about the brewery, which he had known nothing about until then, began to be clear to him and he began to take notice. Perhaps his mother-in-law's suggestion to put him into the business was not such a bad idea...

So the summer drew to a close. The Days of Penitence came round, and the world moved reluctantly into the sadness of autumn days.

XXIV

The Festival and the Fire

F or ages now, it had been customary to send the Scroll of the Law which was housed in the brewery to the Husiatin prayer-house one year, and to the Belzian one the next, to take part with the rest of the Scrolls in the general processions to celebrate the Rejoicing of the Law. This year, after the death of Reb Naftali Zvi, it was the turn of the Husiatin prayer-house, so the Scroll went there. The members of the household also went, in the evening and in the morning, to see the rejoicing over the Sefer Torah, *their* Sefer Torah, to carry it joyfully and kiss it with awe.

All day, Hassidim — big and small alike — went from house to house to taste of the pottage of sweet cabbage cooked with fat and raisins and, especially, the stuffed cabbage fried in honey. In houses where there was wine, they drank wine; where there was beer, they drank beer; and in the houses of the poor they contented themselves with a little spirits — pure or diluted with water. All their faces were jubilant and their overcoats were grease-stained and open. Their kerchiefs trailed from their back pockets and they stamped their feet ecstatically. Their fur hats were pushed back from their foreheads, which glistened with perspiration. And singing filled the air, the fine air of summer's end. They didn't leave out a single house, not even the poorest of them, so as not to put them to shame. The finicky ones, who couldn't eat the crude, simple dishes, only pretended to taste or slip it into their pockets, or gave it to the children to throw out through a hole in the fence. Husiatin Hassidim mingled with Belzian Hassidim in the streets. Although they were on bad terms the rest of the year, today, the day of the Rejoicing of the Law, which was common to all of them, they nodded affably to one another. Sometimes a Belzian Hassid found himself in the house of a Husiatin Hassid, or vice-versa, and there he would be given an extra large portion to taste, it all being an excuse for good-natured merriment.

When the sun set, and after the people had gone back to the prayer-house for the afternoon and evening services, they didn't go home as they normally did, but began a new celebration which some enterprising spirits had been planning all the previous week. The Honorary Officers of the congregation sent the beadles to bring fresh drink and plenty of it. The wine-tax agent donated one hundred bottles of white wine and the enthusiastic Hassidic bartender, who sold half his cellar on this holiday, contributed a small cask of Hungarian wine, and from the brewery they brought several barrels of vintage beer, donated by Mrs. Aberdam — and the celebrations began all over again.

The hall of the Husiatin prayer-house was packed from wall to wall. Only the women's balcony upstairs was almost empty for most of the women were down in the hall (great is the celebration that brings far ones near!) crushed together against the west wall, some sitting on the stone floor, some on the benches, their arms linked. Their cheeks were rosy and their eyes shone brightly and they tapped their feet in accompaniment to the dancing of the men.

A number of pleasant surprises had been prepared in advance. Lazer Isser, the watchmaker, who was known for his clowning and his Purim disguises, dressed up as a doctor this time. His yellow beard was nicely washed, combed and divided from the chin up to his cheeks, a top-hat was pulled down over his ears, and pince-nez attached with a string sat on his small nose. (To tell the truth, he looked more like a little tax-collector, with his short, tight coat and his large brief-case under one arm.) He spoke in an affected voice, in a funny kind of German Yiddish, and all who saw and heard him were convulsed with laughter. He walked stiffly through the crowd, which made way for him as he passed, taking pulses and tapping people on the back and writing out prescriptions with a stick on a piece of paper and generally giving non-sensical directions. Another man was dressed as an old woman, crying out supplications in the language of the Gentiles. A number of people began to tug at his dress, roaring with laughter, but the Rabbi and the ritual cattle-slaughterers and the Gemarra teacher scolded him roundly and chased him out of the prayer-house. *"Tfu! dressed in a woman's gown!"* Some energetic young men climbed on to the stove and suspended lanterns with Biblical verses round them from the cornices. Groups of people stood singing the new melodies that had been brought from Husiatin that year — some were sung devoutly, others boisterously. Then they brought in musical instruments, half the band that was used for weddings, and only then did the dancing really begin. The girls sitting on the benches thought they would go mad. They hugged their knees

H

tightly to stop their feet from jumping on the floor. Suddenly an announcement was heard. The dancers stopped and drew apart waiting for what was to come. The First Gabbai entered from the study-room at the head of a procession of young students and beadles, clutching against his chest with both arms a large deep basin like a washbowl, from which a hot, sweet, fragrant steam rose into the air and pervaded the whole hall. In the bowl, there was white wine cooked in sugar, a favourite drink but dangerous for anyone who didn't know to drink. All eyes filmed over and mouths began to water.

"Glasses! We — want — glasses!"

"Easy, take it easy! They're just bringing little beakers. A precious drink like this isn't drunk in glasses."

"Don't push! Everyone will get his share!"

"It's Reb Zalman Leib's donation — for the recovery of his only daughter."

"To the only daughter of Reb Zalman Leib! May the Lord grant her long life!"

"And a good husband."

"Ah, what an aroma!"

"A heavenly smell! It spreads right down the limbs."

"Ignoramus! Hoh! You don't drink it all at once."

"Where's the Rabbi? Where is he?"

"And Reb Hirtzel Pallan?"

"We want Reb Hirtzel!"

"Where is he?"

It didn't take long before the bowl was empty. Some gluttons brought it up to their mouths and sucked voraciously at the leavings. Polite students and cultivated young men handed beakers to their wives and some of the young girls. The beadle removed the empty, sticky beakers, and the pieces of the ones that had been broken, and the band began to play with gusto. This time, they played the tune to which the bridegroom is led to the wedding. The men formed a large circle, linking arms, and began to move and sway around the platform, some lowering their beards on to their chests, others lifting their faces to the lighted chandelier. And inside the circle, singly and in groups, danced little boys with sweet faces, long coats and long side-curls. Laser Isser had changed by now from a doctor to a Gentile shepherd, with a torn shabby straw hat on his head, a long stick in his hand and a cloth knapsack on his side full of nuts. He got on to a bench and, waving to the children, began to scatter the nuts among them, shouting: "Come on, little sheep," and they clamoured around him, bleating: *Me–e–eh, me–e–e–eh!* in soft, appealing voices, as they squealed with glee and fell over one another to get the nuts.

The dancers were too engrossed to pay any attention to them. Let the joker amuse himself with the kids.

Most of the brewery people stayed on for a short while after the evening prayers and then went home. From the day that Reb Naftali Zvi died and Bracha's crying began and the dread of Pan Lasoti hung over them, they found it hard to be gay. To them, rejoicing by command was only half-rejoicing. Mrs. Aberdam was already closeted with Reb Simha and his account books in her apartment, Bracha didn't join the revelry at all, and only Reb Hirtzel and the three children stayed on. The Hassidim surrounded him and the children affectionately, as if hoping to rub some of their nobility off on to themselves. The children grew so absorbed in the performance that it was hard for them to tear themselves away to go home, so they kept pleading with their father another minute and another and another. What they most enjoyed this time was watching Israel Elia and Sosele. The two of them threw off all restraint and mingled with everyone as naturally as if they were regular residents of the small town rather than the brewery. Several times Reb Hirtzel was pulled out of the crowd towards a place of honour and the Rabbi placed his hand on his shoulder and pressed it affectionately. But he simply could not mingle with the merry-makers and would shrug them off with a joke or a mere shake of the head. When it began to grow late and it became evident that the revelries were likely to continue into the dawn, Reb Hirtzel collected the children, pressed them to his huge body, stroking their heads and their cheeks, bent down and whispered to them, and afterwards they all slipped out of the prayer-house and set out for home.

In the prayer-house, the drinking, the singing, and the dancing continued. Fresh wine was brought in and they sent to Mrs. Aberdam for two more barrels of beer. The Scrolls of the Law in the Ark were forgotten, as if the celebration had nothing to do with them; the lanterns on their cornices kept revolving and displaying the verses; the music went on and on and the dancers continued dancing. The women had already gone. Behind the prayer-house, in the dirty, smelly square, two or three couples of girls and boys stood talking in the light of the lately-risen half moon, and seemed to be enjoying themselves immensely.

While the lights still burned brightly in all the high windows of the prayer-house building and the whole town danced to the blaring music and the midnight was drawing rapidly near, — an enormous Jewish woman burst into the hall (the "Nachmanit" they called her), an awful sight with her size and her bulk, her dark clothes and closely-cropped hair, the little cap on her head and her rough grating voice (everyone knew she stole from her husband and drank several glasses of spirits every day). She mopped her face with her apron and cried out:

"A black year on you Jews! With you it's Simhas Torah and out there the town is burning with the fires of hell, a black year on you! Quick, save the Sifrei Torah! Help, Jews! Fire, fire!"

At first, they thought she was just acting drunk and laughed uproariously and applauded her. Someone threw her a wet towel. She pushed a way through the bystanders with her massive arms, holding on to the cap on her head with both hands, and blared in a fearful voice:

"*Gewalt*! Jews! Fire, fire! Save your homes! Save the children! Save your lives! Save the holy books! Fire! Fire!"

When it eventually dawned on them that a catastrophe had indeed occurred, pandemonium broke loose. Women began to scream and tumbled off the benches; they pushed and crushed, crying out to husbands, fathers, sons, brothers. The congestion was awful, everyone pressing for the door, falling, getting trodden on, getting up again and pushing wildly to get to the exit. In a short while, the whole crowd was outside, running hither and thither, standing and looking, shouting and trying to hush others. Celebrants from the Belzian prayer-house came hurrying towards them, enquiring, shouting, wringing their hands over the calamity that had suddenly befallen them.

And in the dark sky, over the houses and beyond, rose a high cloud of smoke, part black, part pink and moving, illuminated with flying sparks, and beneath it the flames

213

hovered in wisps over mounds of debris and hot ashes, the picture became clear to everyone: of the one hundred Jewish houses in the small town, about thirty had been wiped out by the fire. Others were damaged. The prayer-house building, too, which had been rebuilt only three years ago, was half destroyed by the fire, the firemen having destroyed the other half. Every face was covered with ashes. The victims of the fire wandered about or sat grieving on a stone or girder beside the ruins of their gutted homes. And at ten o'clock in the morning there were already some twenty families in the courtyard of the brewery, with whatever meagre, broken belongings they could save.

XXV

Mother to the Distressed

E very apartment and every room, including Bracha's luxuriously appointed rooms, were opened to the unfortunates who were left facing the winter without a roof over their heads. They even billeted an old, sick man with an orphaned grandson in the room of the paralyzed Mende, to his mute outrage and fury.

Reb Hirtzel, although very badly hit by the fire himself (two flour merchants who owed him large sums of money for wheat were rendered penniless, their stores and their homes having burned down completely), shut his mind off from his private affairs and applied himself to helping the fire-victims. Mrs. Aberdam declared that everyone must give the destitute food, somewhere to sleep and a few clothes – if they like, at her expense, against chits which they should receive from Reb Simha. But she didn't content herself with that: she got in touch with the Rabbi and with the honorary officers of the two prayer-houses (all differences being forgotten in time of trouble) set up an aid committee. They even set aside one of the store-rooms of the brewery as an office to which all donations and gifts in kind could be brought, and distributed from there to the needy.

Sosele attended to the sick women, particularly a woman in confinement who was ensconced in the old lady's

215

apartment, for whom she cooked milk soup or chicken soup every day, including the evening. She emptied the chicken-run and the dove-cote within a few days and began to buy more from the villages.

The biggest surprise of all was Brachele, who had never done any social work in her life and never took any interest in the lives and affairs of others. In the face of this misfortune her hardness suddenly melted. Not only did she open her apartment (asylum of her grief) to these roofless people: she was stirred to great compassion for them and tended each and every one of them without distinction, enquiring solicitously what they and the other people on the premises were short of, and she herself provided what they lacked. Those who had the good fortune to be accommodated in her apartment had never had such a good time in their lives. Bracha and her twin daughters toiled all day to improve their condition and provide them with food and rest. These people didn't stop blessing her and thanking her. They offered to help, protesting at the excessive trouble she was going to for them, who were not worth it and not used to being pampered like this; she also wasn't strong enough for it, being so soft and delicate, and they were very concerned for her health. But she always answered with a charming gesture and a sweet smile and doubled her attentiveness. In no time, word of her charitableness and good deeds got around the place, and they began to call her the Good Angel. From there, the name spread to the town, and from then on no one ever called her anything else.

The brewery people, and most of all Mrs. Aberdam and Reb Hirtzel, saw the fine deeds of their loved one and were delighted. There was another reason for their exultation, and that was the main thing: from the day the fire-victims came to the brewery her crying ceased, and she was tranquil and alert and mingled with the people as if she had grown up amongst them all her life. Others too, who had known her since she was a child and had seen her in the various stages of her mental and physical development, couldn't take their eyes off her. A sort of radiance, not of this world, seemed to emanate from her face, her limbs, and her body which had retained the lightness and delicacy of that of a young girl, invoking the blessings of all who saw her.

She also became a mother to her children. She sent them on errands, mainly for the requirements of the fire-victims, and ordered them around in a motherly voice, gentle and firm, which it was quite impossible not to obey. Often the daughters of Pan Yashinski and even Pani Yuzia herself, were drawn thither and came and helped her. The Polish language sounded like the music of a harp when she spoke it.

The boy, Shalom, worked mainly at the side of his father and grandmother, 'going on missions to the Aid Committee and consulting with the grown-ups about the distribution of the gifts. He too would often cast a loving glance at his mother, and his heart rejoiced and swelled with pride, doubling his desire to help, to improve conditions, to ease their lot, and he applied himself to it with an even greater will than before. He had matured in a matter of days and was a grown-up person to all intents and purposes, to such a degree that people began to bring him difficult problems too.

Herr Lieber alone insisted on his right to privacy and refused to let anyone into his apartment. After much pleading, particularly on the part of Bracha, he agreed to let only the husband of the woman in confinement sleep in the anteroom on the same bunk where his Ruthenian hunchbacked servant used to sleep until he died of small-pox and no one was taken on in his place. His dogged refusal to receive the poor seemed despicable in the eyes of the members of the establishment, both old and new, and they nicknamed him *Amalek*. When he heard his new name he was furious, although he didn't know what it signified, but he refused to budge. When Reb Hirtzel took him to task for it, he replied: "A man's home is his castle." "Woe to the castle in which Amalek dwells," growled a Jew who happened to overhear him and made off fast.

They put Reb Simha's family, his wife and his two unmarried daughters, in his office, to his extreme regret, because he now had no rest from their tongues, neither by day nor by night (in the course of the many years of their life together in penury, they had grown peevish and quarrelsome), and it was only because of that that he stayed away from the house and occupied himself with the poor, whom – in his heart of hearts – he disliked intensely.

Pan Lasoti and the new contract were almost forgotten. The day after the fire, and for days afterwards, carts kept coming from the neighbouring towns: one brought loaves of bread, another used clothing; one potatoes and another jugs and pots of milk products. From Brod came an elegant carriage, and in it two young men wearing high-school uniform, who had been sent by the Jewish community and brought some money. All the carts were sent to the brewery and their contents off-loaded into the storehouse, where Shalom took charge and wrote it all down in a small notebook. Reb Hirtzel received the students from Brod, spoke to them in German and gave them receipts signed by him and Mrs. Aberdam. He also wrote out an announcement for the Jewish newspaper in Lwow, to be published over the name of the Aid Committee, appealing to the compassion and generosity of their fellow Jews. And everyone was full of wonder for it was the first time that the name of their town had been printed in a newspaper, and they were most impressed, as always, with his education and his knowledge of the ways of the world.

They also forgot entirely about the two Jews, the merchants of Oszpiechin, of whom they had talked so much before. Once, in the course of a meeting, one of the Committee members was reminded of them and said: "Perhaps it would be worth while to send an urgent letter to the merchants of Oszpiechin? They were received with great honour here and there's no reason why they should not help the fire-victims." But another member shut him up: "Good-for-nothing! who knows their address?" and they forgot all about them again.

The rest of the unfortunates, who could not find a place at the brewery, crowded into the passages and cellars of the houses that had been spared, generally paying full rent. Some lodged with Gentiles outside the town and they and their children suffered considerably from the pigs and their numerous offspring and the other animals about the place. But most of them used to come daily to the brewery yard to get a jar of *menthe* cordial or a jug of beer, a loaf of bread, a piece of kosher meat, or money.

It was impossible to think of putting up new houses at this time of the year. After the autumn rains and the mud, came the snow and ice, and no building can be done on days like that. Only the well-to-do began to bring beams and logs from the forest in preparation for the spring. Some also got in touch with builders and workers and with the brick-kilns in the neighbourhood. The Aid Committee, run by Reb Hirtzel, collected several hundred silver roubles, but on his advice and insistence the money was set aside until the spring, for distribution among those who needed it for building purposes, and not spent on living expenses in the meantime. They'd manage to keep going one way and another, he said.

Hardly a month had gone by, and Brachele began to look so bad as to be almost unrecognisable. Her face grew thin and gaunt with sharply-protruding jawbones, and burned with an unhealthy heat. Her eyes were sunk in deep holes but their inner light blazed stronger every day. Reb Hirtzel, who happened to glance at her one day, got a terrible fright. He tried to persuade her to rest a bit from her hard work, because the poor were more or less fixed up by now: they had bread to eat and clothes to wear and – the main thing – a dry warm place to lay their heads, and there was no longer any need for her to expend the little, precious strength she had on attending to them. The woman in confinement was now up and about and able to attend to her child herself, and the sick were getting on nicely. Moreover, her mother and Sosele and the girls were doing their duty with the utmost devotion . . .

Mrs. Aberdam was also very concerned and anxious about her daughter's health, which was certainly being undermined by her overworking with the fire-victims. She came to her several times and spoke to her gently but firmly and told her that even in good deeds a person must keep a certain proportion and it is a known fact that the sages forbid expending more than a fifth-part on charity. It doesn't matter if you give more money, but health, my child, is a gift from God which no one has the right to abuse. The Lord does protect the simple but she was no simpleton.

But Bracha would simply gaze at the person talking to her with intelligent, kindly eyes beneath a lofty forehead, a sweet smile on her lips, and shake her head. "Can't you see," she'd say, "I have no other happiness in the world. Let me do what I want to do."

There was nothing they could say to that, so they left her to her own devices. And as her body sank, so her soul soared, gathering strength as her arms went out to gather in all the afflicted.

XXVI

The Final Payment

It was winter. The time had come to pay. Mrs. Aberdam put on her best clothes, the long black dress with the yellow petticoat like the colour of gold, and the ornate coif. She put on her long, diamond earrings and tied the white silk three-cornered shawl round her shoulders. Over it all, she put her warm coat with the stone-marten collar, because winter was at its height. She put the money in the long, cloth bag as well as the receipts from the previous years, pulled on her high boots (Petersburg boots!) and went to the palace, to Pan Lasoti, to pay the last third of the money owing for the lease.

Today was the fateful day — either she'd be the lessee of the brewery for four more months and then have to go out into the world like a newborn babe, or — she'd renew the contract for a few more years and carry on as before until the Lord thought fit to summon her unto him. An air of great composure concealed the dread in her heart. On going out, she kissed the mezuza nailed to the doorpost, as she always did, and nodded her head to the empty room. She went and knocked at the door of Bracha's apartment and said goodbye to her. Reb Hirtzel had gone away on urgent business two days before and wasn't back yet. It was morning. The children were already at their studies and the cooking was well under way. The snow covered the ground in a thick, solid layer, after freezing hard for twenty days. In the yard stood a number of waggons, unloading empty barrels and waiting to load full ones. A cold sun gleamed low in the eastern sky and a chorus of noisily-chirping sparrows filled the branches of the bare trees. It was Wednesday.

She said her morning prayers, as usual, and recited the daily psalm for the Levites. And as she read the verse: *They slay the widow and the stranger and murder the fatherless*, she shed a tear. But when she reached the end of the verse: *But the Lord is become my stronghold; and my God the rock of my refuge*, she raised her head with renewed confidence.

She crossed the road and walked alongside the frozen hedges under the bare chestnut trees, the hem of her dress trailing in the snow. A Ruthenian peasant who passed her took off his cap and bowed to her respectfully. A dark-eyed Jewish youth with long side-locks whom she encountered on the way simply stared at her, not saying anything. And as she passed, he stopped, turned his head and followed her with his puzzled gaze. The big purse was wrapped in a white handkerchief and she held it in her hand like a prayer-book. The boy wondered if Mrs. Aberdam hadn't possibly made a mistake and was going to pray on a weekday in her Sabbath finery. At the end of the line of chestnut trees, she turned left, passed through the finely-wrought iron gate and walked along the snow-covered sidewalk to the palace.

She was made to wait for about half an hour with several squires, all of them silent and morose, before Pan Lasoti had his servant bring her into his room: that is to say, Pan Grabinski's room, but so many changes had been made in it that it was almost unrecognisable. New furniture, new pictures on the wall. Pan Lasoti sat behind an enormous desk, piled with papers and all kinds of gadgets, and as she entered the room he turned his cat's eyes on her as if surprised to see her. He waved her to a chair. With a sly smile on his thin lips, he said politely:

"Pani Aberdam has no doubt brought the rent?"

"Yes, Your Excellency. The payment for the last third, under the *old* contract," putting special emphasis on the word "old".

"Good, good. We'll give you a receipt right away. One moment."

He rang a little bell on his table. The door opened slowly and a meek, self-effacing clerk came in.

"Prepare a receipt at once for Mrs. Aberdam, for the last payment on the brewery lease according to the books."

"At your service, Your Excellency."

The clerk retreated, slipped into the next room and closed the door carefully from the other side. Mrs. Aberdam's heart gave a jolt. Was this really the *last* payment? It was hard for her to sit still. She kept turning over the purse in the handkerchief between her hands. Finally, she summoned up courage and asked:

"And what about the renewal of the lease?"

"Ah, so... About the renewal of the lease... I think Madame is a bit late: Yes, I'm sorry."

The mask of composure that covered the dread in her heart was ripped away. An abyss opened up before her. All the pent-up bitterness that had accumulated in her since the day of her first husband's death and before, clamoured for an outlet. In a dry voice which she herself could hardly hear, she asked:

"How so, Your Excellency? My son-in-law and I tried time and time again to see you already in the summer... Didn't my son-in-law, Pan Pallan, speak to you?"

"Yes, yes. I think that the gentleman you refer to did speak to me once, but we leased the brewery to someone else in the meantime. I'm sorry, but I can't go back on it."

The room suddenly grew dark. Everything began to turn over and revolve in a changing flash of colours, and out of this terrible darkness Brachele's tearful voice came back to her: *the two Jews from Oszpiechin...* It was all as clear as daylight now. Her face was deathly pale as she addressed the cruel, alien Gentile seated opposite her, leaning on his hand propped up on the table.

"After thirty years? And without any negotiations? Is that the behaviour of a gentleman, representative of His Excellency the Graf Molodetzki?"

She fought back the tears that were beginning to suffuse her eyes and looked at Pan Lasoti steadily. Again the verse went through her mind: *They slay the widow and the stranger and murder the fatherless* . . . There was not a flicker on his face. He didn't move. Still sitting with his chin resting on the palm of his hand, he answered evenly:

"Yes, new times, new people. I am making reforms in everything, everything. Mrs. Aberdam is a fine but (pardon me) elderly lady of an earlier generation and she must be replaced by others younger than herself. They also replaced Pan Grabinski. That is the way of the world. I leased out the brewery during the summer to the two gentlemen from Oszpiechin. Rich Jews. They will expand the business and increase the profits. I'm sorry, it can't be undone." (Could it be that the words: *They slay the widow and the stranger...* apply to their own people, to Jews?)

226

"But why didn't you tell me at the time? Actually, according to the contract each side has to give six months' notice. Your action is a breach of the law."

"Ah, indeed. About the legal aspect, I am prepared to argue with you in a different place, Pani Aberdam. When you take me to court . . . The only point at issue here is equity..."

A change came over Mrs. Aberdam as if something had clamped down into place within her. She straightened up, opened her purse and began to take folded bills out of it, in a properly dignified and business-like manner, although her fingers trembled slightly. She counted them out before the eyes of the murderer, arranged them in a neat pile on the table, adding a few silver and copper coins, and when she finished she said in a flat, expressionless voice:

"Please count it and give me a receipt...I am only a weak woman, an old Jewish woman. It is not in my power to fight Pan Lasoti, the all-powerful governor of His Excellency Graf Molodetzki's estates. So I am handing over my case to someone strong, into the hands of our Father in Heaven, who takes the part of widows and orphans that are being killed and murdered, for justice is His — Pan Lasoti!...My receipt, please."

Pan Lasoti's smile contorted his thin lips as if they were seized by a spasm. He extended a long arm covered with freckles, swept up the money with a swift movement, and put it in the drawer. Then, drumming his fingers on the table, he said:

"Well, on...(such and such a date), the gracious Mrs. Aberdam must vacate the brewery premises completely, for the new lessees will come to take legal possession of it the following day. I hope I shall not have to resort to any unpleasant measures..."

"Let's hope so, Pan Lasoti. Let's hope so... The Rabbi of Belz will also stand by me."

"Who?!"

"The Rabbi of Belz. He's a holy man. Princes hang on his word."

"Mrs. Aberdam is jesting! I didn't know she had such a sense of humour."

"Goodbye. Perhaps God will still give you a change of heart. We Jews are a people who have had a lot of experience of suffering – and deliverance, too. Goodbye, Pan Lasoti!"

She pulled herself up to her full, aristocratic height. At the same time, the door opened slightly. The clerk came in with the receipt at a sign from Pan Lasoti, and gave it obsequiously to Mrs. Aberdam. She folded the slip of paper, stuffed it into the purse which she wrapped up again in the handkerchief, and turned to go.

"Goodbye, Pan Lasoti. We have a great God. He won't desert us."

As she went out, she saw neither the snow-covered garden nor the charming buildings in the palace grounds. Her eyes were blinded with tears and her heart pounded like a hammer. She had never been so upset in her life. Not even when she was young, when Reb Shlomke died, did she experience so devastating a pain in the heart.

She walked down the snow-covered pavement, turned automatically down the chestnut avenue, and entered the brewery yard. It seemed to her that she hadn't encountered a living soul on the way; the whole world had died. From some obscure corner of her heart, a defiant resolve arose: *No, I won't give in. I'll raise heaven and earth and not keep silent. As long as I'm still alive, no one will get me out of the brewery!*

In her apartment, she quickly removed her jewellery and changed out of her holiday clothes, folding them neatly and with more than usual precision, putting each thing in its exact place. No one was at home. Only Pearl, who was chopping meat in the kitchen. She could hear the ticking of the clock on the wall and the splutter of the *menthe* cooking in the cauldrons. She was alone in the large, deserted rooms. She collapsed on to the black sofa, dropped her veined hands into her open lap, and murmured brokenly to herself: – After thirty years, in my old age . . . And Hirtzel's position isn't too good either. How will I be able to bear the sight of Brachele and the children in trouble? What will become of Shalom, grandson of my precious, saintly, one and only Shlomke? Is it possible that he'll keep silent up there? Can it be that he doesn't remember me any more? . . . Is it possible that there in heaven too he is so busy studying the Torah that he isn't aware of me, as when he was alive? Is it necessary to study Torah in heaven as well? . . . Perhaps he has a grudge against me because I married Reb Naftali Zvi. But he knows I didn't do it for myself. His image hasn't faded from my mind for a single day. In everything I did, I was preparing to come to him. Everything I did for my future world, I did in his name . . .

And sitting there alone, stricken, lost in thought, with the clock ticking on the wall and the *menthe* bubbling away in the brewery, she is borne in her smiling imagination to the world of the spirits and of light.

XXVII

The Misguided Heart

While she still sat dreaming and smiling to herself, Reb Hirtzel returned from his trip to one of the villages. He pulled up his small snow-cart before his mother-in-law's apartment, jumped from it like a young boy and hurried upstairs. Mrs. Aberdam, roused out of her reverie, sat waiting for him.

"Have you been to the agent's?"

"I've just returned from there. There's nothing to be done here. Brachele was right. She was right, as she always is. The spirit of her sainted father spoke out of her mouth. Those two Jews leased the brewery while they were here in the summer."

Reb Hirzel went as white as a sheet of parchment.

"What swinishness! Those same two pious people! And how is it that the agent didn't tell us anything? According to the terms of the contract, the Graf or his representative has to give notice six months in advance if he wants to cancel."

"That *Haman* said he's prepared to go to court with me. Lawsuits with the Graf! We know the outcome in advance. Tomorrow, I'm going to Belz."

"What will Belz help? Better send a telegram to the Graf. He's at least a gentleman."

"But you know what he answered to my letter. Everything has been entrusted to the hands of the Haman. I shall go to Belz and I won't leave the Rabbi alone until he promises me he will get the decision reversed, and I don't care who he has to exert influence on: the Graf, the agent, or the Jewish trespassers. I shan't budge from there until he promises me that I'll remain in the brewery. The Zaddik, his father, put me into it and *he* has to see to it that they don't put me out. You, Hirtzel, will remain here. You'll supervise the business, and look after Brachele and the children. And don't forget Mende the deaf-mute. Pay my charity contributions to any collectors that come around. See to the wants of the fire-victims. The list is with Reb Simha. It is my wish that in my absence nothing should be changed anywhere. I believe everything will be all right. If the Rabbi can set aside what the Lord decrees – can't the Rabbi annul what Pan Lasoti decrees? I believe in his power. He has his father behind him. Besides, he's a relative and can't wriggle out of it. Even if I have to sit there a month – I won't move from there until we're safe. That's what I say, that's what I shall do."

In all her life, she had never shown so much forcefulness. In all her life, she had never had so much faith. Reb Hirtzel looked a little uncomfortable. He wasn't used to seeing her like that.

Early next morning, Mrs. Aberdam set out in a hired snow-cart for Radichov, and from there by way of Witkov and the frozen River Bug, to Krisnipoli. She spent the night there with a distant relative, pouring out to him all the bitterness of her heart. In the morning she went by train to Belz.

A sombre, brooding atmosphere pervaded the whole brewery establishment. It was the winter days before

Hanukka. At night, the roofs popped with a sound like a shot, from the freezing cold; and in the daytime the sun shone crystal-clear and everything sparkled in festive silence. Beer was brewed once in two days. There was a good deal of coming and going on the place. Apart from the families that had been squatting there since the fire, a number of guests also came, among them Reb Reuvele the pedlar. With some difficulty, they found themselves a place among the fire-victims and the two categories treated one another as mortal enemies. The rescue work had practically died down, as everything was now running in a routine and orderly manner. The children were quiet and a little sad because of the absence of the beloved old lady. And Reb Hirtzel went around with a perpetually preoccupied air, and although in his heart of hearts he didn't believe in the power of the Zaddik of Belz to lift the decree, that is to say – to cancel an agreement made by the Graf's agent – he nevertheless waited anxiously for news from his mother-in-law.

Bracha's condition changed for the worse again. Although the weeping fits didn't return, she was very sad and never spoke to the members of the family at all. She went on attending to the fire-victims, but she seemed to go into a total decline. There were blue rings under her eyes and dark furrows ran down both sides of her mouth. Her body was painfully thin and looked as if it could snap in two. Little by little, the people's love for her changed to an aching compassion. Reb Hirtzel, who saw her sinking from day to day – and his mother-in-law, her mother, not at home! – was almost out of his mind with grief. Once, when he was standing over her in the bedroom, thoroughly wretched and depressed, he stroked her head and kept importuning her with his repeated questions:

233

"What is it, what is it, my child? Why don't you tell me? Why not? You must know what's wrong with you..."

She turned her large eyes on him and said with a bitter smile:

"I shall depart this life soon, and be a nuisance to you no longer."

He didn't pay any attention to what she said, for her voice alone was like a caress to his tortured heart, and without taking in what his ears heard he said:

"Never mind, Brachele. Mother will be back and things will brighten up again. Think of the children: there aren't many people who are blessed with such lovely children. Whoever sees them envies us. We'll still see life, Brachele. Calm down, child, calm yourself. Take care of your precious health – we're not young any more. If you'll want to be well, you will be."

He sat beside her, held her hand and played with it on his knee, and looked at the blue veins throbbing in her wrists. Then he bent over and put his lips to the veins and could not restrain the tears that poured down on to the beloved hand.

But he could not break down the hidden barrier, and the woman's soul seemed to be chained to the underworld.

Letters began to arrive in the mail from Mrs. Aberdam. Each one differed from the next. After a letter full of anger, complaints and reproaches there would be one full of faith, hope and encouragement; all according to how the Rabbi treated her. But even taking all the letters together, it was still impossible to make out anything concerning the matter in point.

Ten days later, Mrs. Aberdam came home in high spirits: at last she had got what she wanted. She carried a letter, written in Polish, signed by the Zaddik in his own hand, addressed to the agent, Pan Lasoti. She had changed so much that Reb Hirtzel and Shalom didn't recognise her. All her dignity seemed to have been taken from her. She spoke a lot and laughed in an unpleasant way and was so distracted that she didn't see anything that was going on in the place.

That very day, she put on her best clothes and went to the palace. The agent received her as before, invited her to sit down and asked what she wanted.

"I've brought Your Excellency a letter from the Rabbi of Belz."

Pan Lasoti was never so surprised in all his life. Mrs. Aberdam, completely oblivious to the fact, held out the letter, adding:

"The Rabbi of Belz is a holy man. Princes heed what he says. For him nothing exists except righteousness and justice and love of his fellow men, and God is with him."

At a loss, Pan Lasoti stretched out his hand, took the letter, opened it and read it cursorily. Afterwards, he handed it back to Mrs. Aberdam, unfolded, together with the envelope, saying:

"I do not have the privilege of knowing the personage who wrote this letter. Will you please write to the Rabbi of Belz and tell him to address his letter to those leprous Hassids of his!" he said, raising his voice to a roar on the last words. "Excuse me, Pani Aberdam. I'm very busy." And he nodded his head towards the door.

A storm of contumely rose to Mrs. Aberdam's lips, intended for this wicked enemy of Israel who sat there looking at her with mocking eyes. She didn't want redress for the insult to herself, but to the all-powerful Zaddik —

235

for the insult to the Rabbi of Belz! Her blood boiled and she shook all over as if seized with a fever. She had already risen from her chair and was about to spread her arms in the air and open her mouth in a loud cry, when suddenly some inner force restrained her. A shining, familiar image passed before her eyes. There was perfume in the air. A wonderous peace came over her and pervaded her entire body. No, this evil man would not see Mrs. Aberdam degrade herself. She looked him straight in the face for a moment, smiled and said:

"From now on, Your Excellency will have to deal with the Rabbi of Belz himself," and stalked out of the room without another word.

She had barely gone fifty yards from the palace, when the agent's three hunting dogs came bounding after her, yelping wildly. She waved her hands to drive them off, but they seized her dress in their teeth and tore it. She turned around several times, with the dogs hanging on to her dress. They made circles around her, looking straight into her eyes and wagging their tails with a peculiar roguishness, as if making fun of her. She was just getting ready to shout, when a loud laugh came from the side of the palace, followed by a whistle, and the dogs suddenly left her and ran back the way they'd come, the three of them in a row as if harnessed to an invisible sleigh.

Mrs. Aberdam leaned against the fence for a few minutes, listening to the palpitations of her heart. Then she looked down at her dress, hanging on her in tatters. A yellow strip from her underskirt was also dragging on the ground, and one black-stockinged leg was showing. Her face twisted into a wry smile. She straightened up and began to walk home. She walked slowly, without caring any longer if anyone saw her.

When she came into the yard, the people were shocked to see what had happened to her and began to ask her what it was all about, but she went straight up to her apartment without a word. The members of the household, Reb Hirtzel and Shalom among them, followed after her, shaken and silent. In the room, she sat down, as she was, on the sofa, and told all the people standing around her how the agent had treated her and how he had turned his dogs on her when she left.

"Now the Rabbi of Belz will believe me. Now he'll know. This wicked man has not treated *me* with disrespect, but him himself. Now I'm sure he'll bestir himself to punish him. It's impossible that he shouldn't. Tomorrow I shall go to Belz again and give him back his letter which has been polluted by the hands of that monster. Here it is, in my pocket." And she patted the pocket of her mantle.

All the laughter suddenly went out of Reb Simha. His lips went grey like the hairs of his beard. He was so worked up that his voice shook:

"What did he say? *Leprous Hassids*? About that, the Zaddik will not be silent. Impossible! No!" he said, and left the house.

XXVIII

Death of the 'Good Angel'

Mrs. Aberdam stayed in Belz for about three weeks. The winter weather worsened and there were days when it was impossible to do any brewing for fear that the *menthe* might freeze in the cooling-vat and spoil.

The whole town now knew that the two fine Jews from Oszpiechin had done a despicable thing. They had trespassed on Mrs. Aberdam's property and stepped into her shoes and in the spring she and all her household would have to vacate the brewery; and with her, no doubt, all the fire-victims under her protection would be driven out. This subject now took precedence in the minds of everyone, the fire and the houses that were going to be built taking second place. The recent acts of kindness by herself, her daughter, her son-in-law and her grandson, had won all hearts, which was why they sympathized so much with her distress and her unhappy fate and cursed the trespassers roundly. The refugees from the fire who were living on the premises, kept whispering together and enquiring how matters stood, what news from the old lady, what the Zaddik said. They knew everything: that the Rabbi of Belz had written to the Rabbi of Viznitch asking him to try to influence the two Jews, *his* Hassidim, to drop the disgusting business; that the Rabbi of Viznitch did actually try to intercede but the two Hassidim answered, without mincing words, that if the Rabbi (may he live a long and happy life) continued to interfere in their business affairs they'd cease going to him and hinted that the people of Israel were not, thank God, short of Rabbis. From then on, the power of the Rabbi suddenly waned and he occupied himself in writing long letters to the Rabbi of Belz about the tribulations of Israel and God's problems in the diaspora, and the like. The Rabbi of the small town of L. roused himself to action and wrote a flowery letter to the Rabbi of Oszpiechin (they found his name in the almanack of several years back), demanding that the two most learned, wealthy, powerful etc. etc. Jews, Reb Akiva Holtzhendler and Reb Gedalia Nussenbaum appear before a rabbinical court in the matter of the trespass. But the Rabbi replied smoothly that to his regret the learned etc. etc. gentlemen refuse to comply, maintaining that they litigate in the regular courts only, and because of our sins we Rabbis have no power today to compel anyone to do anything, and woe to us this affront to the Torah and so on and so on . . .; particularly as the litigants are very determined men and well in with the authorities – need one say more?

The letters which arrived at frequent intervals from Mrs. Aberdam and were read without fail by Reb Hirtzel and the boy, Shalom, were infuriating and depressing at the same time. One letter would contradict the next. It was impossible to recognise Mrs. Aberdam in them: her sense of balance, her moderation, her refinement and gentility, her respect for her standing and her infinite patience, were all gone. Apparently, there in Belz, she was in a perpetual state of anger, pain and frustration. In one of the letters she asked most particularly that they should let her know, in the name of God, Pan Lasoti's first name. The Rabbi wanted to know. Reb Hirtzel, and the boy as well, already knew that theirs was a lost cause. There was positively nothing to be done about it. There was only one way: to take legal action against Pan Lasoti, the Graf's representative, but it was quite evident that he would have the upper hand, even if they put up the best advocates. It had not yet happened that a Jew should win a case against the Polish gentry. It was also a long drawn-out business. In trials of this sort, delays in giving judgement, postponements and a deliberate drawing-out of the proceedings were quite the usual thing. It can go on for years: collecting evidence, swearing people in, judgments, appeals from one court to another – there is no end to it, nor to the costs. A trial like this can bring a man down to his last penny, his last bit of bread, and the grave. No, Hirtzel Pallan will not let his mother-in-law, an old woman and by no means well off, get involved in such a nasty business. Under no circumstances!

His own business was declining rapidly. The business trips to the surrounding areas were becoming so few and far between that he was thinking of selling the horse. There simply wasn't any need to travel any more. The Russian Jew, Spudik, who had settled in the town several years ago and opened a small flour shop, and grew rich while no one was looking, had begun to deal in produce – secretly at first, and then openly – bought himself a horse and cart and went travelling around, making enormous down-payments and – incidentally – practising a little usury on the side. He also got rich from the fire, because everyone needed his services. But Reb Hirtzel couldn't do those things. Even if he wanted to he

I

couldn't. Some of the squires had grown old, or died, and their heirs didn't know Reb Hirtzel and didn't prefer him and his fine manners and cultured way of speaking, to Spudik's cash, for all his corrupt ways and appearance. Nor did he have any other resources from which to replenish what he had lost through the two merchants who had been hit by the fire. And the moneylenders in Lwow became importunate and hard, demanding repayment exactly on time and giving no new loans, even at high interest, as information had reached them of his rapidly deteriorating position.

But he regarded all these troubles as negligible compared with the distress over his wife, whose condition grew worse from day to day. Latterly, she had even stopped eating. She lost her appetite completely and at mealtimes would no more than peck at her food and then put down her knife and fork: she was already full. On the other hand, she kept pressing him and the children to eat more and more, as if thereby satisfying her own needs. To her husband's solicitous enquiries, she would reply that she was, thank God, fit and well but didn't feel any need for food. In her opinion, one can live without food altogether. Her late father also used to eat like a bird, her mother tells her. She's like her father in this respect. The main thing is that she's actually feeling quite strong, stronger than she's ever felt in her life.

The people sitting round the table were surprised at this unexpected eloquence. As she was speaking, they looked at her emaciated body, at the thinness of her face and the abnormal brightness of her eyes, and their hearts trembled.

In the fourth week of Mrs. Aberdam's absence, the wife of a poor shoemaker, one of the fire-victims living on the

premises, fell ill (she was the mother of three small babies).
She complained of a sore throat. When Bracha learned of
this she immediately went to her. The family occupied a
small room next to the prayer-room (the minyan was now
bigger than ever before. Besides the fire-victims living in
the brewery, a number of people from the prayer-house
that had burnt down in the town came there to pray on
Saturdays and even placed there, temporarily, two Scrolls
of the Law which they had managed to rescue and for
which there was no room in the synagogue). When
Bracha came in, the woman pulled herself up in the bed.
Bracha went up to her, felt her forehead and her neck and
asked where it hurt. She promptly sent for a spoon, asked
the sick woman to face the window and looked into her
throat. It was all red, as if on fire. It must be rinsed out
with salt water. She asked for some salt, and when she
found there was none in the room, she ran to her apartment
and brought a glassful of luke-warm salt water. She stood
over the sick woman until she had rinsed her throat
several times, spitting the water out into a basin which she
held in front of her. She told her to do this every half
hour, and stayed on to dress and feed the children.

A few days afterwards, in the middle of the night,
Bracha woke up in a panic, groaning very hoarsely. And
between groans, a sort of hollow, barking cough was torn
from her throat. Reb Hirtzel, who lay in the bed opposite
her, unable to sleep because of various torturing thoughts,
jumped to the floor and hurried barefoot to her side. He
lit a candle and wiped the perspiration from her face and
forehead with the sheet. He asked what was ailing her.
She just gripped her thin neck with her hand and shook
her head weakly, for she couldn't utter a word. Her voice

seemed to stick in her agonising throat and she couldn't release it from there, although he could see she was trying very hard. The twins in the next room also woke up (Shalom slept in the old lady's apartment) and stood shivering in their nightgowns outside the door, listening to what was going on inside. Their father's whispers made their hair stand on end with fright. He opened the door and asked them to prepare a little hot water, because their mother had a very sore throat and it was difficult for her to talk. Both girls rushed to the kitchen, lit a fire in the stove, and in a short while brought their father a hot kettle, a basin and a small towel. He packed them off to sleep, closed the door and stood by his wife applying hot poultices to her neck, until her voice softened somewhat and she could say:

"Thank you, Hirtzel. I feel a little easier now. It's like needles pricking in the throat."

But suddenly she felt bad again and the poultices no longer helped. When the dawn showed grey in the window, Reb Hirtzel got dressed, harnessed his sleigh, and came back with the old doctor within half an hour. The doctor took off his coat and began to crack a joke, as usual, but when his experienced eyes saw the woman's face he suddenly fell silent. He held her hand and felt her pulse. Then he asked for a spoon and told Reb Hirtzel to give him a lighted candle and hold up the sick woman's head. He forced her mouth wide open and glanced into her throat. Then he took out a small notebook, tore out a piece of paper and hastily scribbled a few words on it, and in a gruff, authoritative, snappy voice ordered him to run and bring him from his home, immediately, the things he listed on the paper. One of the twins snatched the paper from his hand and ran like mad. When his instruments arrived, the doctor bent over the sick woman, bared her arm and gave her an injection; bared her ribs, and gave her another. He worked as if possessed. When he finished, he turned to Reb Hirtzel, his white hair and beard in disarray, his eyes frightened.

"She's in great danger."

Reb Hirtzel didn't grasp what the doctor was saying. He transferred his gaze from the doctor's wild appearance to the burning face of his wife. Her head-band had fallen off and her black hair, which had not been out for a long time, glistened wet with perspiration. When there was a pause in her coughing, her face was like a burning rose in the middle of the pillow, her lips slightly parted, her eyes screwed up tightly with the pain.

And at ten o'clock, a great cry, as of many voices, went through the whole establishment. Bracha's gentle body lay peaceful and composed upon the bed; and on her face – a set smile with a touch of mockery in it. She said she would depart this world shortly, and you see – she kept her word!

XXIX

In the Glistening Snow

I t was early afternoon of the following day, at the beginning of the month of Adar, a day full of glitter and enchantment. The orb of the sun stood high in the pellucid sky and shed its cold light over the snow which covered the whole earth. Everything seemed to be enveloped in a shroud, and the tinkling of sleigh-bells flying over the road sounded strange and remote. After the wailing that pervaded the brewery, a brittle silence prevailed in the yard. The heavy door of the brewery was bolted. Only once every half hour a snow cart would glide into the courtyard loaded with large blocks of greenish-looking ice, unload them into the empty ice-house and return to the lake quarry.

From the courtyard gate, a lad of about twelve emerged. He was small, dressed in a short, light-blue winter coat, high boots and a black fur hat on his head. He stood a moment at the gate, looked this way and that, then turned left and began to walk along the side of the road, trampling down the soft snow, at every step pulling out his boots with the snow adhering to them, especially round the heels. He walked with his head down, his eyes fixed on the particular patch of snow that he had to crush underfoot. He didn't walk on the side where the palace and the small town lay, but on other side, where the bath-house and

the few Jewish houses were, and beyond the houses of
the farmers, a sort of village in itself, and the road that
leads to the water mill and the pine woods of the farming
community. Between the brewery and the houses of the Jews
was an empty square and in the middle of it a fenced enclosure of about four square yards, inside which was a big
wooden cross with a small suffering Christ made of metal
affixed to it. The enclosure was so full of snow now, that
the hammer and the pliers and the nails that always hung
there in holy display were no longer visible. The boy
crossed the square diagonally without looking at the
cross. The windows of the distant houses were sealed with
a thick covering of ice and frost and the ancient doors were
warped and swollen-looking. Were it not for the smoke
that curled over the roofs one could have thought that
the dwellers had also frozen and there was no living soul
inside.

The boy walked along the side of the road and did not
see the snowy line of the boards on the other side, which
were meant for people to walk on. He felt a need to crush
his boots into the virgin snow.

In his brain was a single thought – cold, sharp and keen:
I won't go to her funeral! I won't go to her funeral!

As much as he tried to add words to this thought, he
could not. Just these six words kept repeating themselves
over and over again. And when he tried to think beyond
this, it was as if he touched the walls of pain and he
recoiled.

On the narrow sidewalk and in the middle of the road
he passed at varying intervals a farmer in an orange-
coloured sheepskin, a peasant woman enveloped in a
large, woolly shawl, a farm-girl in a man's high boots, a

248

Jew huddled up in a crumpled overcoat, and a flat, empty sled – but he didn't see them. He kept walking on, head down, trampling the snow underfoot. He quickened his pace, as if running from someone. He was already passing the bath-house. A big pile of wood lay outside it and the bath attendant was standing there with his foot on a log, axe in hand, scratching the back of his neck, as if trying to puzzle out how to get the better of this stubborn log. The boy ignored him and took the road leading to the village. In the farmyards there was a bit of activity. A dog barked, waddling geese cackled as they sank into the snow, pigs grunted and farm-girls carried steaming tubs to feed the animals. In some farmyards they stopped to look with some surprise at the boy walking alone along the way.

He was not aware that his hands, hanging down his sides, were already blue with cold, and only when he felt the pins and needles at the end of his fingers did he put them into the pockets of his coat.

I won't go to her funeral. No, I won't! – He kept repeating in stubborn revolt. He continued walking until he came to a crossroads: the road to the right wound along to the mill and the big lake that worked it. In the summer it is a sandy track, heavy underfoot and scorching hot. The one on the left goes down to the woods. In summer, it passes between green meadows where the good wood-sorrel is to be found. He'd been on these roads more than once in the horse and trap with his father. He raised his eyes and looked around him. The vast expanse lay pure and gleaming under the snow, broken by an occasional cluster of bushes, some white, some black, that stuck out above the surface. The whole terrain appeared to slope downwards and at the end of the slope, far, far away, lay the cluster of snow-covered buildings belonging to the mill. The lake was not visible because of the ice and the snow, and no sound issued from the mill. On the other side stood a wall of forest weighted down with frost. The boy stood considering for a moment which road to choose. Then he remembered that there were no houses or people in the wood, so he headed for it.

Because of the slope, his progress was fast, a sort of skating run. A strong wind was blowing and the carpet of snow seemed to move before him. It sparkled in the sun with myriads of tiny, glittering particles. The boy bent forward because of the driving wind behind him. And because of the biting cold he pulled his hat down over his ears, put up his collar, and stuffed his hands into his pockets. The snow was very deep here and every now and then his boots would sink into it up to the rim. On one occasion, some snow even got into them and after a few moments he felt the cold dampness touching his ankles, but he kept hurrying further and further on.

On this route, not a living soul appeared. Only once, a flock of ravens passed over his head. They came down and stood like dozens of black, moving spots on the snow in the meadow. The wind howled in his right ear and stung his face which was still smarting from the hard particles of snow. He wanted to think now, to think a lot, but the walls of his brain still hurt as before, and would not allow his thoughts to expand. When he saw that he was nearing the wood he began to run towards it. His heart beat hard in his breast and it seemed to him that he was running after his heart. He was now twenty paces from the trees. He had to go up a slight rise. On the left, there was a sloping piece of fenced-off land with a few trees on it.

He remembered that this was where they buried dead animals. In the summer the sandy soil in the spot was upturned and scrabbled about and bones lay strewn on top of it most of the time. Now this spot too shone in perfect purity. He stood blinking his eyes in the too bright light and gradually felt the seething tumult in his brain subside. His heart stopped its furious pounding, and his mind began to clear. He started to climb slowly and carefully so as not to slide back down the slope, until he came to the first of the trees. He turned and leaned his back against the trunk, so that he could look back over the fields that he had crossed. The trunk was thin, and from the contact of his back it moved, shedding a mass of snowflakes that covered all of him with a white powder. The sudden, soft contact felt very pleasant. It had life in it and movement. He knocked his back again and again against the tree and the snow kept piling softly over him until he stopped.

"I'm a snowman!" he said to himself, reluctant to move from here again. Suddenly he remembered why he had come. His thoughts now flowed freely, serenely, unchecked. The funeral would be at three. That's what the old doctor said to Israel Elia in the courtyard. As he passed there he heard him say it. It must now be half past one. When he went out it was twelve o'clock. He must stay here until evening. At four o'clock it already begins to get dark. No – actually he can leave here at three and walk slowly so as to reach the courtyard at half past four. He doesn't want to get back earlier than that. He must be sure that she isn't in the house any more. He'll come back after everyone gets back from the funeral. But what will he do here until three o'clock? There are no

251

wild animals here, he knows that for certain. One can walk the whole length and breadth of the forest in three quarters of an hour. At the most, a hare or a hungry fox may stray there. Nor is there any fear of snakes in the winter. They are asleep in their snow-covered nests. What will he do in this deserted spot for an hour or two? He was at a loss. Never mind, he'll walk around a bit and look at the trees. Each one had a different structure, from the swollen, frozen base to the snow-laden treetops. He could also climb up one of them, sit on a branch, swinging his legs and hitting them against the tree to warm them. If it were summer, he'd have made a bonfire and sat in its glow!

While thinking, he began to move among the trees. The layer of snow on the ground was interspersed with mounds and bushes, because the snow fell through the branches which broke its fall in many places. But it was soft and fine as if it had passed through a sieve. His boots sunk into it wondrously lightly. Suddenly he came upon a series of small confused footprints. Yes, those were a hare's footprints, for this is what it does: as it kicks out its hind legs it sends up a spray of snow. Perhaps it might be worthwhile following these footprints until he finds the hare. Perhaps it is freezing somewhere in the snow and he can save it from death!

But he turned away and went even further in. And the further he went, the more the wind died down. A vast unbroken silence lay over everything. At every two or three steps he stopped to feast his eyes on the pure, silent vistas. He touched the thick tree-trunks with his hand, but the ice made it wet and he immediately felt the skin contract until it hurt.

He went on, stepping over the pale shadows of the

trees, and felt on his back the sun-rays penetrating into the thickets, and it seemed to him that it had grown less cold. "How good it is here!" he said to himself. "Why don't people come here to be purified and cleansed?" He remembered clearly all he had heard and read about the purification of the soul, as well as the verse in Isaiah: "Though your sins be as scarlet, they shall be as white as snow." Like the snow in the forest. But peoples' houses are sealed and boarded up against the snow, so how will their sins get white as snow? . . . And a great desire came over him to roll in the sifted snow, until he got white all over. He found a clearing, stood in the middle of it, and threw himself full length on his back. Not in order to leave his imprint in the snow, as children do in play, but to envelop himself in it altogether. And he stretched his arms close to his thighs and put his feet together and began to roll over and over until his shoulders began to hurt. He sat up and took a look at himself. He was completely covered in snow, but the colour of his clothes was still visible, because the snow hadn't stuck to them properly.

What's that?! – His ears caught a sound like the yelp of a puppy that's been kicked. He strained his ears in the direction of the sound, but it was not repeated. "Probably just the bark of a hungry fox." And he sat like that and gazed up at the sky suspended between the white branches. "It is possible to look at the sun without screwing up your eyes." And the discovery of this fact pleased him so much that he kept staring into it. Again, the cry of the kicked dog reached his ears. He got to his feet and looked all around. Then he started on the return journey. As he emerged from the forest saw a large shape covered in rags plodding along the road in the snow and approaching the

253

wood, dragging three dogs – two large and one small – after him, each at the end of a cord.

"Stril!" recognition flashed in his mind. "Stril the skinner."

The large shape drew nearer. Another thirty or forty paces and he'd reach the wood. One of the dogs ran ahead but the skinner kicked him and the dog recoiled with a yelp of pain.

The boy remembered that Stril also caught dogs that had no identity discs tied to their necks. He had caught these three, evidently, and he was going to kill them in the enclosure. And indeed Stril made for the fenced-off plot, pushed the fence with his foot and some kind of gate opened in it. He turned and pulled the dogs inside one by one. The dogs sat down on their haunches in the snow, and howled and refused to go in, but he dragged them in by force.

The boy descended slowly to the fence of the square, leaned his chest against it and looked inside.

Stril went up the square with the dogs until he reached the first tree. There he tied all three ropes to the trunk. He took out of his bosom a small flask, pulled out the cork with his teeth, and took a long swig, with his head thrown back. Then he put the flask back in his bosom and took a big loaf of bread out of there, kneaded it with the fingers of both hands, flattened it, took a few bites out of it and put it back in his bosom. Now the boy could see his red face covered with a dirty stubble of a beard, and his small glittering eyes under thick eyebrows. Stril detached one of the cords from the tree and led the brown, hairy dog to another tree, which had low branches. He threw the rope over a branch and pulled. Immediately the dog rose

254

stiffly into the air, its body lengthened and jerking, its paws stretched out before it; it spun around, eyes rolling in the head, and thin tongue sticking out. Stril wound the rope round his enormous hand, and with one leg extended for better balance, held on to the rope for several minutes, watching the writhing dog. When the body grew still, and the legs dropped and hung down limply, he went up close, looked at the protruding eyes, and took the animal down slowly. It fell in a heap on the snow. There was still a faint flutter behind the ribs, but the rest of the body was lifeless. Then he left it and went to take the second dog. It was a farm dog, black and hairy.

The boy put his head on the wooden post of the fence and looked on with half-shut eyes. Every now and then he had to shift his legs because of the cold. The second dog was strangled in the same manner as the first. Then Stril went and took the little dog. It was a dainty little reddish-brown puppy with white spots. The boy raised his head. The puppy got itself all entangled in the cord and gave a soft little bark and then began to whimper. Stril raised a foot to kick it but at that moment the puppy disentangled itself and began to run round Stril's legs. He chased after it, making circles in the snow, panting for breath and cursing roundly. Eventually, he caught up with the puppy and sent it flying the full length of the cord with the end of his boot. Then he began to drag it to the tree.

"Leave that puppy alone," cried the boy angrily from the fence. Stril turned in amazement. But when he saw the boy and his refined face, he gave him a broad smile, bowed slightly and touched his hat.

"Good-day, Panitch! What are you doing here?"

Stril didn't recognise the boy, covered with snow as he

was, but he had a great respect for all gentry and the boy, judging by his clothes, looked like one of them to him.

"Untie the puppy and let it run home. I'll pay you tomorrow."

"How much?"

"Half a gold ducat."

The skinner walked up to the fence, dragging the cowed puppy after him. The nearer he came, the bigger and more uncouth he seemed.

"Show me your money, Panitch!"

"I'll give it to you tomorrow. Come to the brewery and ask for me. I'll give you some beer to drink too."

The frost had begun to thaw on the killer's short mustache, for his breath was like a bellows. He could already taste the good, bitter beer on his tongue.

"When I've skinned those two over there, I'll go with you, Panitch, and you'll give me the money and the beer and then I'll let the puppy go."

His tiny eyes, buried in the fat of his face, glinted with the cunning of an idiot.

"No, let him go at once and you'll get the money and the beer tomorrow."

(He reminded himself of what was going on at home at that moment, and felt a stab in his heart.)

Stril shook his head and turned to go back to the tree. The boy jumped clean over the fence, caught hold of the cord and began to tug hard, to get it out of the hands of the skinner.

"Let go, I say! Let the puppy go!" (If only I had my penknife with me, he thought regretfully.)

Strill held the rope in his large hand, looked at the boy, and grinned slightly.

"It's a pity to spoil your hands," he said. "In a little while I'll give you its skin. It's a nice skin, with white spots. You can have it cured and put it next to your bed."

The boy, knowing it was useless to try to hang on, cudgeled his brains for some way of getting around him by cunning.

"Do you know whose puppy this is?"

"The devil knows!"

"It belongs to the *Wachmeister*" (head of the police).

"That's a lie!"

"It's true! If you kill it—the owners will shoot you, like a dog. Just three days ago his son-in-law sent it to him from Brod."

The skinner stood thinking for a moment.

"Good. When I've skinned the other two, you'll go with me to the *Wachmeister*, Panitch."

He tied the puppy to another tree, took a broad knife out of his high boot and a scythe-sharpener (a piece of wood dipped in tar and sand), honed it a few times, and then bent over the body of one of the dogs, turned it on its back, slit it down the chest and began to strip off the skin with the care of a devil, cutting with the knife and pushing with his fist, until the skin came away from the hot, quivering, still steaming flesh. When he cut the veins it began to bleed. He finished skinning one animal, threw aside the naked carcass, and began to work on the other. Twice the boy tried to get to the rope of the puppy, but each time Stril's eye caught him he straightened up and fumed:

"If you touch that dog—I'll hang it from the branch. 'Pon my word I will.'" And the knife flashed in his hand.

When the job was done, he buried the bodies (they

257

looked so small and pitiful!) in a snowdrift (*In the cemetery they're digging now*), unfastened a long coil of rope around his waist, and took off an old sack. He rolled up the soft skins and pushed them into the sack. The he sat down on it, took out the flask and the mauled bread again, swallowed a good swig of brandy and began to gnaw at the bread as he did before. With a full mouth, he growled something to the boy and indicated the flask.

The boy shook his head and drew away a little. The smell that Stril gave off was murderous.

"Give the puppy a bit of bread." (It was trying to gobble bits of snow.)

It was Stril's turn to shake his head.

When he finished eating, he picked up a fistful of snow and put it in his mouth. He hauled the sack on to his broad back, tied the cord around his waist, took hold of the puppy's cord and signed to the boy to follow him.

All of a sudden, Shalom began to feel ravenously hungry. His insides seemed to turn right over. But his hunger made him remember something else and all went dark before his eyes. He thought he was going to faint. He pulled himself together and began to walk.

"What time is it?" he asked the skinner, who looked up at the sky and answered:

"Almost three. The sun is already low. The day is short."

The skinner started on the descent. The boy followed behind him. Stril took big steps and the boy, who was very weak by now, had difficulty keeping up with him. Every time the distance between them increased, the skinner waited for him with a stupid laugh.

In less than half an hour they sighted the first house of the village.

An awful fear came over the boy. By going so fast he would get home at four, or even earlier, and he might still find the funeral in the yard, or on the way. He began to shake all over. "No! I won't be seen at her funeral! No, no, no!"

And when the skinner was a little way ahead, the boy slipped aside and ran behind the house. Farther on, Stril stopped and turned to wait for the boy, but he wasn't there. A look of great surprise spread over his heavy face. Had he been tricked? Perhaps it wasn't a boy at all but a demon? . . . He stood there for a few moments, debating whether to go back or not. Then he nodded to himself: "Maybe it *is* the *Wachmeister's* dog after all," and continued on his way to the small town.

One of the Jewish fire-victims who lived with the farmers brought the boy home to the brewery. He had found him huddled behind one of the hedges, half frozen and on the verge of collapse. The Jew carried him in his arms all the way, for the boy was almost dead with cold.

XXX

The End of the Tale

The Zaddik of Belz found that as the name of the agent was Frantisek Josef, the same as that of the Emperor (may the Lord enhance his glory), he couldn't do anything to harm him as he would thereby provoke the "minister" of the gracious Emperor and bring misfortune (God forbid!) on the Jews. When the old lady heard this, all the fight went out of her, and the feeling of anger and vindictiveness that invaded her every time she thought of the wicked agent, was replaced by one of utter dejection and defeat. She left there the next day and when she came home she was greeted with the terrible news of Bracha's death. It was already the third of the seven days of mourning. Like a woman possessed, she ran straight to the cemetery in the wind and the snow (Reb Hirtzel got dressed quickly and went after her) and threw herself on the snow-covered grave, spreading her arms and her shawl over it like giant wings. She wept and she wailed and she fainted and she revived and started weeping again. But there was a sort of emptiness in her voice. Her son-in-law led her gently home to her apartment, and she sat down with the rest of the mourners, on a small stool. She sat like that day and night, in the clothes that she hadn't removed since she came back. She neither ate nor drank nor slept – not even when the rest of the household slept soundly. She looked terrible. Under her eyes, there were two dark hollows. She suddenly aged ten years. She also seemed to have shrunk a little in stature.

Next afternoon, the flood-gates of her heart suddenly opened and she began to tell them what had gone on in Belz with the Zaddik. Her story was long and tedious and she kept repeating, in all innocence: "If only the wicked man had another name and not the same one as the Emperor, may he live long!" She didn't mention Bracha at all. She asked no questions about her illness, her death, her last words; she did not enumerate her virtues nor lament her youth – as if this wound, the most terrible of all the wounds she had suffered in her life, had been destined to scab over immediately with a thick layer of skin. The day after that, she began to talk about the family, about vacating the brewery, about the accounts. She asked Reb Simha to come to her with the ledgers. She made a special point of selling all the beer in stock in the cellar. They were not going to leave the full barrels to those Jewish rascals. To the people who came with muffled steps to offer condolences, she spoke shortly and with a stern, almost unfriendly expression, as if she suspected them of wishing her ill. She also gave orders to cut down a little on what they were spending for the fire-victims. She was no longer so pleasant and open-hearted because the Almighty had "dealt very bitterly" with her.

The seven days of mourning came to an end and everyone grew busy with preparations for vacating the brewery, which they were going to have to do, whether they liked it or not, in a few weeks' time.

And on the appointed day, about a week after Passover,

two young men came to the town: one was the son of
Reb Gedalia Nussenbaum and the other an expert brewer,
also a Jew from Bohemia. They spent the night at the inn
and next morning they came to the palace with their
fine briefcases. The agent, Pan Lasoti, received them
graciously and informed them that the previous tenants
had already left the brewery. Everything had been handed
back to him in perfect order, two days before. And after
Nussenbaum Jr. had spread out before him the notarial
permit and the brewer's certificates, Pan Lasoti sent the
clerk with them, and a servant to carry the heavy bunch
of keys which he would hand over when the inventory
was drawn up and signed.

In the town, there was a certain feeling of disappoint-
ment. They'd been told that the two merchants would be
coming themselves, and some of the people who hated
injustice were getting ready to give them a reception
befitting dastardly Jewish trespassers. But the Jews from
the "big world" were shrewder than the townspeople
and sent the young man instead. He was clean-shaven and
smartly dressed and walked through the town as if he
had nothing to do with the Jews. Someone stopped him
and tried to get him into an argument, but the young
man pretended not to understand what he was saying.
So the Jew spat and went away.

There was a weeping and wailing when they left the
brewery. The fire-victims, who also had to vacate the
premises by order of the agent, ran hither and thither
assembling their meagre belongings. The women wept
loudly and cursed the agent and the new lessees. Pearl, who
decided to go with Mrs. Aberdam and the Pallan family,
to be with them wherever they went, ran from room to

263

room, from apartment to apartment, taking leave of them with great lamentations, slapping her contorted face with her apron and kissing each and every mezuzah. Sosele too ran from place to place with outstretched arms. She collected the holy vessels in the prayer-room and told Israel Elia to take them, for the time being, to the apartment they had rented in the town. Then she came to Mrs. Aberdam and asked her to give her the deaf-mute. She wants to take him to her home and care for him like a son. She knows he is a difficult person, a grumbler and a crosspatch, but there's no one who'll take him in, poor cripple, and she has no children. (At this point she suddenly remembered the Jew who came and "stole" the orphan girl from her and began to grieve all over again.)

Mrs. Aberdam agreed and also promised to contribute something to his keep now and then, to the extent that she was able. For the accident had happened to him at her place and she couldn't just wash her hands of him. But Sosele insists that she will not accept anything. She wants to do a whole mitzvah, not a half one. Israel Elia is going to get a post as bailiff in the neighbouring forest and they won't be short of a livelihood.

Only Reb Simha went around looking like death. His face had gone sickly white and he didn't know where he was in the new order of things. His wife, who was suddenly faced with the problem of finding a new apartment at a time when there was such a shortage of housing, now took complete control over her husband. Luckily, she had several thousand silver roubles in hand, which she and her daughters had saved, and with this money she proposed to open a restaurant – when the new buildings went up. Her husband would help to attract people there.

She just had to get him out of the habit of making caustic wisecracks. Never mind, *she'd* teach him manners. And the girls would help. When he stopped being the bread-winner he would do as he was told. Herr Lieber refused to admit that he was getting old. He stoutly declared that he would pack his knapsack and go out and look for work. Never mind, he was used to it. Forty years ago, he also wandered from place to place – until he found something. He has his small savings, and an artist like him won't be lost. The labourers all remained at their jobs: good working hands for any master. Vanka the stoker was very silent. Only when he was tipsy on his day off did he roar: "All the same, they wronged the old lady. When I'm a stoker over there, in the other world, I'll know for whom to add an extra log of wood . . . Ho, ho! I'll know!"

Pan Yashinski and his family left the estate that same winter. The agent did not dismiss him, as he feared he would, but transferred him elsewhere, to another of Graf Molodetzki's estates. For a week before they departed, Pani Yuzia's face and eyes were swollen with crying. She knelt before Mrs. Aberdam, like those village brides who kneel before the neighbours before going to their wedding, hugged her knees and called her "mother" and said it was hard for her to leave the soul of the young lady which still hovered there. She kissed the twins a number of times, and even Shalom gave her his hand this time, which she held for a long time, gazing softly, lovingly into his face.

And Reb Hirtzel, after liquidating all his mother-in-law's debts as well as his own, and after selling the greater part of the excellent furniture to a Pole, the postmaster, was left with about a thousand silver roubles. With half the money, and with his mother-in-law's agreement, he bought the house of Potchbani, a clerk in the tax-office who had to sell because of his many debts. It was a nice, wooden house with three rooms, a kitchen and a hall, and a garden of trees and flowers in front.

By the summer, the family was already installed in the house. The twins, who finished primary school that year, worked in the house and tended the garden as they used to see Pani Yuzia doing. Pearl did the cooking and the washing. Reb Hirtzel now worked a little as a broker as he didn't have the money to do any business and he feared loans and interest as he did the plague. Brokerage was not much to his liking, but he did the work with his usual delicacy, good taste and honesty, with the result that the income from it was small and most of the time there was nothing for him to do. So he got used to staying at home and reading: the Gemarra, books on ethics and researches. He was surprised at himself, that he, son of the Rabbi of Radichov, could have been cut off from the good books for so many years. They brought back things he had learnt in childhood and revived his spirit. It was as if he had begun to bloom again. On several occasions he got into a discussion with the local Rabbi and an educated young man on matters of religious theory and investigation, and they were amazed at his knowledgeability. He also headed the building committee for the gutted prayer-house, and managed to start collecting building materials. He even went once to Husiatin, because his father, the Rabbi, who also died that year, had extracted a promise from him before he died that he would make the journey to the Zaddik in his stead.

Mrs. Aberdam spent the whole of the beginning of the

summer, until after Pentecost, on erecting tombstones for Reb Naftali Zvi and Bracha. She set aside a special sum of money for the purpose, and went twice to Brod to see a master stonemason in this connection. In the whole of the cemetery in the town, there were no tombstones as fine as these, and many people came to see them put up. After that, she sat idle for a few weeks until she was overcome with extreme boredom and fear of approaching death. One day, she came home and announced that she had rented a tiny shop, two metres by two, and bought a few sacks of flour, and she would sit there and sell the flour to a few customers by weight. She can't rest, and as long as her legs can carry her she must earn her bread. She doesn't want to be dependent on others, not even on her own children, as long as she can bring anything in. The housekeeping can be left to Pearl and the girls. So she began this little retail business. From early in the morning to late in the evening, she'd sit in her airless cubicle, knitting or mending socks, and only when a customer came in would she lay her work aside and weigh a little flour out into a cloth- or paper-bag. She no longer worked for charity, maintaining that a person who can't give has no right to make others give. Nor did she ever go to Belz again, although she paid her dues regularly, and spoke neither good nor bad of the Rabbi.

Her whole world was now concentrated in her grandson, Shalom, He was all that interested her, as if he was all that remained of her past. He was her only consolation in life. She didn't show her feelings, but at home she always managed to twist things to his benefit. When he sat reading, or writing in an exercise book, she'd watch him all the time, trying to find in him some resemblance to her first husband, the late Reb Shlomke. What she wanted to find, she found: every word, every gesture was Reb Shlomke's. Therefore, she wanted him to learn a lot of Torah and be a pious man like him. She arranged matters so that she succeeded in getting him to learn two hours a day with the Rabbi. The boy took to it with a will and became very attached to the Rabbi. For he was a gentle, kindly man and explained things in a pleasing manner; and not only was he never strict with him, but he also treated him like an adult. He was particualrly impressed with the fact that the Rabbi often turned to him, as if in doubt, and asked his opinion. He was now the only one learning with the Rabbi, because the rest of the boys were busy building their fathers' houses, and the Rabbi regarded him as a sort of brand snatched from the fire and showered him with affection. Apart from his study-hours with the Rabbi, Shalom spent his time reading the books in the house, and began to dip into research. Although at first he didn't understand everything he read, he gradually began to get the idea and weigh every word, every thought. He also went on learning the languages of the country by himself, from grammar books that he obtained from the lady principal of the school.

He had entered his thirteenth year, his Bar Mitzvah year. Mrs. Aberdam took note of it and reminded the boy that he should begin to learn the principles of the use of phylacteries. She showed him the small phylacteries belonging to the late Reb Naftali Zvi, written by a pious scribe who was a real artist. She was going to have new leather boxes made for them, and they would become his. The boy thanked her with a sweet smile.

Mrs. Aberdam had calmed down by now and begun

to behave as in the good old days. She walked erect again, and because of her thinness it was even more impressive than before. Under her pillow, she kept a box of snuff which she sniffed when she was at home (she didn't do it in the "shop" because she was afraid that crumbs might fall into the flour). She wasn't as well-groomed as before. Her white, short hair often stuck out from her kerchief or her coif and showed how she was aging. Only on Sabbath did she dress up in her best clothes and long diamond earrings and go to prayers with her son-in-law and her grandson. At the end of the street, she would go off to the prayer-house where she was a member, and they would go to the temporary Husiatin premises. Afterwards, she would have to wait for them at home because the Husiatins are always late with their prayers.

Reb Reuvele sometimes came and stayed over as he used to do at the brewery. Sometimes, other guests would also come round. But Reb Hirschele Merubeh never came again because he had died suddenly at some place on his roamings. And when they gathered in the evening, they'd tell stories again, and Mrs. Aberdam would tell the ones about the burning bed and the hobgoblin. Those were now like legends of long ago, full of nostalgia for the days that were gone.

Once, on a hot, close summer night, they all kept tossing on their beds, unable to fall asleep. The men, Reb Hirtzel and Shalom, slept in one room, Mrs. Aberdam and the girls in the other. The door was slightly open and the old lady's bed stood opposite it. About midnight, a terrible cry was heard coming from her:

"Shalom! Shalom! He-e-e-elp!"

Reb Hirtzel sprang out of bed and stood in the doorway.

"What's happened, mother?"

"Didn't you people see? Woe is me! I woke up and saw Shlomke's bed all on fire...just like then...The bed is burning...and the boy is in it!"

Shalom, who had heard every word, laughed to himself at his grandmother's dream. But suddenly his laughter stopped and his heart began to pound furiously as if seeking to burst within his breast.

* * * *

1915–1929

Biographical Note

Asher Barash achieved distinction in a variety of literary fields —
as an essayist, poet, short story writer, translator, editor and
teacher. Born in Lopatin, a town in the Galician province of
Brody, on March 16, 1889, he was connected through his mother
with the family of the famous Rabbi of Belz. His father was a
well-to-do grain merchant, also of rabbinical family, who owned
an orchard and vegetable garden, and they lived in a neighbourhood of farmers, tradesmen, and clerks, of Ruthenian and
Polish nationality. This variegated milieu was etched in Asher
Barash's mind during his early years. His education was traditional, in *cheder* and *beit midrash*, while for his secular education
he attended a Government school. He embarked on a number of
literary ventures at an early age.

When he was fifteen, he left his home town, teaching in various
places till he reached Lvov, where he lived for an extended
period belonging to a circle of Hebrew and Yiddish authors.
Here he completed his secular education, specializing in German
and Polish literature, and it was here that his qualities as an
author were moulded.

Initially he published poems, stories and articles in Yiddish,
Polish and Hebrew. Afterwards, at the instigation of Yosef Chaim
Brenner who came to Lvov in 1908, Barash published a series
of prose poems entitled "Agitations" in the second anthology of
Sifrut, edited by David Frishman. From then onwards, he
devoted himself exclusively to Hebrew literature.

His first Hebrew story, "Terms of Betrothal," was published
in *Hashiloah* in 1910, a date which Barash regarded as the
beginning of his career as a Hebrew author. Later, G. Shofman

published in an anthology he edited, *Shalechet*, a number of Barash's stories, among them "From the Lot," which made a deep impression at the time. In the spring of 1914, when he was twenty-five years old, he emigrated to Eretz-Israel (Palestine), as an author whose name was already known to the public. He taught Hebrew language and literature at the Herzliya High School, at the Teachers' College, at the Haifa Reali School and at the Tel Aviv Commercial School. During that time, the period of World War I, he published poems, stories and essays in the weekly *Hapoel Hatzair*, in the monthly *Moledet* and in the weekly *Ha'achdut*. In the twenties he joined his friend Ya'akov Rabinovitz in publishing the *Heidim* monthly magazine, which was a rallying point for young authors seeking new modes of expression in literature and in public life.

His literary work in the fields of poetry, fiction, translation and editing was extensive and varied, his collected works appearing in three volumes (1952–1957). He was awarded the Bialik Prize for his short story "Strange Love."

Asher Barash was active in public life, particularly in literary circles. He initiated the founding of a publishing house and of various literary projects. He was the chairman of the Authors' Association, one of the founders of the PEN Club, editor of the monthly magazine for youth, *Atidot*, and a member of important public institutions. In his last years he laboured to create the bio-bibliographical institute of Genazim, which after his death was named in his honour. He died in Tel Aviv on June 4, 1952.

* * * *